Michael Abraham

Union, WV

A novel

Pileated Press
Blacksburg, Virginia

Billy — I hope you enjoy this story!

Michael

Also by Michael Abraham

The Spine of the Virginias,
Journeys along the border of Virginia
and West Virginia

For updates and ordering information on my
books, excerpts, and sample chapters, please
visit my website at:
http://www.bikemike.name/

I can be reached by email at:
<bikemike@nrvunwired.net>

Union, WV

This is a work of fiction. Many historic figures are mentioned by name, but any resemblance to any living person is coincidental and unintentional.

ISBN 978-0-926487-53-6

Cover photograph © 2009 by Michael Abraham
Author photograph © 2009 by Tracy Roberts
Book design by Michael Abraham and Josh Wimmer

Printed in the United States of America

III

To Jane and Whitney Abraham,
the two most important people in my life.

Acknowledgements

I am deeply indebted to many people who supported my effort. My editors worked countless hours to help me make my book readable, relevant, and grammatically correct.

Jane Abraham, Blacksburg, VA
Mary Ann Johnson, Blacksburg, VA
Kate McCoy, Blacksburg, VA
Tracy Roberts, New Castle, VA

I am also indebted to the people who helped me understand the Civil War, the culture of Northern Virginia and Union, West Virginia, and other technical aspects of the book. I thank them.

Jay Banks, Union, WV
Jeffrey Chain, Christiansburg, VA
Lee Chichester, Meadows of Dan, VA
Jennifer Copeland, Rock Camp, WV
Michael Gravely, Union, WV
Rod Graves, Union, WV
John Gregg, Blacksburg, VA
Lloyd and Garnett Haynes, White Sulphur Springs, WV
Stuart McGehee, Bluefield, WV
H. Craig Mohler, Union, WV
Mike O'Dell, White Sulphur Springs, WV
L. W. "Doc" Reed, Pickaway, WV
James I. "Bud" Robertson, Jr., Blacksburg, VA
Marion Shiflet, Union, WV
Warren Smith, Sweet Springs, WV
Mark Vanderberg, Blacksburg, VA
Jane Weiseman, Blacksburg, VA
Fred Ziegler, Greenville, WV

Union, WV

Characters

Quarles Immediate Family

Wayne Derek Quarles	Protagonist
Donna Brickman Quarles	Quarles' wife
Willa Angela Quarles	Quarles' daughter
Edmund Thomas Quarles	Quarles' son
Betsy McGranahan Quarles	Quarles' mother

Northern Virginia

Cynthia Menendez	Quarles' paramour
Martin Kneeland	Quarles' friend
Arnie Heckleman	Quarles' friend and insurance agent
Wilson	Quarles' boss

Union, West Virginia

Prof. Philip McGranahan	Quarles' great uncle
Terry Yount	highway worker
Chris Witherspoon	rescue squad member

Renu Ramkija	emergency room doctor
Sheila	hospital orderly
Truman Hankins	Rotary Club member, former banker
Allen Smart	hospital doctor
Stuart Cummings	*Monroe Watchman* publisher
Ansel Cummings	Stuart's son, coal miner
Gibby Robinson	guitarist
Mildred Webb	nurse, caretaker
Sherwood Webb	husband of Mildred
Reed Rathmell	Rotary member, former preacher, falconer
Juliet Rathmell	Reed's daughter
Burton Jones	Rotary club president
Franklin McRoberts III	Rotary club member, former state senator
Clyde McCall	Bozoo storyteller
Fiona McGregor	minister
Christie and Jim Dickson	owners of Phil McGranahan's house
Levi Rubenstein	musician, husband of Isadora
Isadora Rubenstein	pharmacist, wife of Levi

Andy McGranahan's Monroe

James and Annie McGranahan	Scot couple
Thomas McGranahan	son of James and Annie
Katherine Lindsay McGranahan	wife of Thomas
Thomas McGranahan II	son of Thomas and Katherine
Stefan Holtz	second husband of Katherine
Victoria Phelps McGranahan	wife of Thomas McGranahan II
Thomas McGranahan III	son of Thomas II and Victoria
Andrew Jackson McGranahan	son of Thomas II and Victoria, twin brother of Teresa
Teresa McGranahan	twin daughter of Thomas II and Victoria, twin sister of Andrew
Josiah Raney	cobbler
Mordeci Mishkin	pharmacist
Rivka Mishkin	midwife, wife of Mordeci
Alison Larkin Littletree	wife of Andy
Wes Littletree	brother-in-law of Andy, husband of Teresa
Jacob Cox	Union officer
Anthony, Joseph, Silvio Pasko	Union soldiers
M. & M. Walker Crain	Goods Mill residents

Union, WV

Part 1

August 27

Soaring, Pristine landscaper of white,
creamy. Undulating, sensual. Tequila. Tits,
luscious tits. Cream rivers of white milk.
Ripe, red strawberries atop meringue tips.
Soaring. Pink-brown Nipples. Tits. Round
luscious Tits.

"Mmmm!" sighed Wayne Derek Quarles. Before he opened his eyes, he let her scent, a sinful bouquet of woman-sex juice and floral perfume, waft deep into his nostrils. His opening eyelids revealed her right hand, where the tender touch of her fingernails twirled the hairs on his chest. "I must have been dreaming," he said, languidly.

"You deserve the rest. You've been working pretty hard for the last hour," said Cynthia Menendez as she rested lying prone. Her head was near his, with her belly down and shoulders propped up by her elbows. The tips of her breasts rested on the yellow sheets. She had deep-set brown eyes and dark mascara. She wore nothing but a half-dozen rings, two pierced earrings dangling from each ear and a gold bracelet on her right ankle.

Wayne looked at her butterscotch skin, the curvature of her buttocks and legs, and the lascivious tattoo of a rose at the small of her back. He rolled on his side and ran his index finger down the left ridge of her back from her shoulder to the tattoo. She giggled and her skin burst taut into a bronze landscape of goosebumps. He thought this was the most gorgeous sight he'd ever seen. Looking into her doe eyes, his mind flashed back to their first meeting in Baltimore, three-and-a-half months prior, in early April.

+ + + +

April 8

Wayne attended a two-day sales training conference at the Baltimore Harbor Omni a Thursday and Friday in early April. During one of the breakout work sessions on Thursday, Cynthia and he were assigned to the same table. Her dress was short; the neckline was low. Everyone at the table exchanged business cards as they began to work. Wayne read hers. Cynthia Menendez. Kendall Associates, Commercial Real Estate. Glebe Road, Arlington. Her glance at him lingered longer than decorum would dictate. He thought to divert his stare, but held on longer than she.

After the day's sessions were over, Wayne had dinner with a couple of guys he'd met the year before from Rockville. On his way out the door, he noticed her sitting with some women nearby. She looked up as he passed and gave him a friendly smile and wink. He lied to the Rockville guys, telling them he'd left his cell phone at the table. He walked past her again lightly brushing her hair. He nodded at her, and then moved to the bar. He ordered a Lynchburg Lemonade and lit a Marlboro.

Distracted by a NBA playoff game on the big-screen, he didn't see her approach. She lightly ran her knuckle up his spine. Startled, he spun around to see her eyes inches from his.

"Hello again, Wayne. Mind if I join you?"

"Cindy is it, right? Sorry, Cynthia. Please." Her shoulders were broad and pleasing. She wore a yellow dress, with two spaghetti straps wrapped over each shoulder. She had prominent cheeks with a mole on the left and a silver comb in her raven-black, curly, shoulder-length hair. She smelled good, with a familiar perfume.

She turned to the bartender and ordered a gin and tonic. She took a sip. "Are you a basketball fan?"

"Just something to watch. Car racing is really my passion. NASCAR. Grand Prix. Indy. I keep an old Triumph TR-3 at the racetrack at Summit Point in West Virginia for track days. I love speed. You?"

"Art. Jewelry. Clothes. Mostly, I'm devoted to my work. I love sales. I love the hunt, the subtle manipulation, the conquest. I love to see men squirm."

He wondered uneasily how serious she was about this proclamation and whether she saw him squirm when she said it. He looked at her hands. Her nails were polished blue. She had a silver bracelet and there were too many rings to count. He said, "You married?"

"Maybe."

He saw her looking at his hands, perhaps searching for a wedding band. His sat on the bureau at home.

She said, "You?"

"Maybe."

She looked at him for a long moment. He was sure she was sizing him up and he wondered if she found him appealing. He was medium height, perhaps 5'11". He had a cleft chin and hazel eyes, with bushy eyebrows. He had lots of freckles. He had a few more pounds than he should have but was still muscular. He wore designer eyeglasses. Rogaine was beginning to work on his male-patterned baldness. He had a crisp blue shirt and a navy blazer.

She looked at the television. She took a deep sip of her drink and looked at him again. She clenched her teeth. "What room are you in?"

"Four-eighteen"

"I'll be up in a moment," she said, and then left, tapping his knee as she swiveled past. Her bracelets clanged. Her aroma perplexed and intoxicated him.

He left a couple dollars tip on the bar, and then headed for the elevator, wondering to himself whether he was about to get lucky or whether he was the biggest sucker on planet Earth. Reaching his room, he slid the plastic key downward and then upward in the door slot. The tiny green light lit. Inside his room, he sat on the edge of his bed and wondered how to prepare for a fantasy moment that might or might not arrive. His head swam in a flood of lust and guilt, anxious over which was dominant.

He stood again, took off his blazer and draped it over a chair. He removed his pistol and holster and stowed them in a dresser drawer. He unbuttoned the top two buttons on his shirt, and then re-buttoned the bottom one. He turned on the TV, lowering the volume so he could listen for approaching footsteps. Larry King interviewing a Michael Jackson brother. Alexandra Steele on the Weather Channel. Crap! He turned it off. Silence, except some kids screaming down the hall. Raindrops fell on the windowsill and trickled down the glass, refracting the city lights.

Wayne turned the TV back on again and found a Blues music station when the knock came, shave-and-a-haircut. As he walked to the door, a black bluesman belted,

> I was once a boy, so little,
> I found at age eight,

Behind the zipper of my pants,
Was a tool of pleasure, oh so great...

He opened the door and there she was. Her scent of perfume and cigarette smoke reached his olfactory and his eyelids drifted downward as he breathed it in. "Hi." She winked and walked past him.

"Hi."

Now a man I be,
Full-grown and true,
There are wondrous things,
I can do for you.

"Can I get you something?" he said, realizing he had no booze to give her, had she said yes.

She held her index finger to her lips and shook her head. She held her hands on the sides of his ribcage and positioned him standing by the desk. "Here." She took a small glass filled with a scented candle and a cigarette lighter from her purse. She lit the candle. She then turned off the lights, and closed the cabinet that housed the TV. She pulled the chair from under the desk, and motioned for him to sit. She kicked off her pumps. She hiked up her skirt. Lambent light from the candle cast her shadow across the room. She spread her legs and sat astride him, pulling his head towards her chest with both hands. She pushed her lips against his, and her tongue played on the rim of his teeth.

All the sexy women,
Line up for me,
The good things in life,
They say are still free.

He closed his eyes and bit her tongue. He felt her mouth move away. He opened his eyes and watched her slip the straps of her dress off her shoulders and expose her breasts. He closed his eyes again, soaking in the moment, and felt her hands move behind his head as she gently pulled him towards her. When he opened his eyes again, each eyelash brushed against a breast, while the cross medallion that hung from her necklace bounced against his forehead.

The good things in life,
They say are still free.

He reached her damp clitoris and began to rub his knuckles against it, gently side-to-side. She writhed and moaned. Her breasts rubbed against his face, one on each of his cheeks. He felt her heart race and beads of sweat form. She climaxed, but he continued to rub, only stopping when her hand reached his wrist and pulled his hand away.

Moments later, she took a deep breath and lifted her weight from his lap. She tucked her breasts inside the fabric of her dress and looped the straps back over her shoulders. She brushed back her hair with her hands and stepped into her shoes. He grinned a sly grin and she smiled, gave him a peck on the lips, and then walked to the door. "Bye." And she was gone.

The good things in life,
They say are still free.

He shook his head, wiped his eyes, and sighed. "Holy orgasm, Batman." He blew out the candle and clicked on a desktop lamp, not sure whether to feel elated or taken advantage of. He went into the bathroom and took off his clothes for his shower, dropping his soiled boxer shorts into the trash can. Before he closed the shower curtain, he ran his knuckles under his nostril.

+ + + +

April 9

The following day, a Friday, the second day of the conference, Wayne entered the large conference room and scanned it looking for Cynthia. But she was gone. He kept her card in his briefcase, but calling was out of the question. He figured it was a one-time, spontaneous fling. Sitting in an audience of bored people with a PowerPoint presentation on the screen, he furtively held his knuckles to his nostril again, straining vainly to recapture her scent. Her memory aroused him nonetheless.

At the end of the day, he drove his cherry-red Hummer home near Park Avenue in Vienna, Virginia, smoking Marlboros and fighting maddening traffic all the way from Baltimore on I-95. He hated the traffic and sometimes felt that he was drowning in a rising tide of humanity. Whenever traffic stopped entirely, he pulled his harmonica from his pocket and played to himself. He had gotten it as a teenager, a Christmas present. He was never skilled enough to find a paying audience, but playing it soothed his nerves. The numbing, soporific sameness of suburban driving forced him back into the realities of his life.

He and Donna had been married for nine years. Their wedding was more memorable than they hoped it would be, in that it was held at the Alexandria Episcopal Church the Saturday after an airliner slammed into the Pentagon on a gorgeous fall Tuesday in September 2001, a couple miles to the north. A UVA classmate of Donna's was in that burning wreckage and her funeral was the day before the wedding in the same church. Should they call off the wedding just because the United States had been attacked and the smell of burning flesh and kerosene was still wafting through the air?

Wayne and Donna met on a double-date in Charlottesville, a month before he was expelled for Honor Code violations, 30 credits shy of a degree in economics with a minor in history. She was pretty, with dirty-blond hair and fair skin, from New Rochelle, New York. She had finished her degree in accounting, and later earned her CPA license. She worked for a Falls Church accounting firm until the babies arrived. Willa was now 7 and Edmund was 5.

Wayne had slept with Sally, one of Donna's bridesmaids, a week before the wedding. Two years later Donna was pregnant with Willa. Wayne was revolted by the thought of having sex with Donna during pregnancy, envisioning himself tupping the fetus' head. When he ran into Sally at an Annandale bar during Donna's 32nd week, Sally invited him to her apartment where they copulated again.

Wayne and Sally had two more carnal unions during the following week before Donna caught them, tipped off by another of her bridesmaids. With her round belly, swollen ankles, and tears streaming from her eyes, Donna read Wayne the riot act and swore she'd leave him in an instant if he ever cheated on her again. He wondered how the attractive woman he'd married had so quickly come to look so puffy, rubicund, and unappealing. As she ranted, he envisioned a squealing sow.

Still, her threat was enough to keep him faithful, excepting his encounter with the wafer-thin blond prostitute at the automaker's convention in Las Vegas. And he wasn't looking for a new affair when Cynthia came along; at least he didn't think he was.

Their marriage had gone as well as he'd ever expected, given the stresses. But all new marriages waver, he told himself. During her pregnancies, Donna was no more interested in sex with him than he was with her. Once Willa was born, Donna seemed overwhelmed with work and mothering. In his mind, he knew she would never cheat.

When Donna's mother's dementia became worse during recent months, Donna became increasingly detached from him. They spoke less. When they did converse, it was obligatory stuff, plans for the day and so forth, not of aspirations, ideas, or affection. She never flirted nor reached for him in bed.

Donna's dad was years dead, so she began to travel home more often to take care of her mom, eventually every other weekend. Most of the time, she and the kids took Amtrak, leaving Friday afternoon and coming back Tuesday morning.

Donna had left on Friday and was gone by the time he arrived at home. He did some household chores over the weekend, trying to keep the place straightened. He took his shirts to the dry-cleaners and spent two hours at the shooting range in Fairfax, as usual on Saturday morning. He washed the Hummer and the Harley, as he did each weekend. He did some day-trading and posted a blog entry on *www.redhawk.com*, his favorite rant site.

Whenever he thought about Cynthia, he quickly and successfully fought back any signs of guilt. He'd done nothing wrong and had no reason for remorse; he hadn't even penetrated. On Sunday afternoon, he washed the shirt and trousers he'd worn in Baltimore. He smelled her perfume on the collar of his shirt and became aroused. He knew Donna would be able to smell it; women's sense of smell always astounded him. He soaked the sweet aroma into his nose before dropping the shirt into the swirling, soapy water.

+ + + +

April 12

Donna and the kids were already at home when he returned from work on Tuesday evening. He and Donna exchanged dutiful kisses. For an instant, he wondered if she suspected anything. But she seemed oblivious in her exhaustion. By the next morning, they were back to their routine. He assured himself his singular indiscretion in Baltimore would quickly become inconsequential.

+ + + +

April 21

Wayne's office was in downtown Washington, but he only went in on Mondays. He sold fleets of Chevys, Buicks and Cadillacs to rental agencies and other buyers throughout the Metro area. As a salesman, most of his work was on the road. He enjoyed the freedom to go where he thought most lucrative, but that freedom had a cost. He was constantly anxious and angry behind the wheel, increasingly infuriated by all the blunt skulls with whom he was forced to share the road. He put 35,000 hard miles each year on his cars and traded every two or three years. He was currently driving his third Hummer. He'd bought it in February. He used it for work but he felt it was a reflection of his personality and his superiority over the teeming low-lifes of which the area was increasingly populated.

Years prior, his first Hummer had been keyed-up near the downtown office – parking spaces were non-existent anyway – so he stopped driving and started taking the Metro, leaving his car at the Vienna station on the Orange line. He always parked in the same area at the back of the lot. He also figured it would be away from more of the cellphone yakking morons who couldn't even park a car, although the lots were almost always full by the morning rush.

A week after the Baltimore conference, he was first in line at a traffic light on his way to see a client in Silver Spring when his cellphone rang. He gulped the last bite of his Whopper, spilling ketchup on his lap, and threw the wrapper out the window before grabbing his cell phone. The 703 area code was on his caller ID, but he didn't recognize the number.

"Hello, this is Wayne."

"Hi Wayne. It's Cynthia."

Cynthia, he thought. He closed his eyes and remembered the scent of her perfume. Cynthia. Cyn. What an appropriate nickname. "How's everything going?"

"Fine. I've been missing you. Sorry I had to leave the conference without saying goodbye. A friend had a minor medical emergency and I left to help her."

"I wondered if I said something I shouldn't have."

"Not at all."

"I've missed you, too."

"May I see you again?"

"Sure." He thought for a moment and realized Donna would be away that weekend. "How about the day after tomorrow, Friday? Where's good?"

"Meet me at Starbucks at the Rosslyn Metro station. Seven o'clock. We'll take a ride together. Bye!"

In his mind's eye, he saw her full breasts wrapping around his face again. He felt a tightening of his lap belt and looked around self-consciously. He pressed the accelerator and entered the intersection before the light had turned green and was almost nailed by a UPS truck coming from his left.

+ + + +

April 23

Two evenings later, he got home from work early and took a shower to prepare for his second rendezvous with Cynthia. He stared at his wardrobe and fidgeted over what to wear. What the fuck? She wouldn't care what he wore anyway.

He drove to the Metro lot, parked his Hummer in its usual spot and rode the Orange line towards the city. He hated mixing with all the teeming humanity that the Metro meant. But since he got on at the start of the Orange line, he always got a seat. He exited the station at Rosslyn. She was waiting when he arrived, sipping a cappuccino from a Styrofoam cup and reading *Vogue*.

"Hi," she said.

"Hi yourself. Nice to see you again." He sized her up and she was just as sexy as he remembered.

"Didn't your momma teach you not to stare?" she teased.

His eyes darted from her bustline to her eyes. "Sorry! I was reworking an old fantasy. That was quite an introduction we had in Baltimore!"

"Yeah. I'm thinking an encore is in order. But sit for a moment. Let's talk. Tell me more about yourself."

"Must we?"

"Let's not move so fast this time."

"Very well, I sell cars," he said, looking at her intense brown-eyed gaze. "I've always loved them. The bigger and faster they are the better. I sell to the agency buyers. It's a killer competitive world, but it's what I know. I've learned every trick in the book. I read the personalities, assess the weaknesses, and move in for the kill. The strong survive. The money has been good in recent years, but I never seem to have enough. Lately, the recession has hit me.

"What else is there? I also do some day-trading. I read about war history, mostly about weapons. I have a penchant for all things mechanical: cars, motorcycles, tools, and guns. Loud things." He wondered if his display of manhood was resonating with her.

"Wife?"

"Do you want to know?"

She nodded.

"Yes, a wife and two kids. Shall we not talk about them? You married?"

"Yes. My husband is overseas a lot. He's overseas now. I don't know exactly what he does and I wouldn't be able to tell you if I did. We've been married six years. No kids. It gets pretty lonely. Women have urges."

Quiet.

"I've got a place for us to go," she said. "Come."

She led him onto the Blue Metro line towards Alexandria. They emerged on King Street and walked to South Royal Street. They entered a five-story condo, and walked past an elderly couple who Wayne thought looked at them suspiciously, as if they knew what he and Cynthia had planned.

Wayne and Cynthia entered the elevator. A pre-teen girl entered the elevator just before the doors slid shut. While the girl faced towards the closed door, Wayne playfully rested his hand on Cynthia's ass and gave it a little squeeze. Cynthia brushed his hand away. The girl got off at the third floor without looking back at them and Wayne put his hand back on Cynthia's ass. This time, she let it stay.

As they left the elevator on the fourth floor and walked the dim hallway, Cynthia said, "This place belongs to my friend Katie. She splits her time here and in L.A. I watch it for her while she's gone." She turned the key and they went inside. Cynthia adjusted the air conditioning, turned on a ceiling fan, and lit some candles. Wayne felt the warmth of the room and smelled a scent of cinnamon. He felt beads of sweat build on his eyelids. The artwork on the wall looked expensive and had sexual overtones. Cynthia took a bottle of zinfandel from the wine cooler. She poured a couple of glasses.

"The night we met in Baltimore... I guess I owe you an apology. I was a bit self-indulgent with my lap-dance."

"It wasn't anything I minded," he chuckled.

"Still, tonight's yours." She reached over and unbuttoned the top two buttons of his shirt. She put her index finger in the wine glass and smeared the red fluid on his neck under his left ear. She licked it. "What's your pleasure?"

They had sex on the sofa. He was on his way home by 11 p.m.

+ + + +

On the Metro train, he saw six Asian kids mumbling in their rapid-fire, incoherent language. Vietnamese? Cambodian? Damn gooks! They sounded like they just got off the boat. What the hell were they doing in the United States of God-damn America?

In bed at 2 a.m., he couldn't sleep. He got up, lit a Marlboro, and logged onto the *www.redhawk. com* site under his blog name, QUARRELLER, and typed.

> *Who opened the floodgates to every black, Hispanic, Asian, Muslim, or Arab in the world? Our government seems hell-bent to overwhelm us with rights of specific minorities. Prior to the 1960s, the US was relatively homogenous, but*

*today people of the world's races and ethnicities
are streaming in. They resent being minorities
and are actively forcing their culture on us.*

He absentmindedly blew a few notes into his
harmonica as he composed.

*Over the past few years, a church in Chantilly
has begun importing refugees from the war
in Zimbabwe. These people are blacker than
midnight and have no interest in adapting to our
culture. While there are only a few here, their
cultural needs will be easily handled. But when
they procreate and overwhelm the existing society, there will be no ability to force conformity
with the current society. In the name of "political
correctness" they will annihilate us. As chari-
table as this might seem today, the future will
bring strife and mayhem. I don't want to live in
New Zimbabwe, do you?*

*Blacks have never assimilated into American
life. It's all about shucking and jivving, hooting
and hollering. The teenage boys wear their
pants around the cracks in their asses and the
girls copulate with anything that has a dick.*

*What's with all the signs that have Spanish
in addition to English? This isn't Tijuana. The
cost to our local governments to bring a Babel
of languages to every new sign is inestimable.
Anyone who wants to live in America should
speak English!*

*It's time to shut down the borders. Illegal immi-
grants are giving birth to babies in this country
who are automatically American citizens. That's
got to stop! Employers who hire illegal immigrants should be fined, increasingly until they
stop. It's time to end Affirmative Action and
bilingual programs. The deluge of foreigners will
turn you into a minority in your own country. Are
you ready for that? Se habla espanol?*

+ + + +

April 24

Per his usual weekend routine, Wayne drove the Hummer to the dry-cleaners to exchange suits. He stopped at the Exxon station for his weekly fill-up, which came to $88. He bought a carton of Marlboros, cursing the price he paid for them, laden with goddamn sin taxes.

His final stop was the shooting range. He was constantly worried about maintaining his skills. Since he witnessed a drive-by shooting in DC when he was in his teens, he vowed to never be without his gun or the wherewithal to use it. Everyone he saw on the street or in an adjacent car at the stoplight was a potential adversary. He had a concealed weapons permit and kept a SigSauer P220 "Talon" under his dashboard. The sales guy at the gun shop, heavy bars on the windows, said it was likely fatal with one or two bullets. "Hit him before he hits you," the salesman had told him. Wayne always carried a Taurus .38 special either on a holster on his belt or on a shoulder-strap holster.

Back home, he logged in as QUARRELLER on his rant website and keyboarded a tirade against the government lawyers who wanted to disarm citizens.

> *Stock up, my fellow Americans! The President's new appointee to the Supreme Court is a wretched gun-hater. He believes, and his prior judgments amply show, that the Second Amendment means nothing. Gun control is coming to America. First, registration will be mandatory. Any gun not registered will be confiscated. This slippery slope leads to an*

imposition of martial law, and with it a weapons ban. All privately owned firearms will be surrendered to "protect" the public. Private citizens will have no way to defend themselves. It's coming! Pinko groups like the Brady Center are overwhelming our elected officials.

When only the criminals and the government have guns, liberty in America is over. Personal defense is your only defense.

Guns are used in many violent crimes every day, but the crimes are already illegal. Making the guns illegal only disarms the potential victim. Wake up, people! Now is the time to stock up on guns and ammo. They're coming!

+ + + +

May 7

Two weeks later, Wayne and Cynthia met again, this time traveling separately to Alexandria. They met at Vandenberg's Bookstore on Duke Street. Cynthia was thumbing through a Kristin Hannah romance novel when he spotted her, wearing a pink and white dress. She purchased the book and he bought a copy of *Motorcycle Cruiser* Magazine. They walked together to Katie's place. After they'd had sex, they walked to the coffee shop, *The Beanery* on South Washington. She said, "Last time we met, you started to tell me about yourself."

"Not much more to tell. I sell cars to fleet buyers. That means I sell to anyone who buys more than one car at a time. It's a cutthroat job. I got a good order last week for eight cars from Memorial Hospital. I've known the buyer since high school. We played together on the football team. The only way I could get the order was if I gave him $100 kickback for each car out of my commission. I hate this sort of thing, but that's the way business is done these days.

"Dad was one of the last soldiers to die in Viet Nam while mom was pregnant with me, so I never met him. He was infantry. Fell into a booby trap where his leg was sliced by a bamboo spear with feces smeared all over it. He died a few days later from infection. He left for war one day and came home in a flag-draped coffin. Mom has a photo of her standing with my brother by Dad's coffin. She was large with pregnancy. He was an only child, so I have no relatives on his side. Mom remarried and lives in Boston. Her husband is a self-righteous ass. They seem to spend a lot of time overseas, in Third World countries.

"My older brother was killed in a freak accident when I was nineteen. We were driving in a VW Beetle on I-66 when the engine died. We coasted to the shoulder, and he and I were having a look under the hood when a carload of Spics crashed into us and then drove off. My arm was broken but my brother was killed. The driver of the other car was never found."

"That's horrible! I'm so sorry."

"It was a real wake-up call for me, knowing that somebody could kill somebody else and never be punished for it. When something like this happens, you never get over the bitterness."

"What did you do?"

"There was nothing to do. Somebody in a passing car stopped to help and eventually rescue crews arrived, but my brother was dead already. Ever since then, I've driven bigger, more reliable cars and I never go anywhere unarmed."

"Do you have other family?"

"Mom's family had some uncles and cousins. One cousin lives in London, another in Hawaii, but I have no idea what they're doing. We got a

Christmas card from the one in London a few years ago, but that's about it. I tried looking up the other when we were in Hawaii on vacation five years ago, but he just couldn't seem to find time to see us. Mom has an uncle somewhere in West Virginia she was once close to, but he must be a hundred by now. He's an old professor; supposedly he was once a brilliant guy. I saw him last when mom remarried, 20 years ago. I doubt I'd even recognize him any more.

"My wife's mom is still alive, but just barely. My wife's visits with her in New York are what allow me to see you without risk of being caught." He looked into her enticing eyes and realized he didn't know much about her. "How about you?"

Cynthia said, "You know I sell commercial real estate. As I told you, my husband works overseas. No kids. I have a large family in Texas where I was born and California. I'm one of five children but I'm the only one who lives east of the Mississippi. My husband and I moved here when he got a job with a security contractor after Desert Storm. I have lots of girlfriends that I go to restaurants and shopping with. I'm a pretty talkative person. But I think it's best if you and I communicate in other ways."

"Works for me!" he grinned. "Let's head back to Katie's place for a nightcap, shall we?"

+ + + +

May 26

Chocolate. Iniquity's bed. Beach sex and martinis. Chocolate, luscious Cynthia. Harems of nuns and elite, honey elite. Bikinis, honey thighs reduction. Soaring sand sex. Erotica's fingers. Sweet

reduction deep fudge indulgence.
Cross medation CyN this.

Wayne, wake up!" yelled Donna. "You already hit the snooze button twice. It's your day to take the kids to school and they'll be late if you don't get out of bed!"

It was two-and-a-half-weeks later, a Wednesday. Wayne shook with anxiety, fearful Donna may somehow have read his dreams. He wiped tear crumbs from the corners of his eyes and convinced himself that his dreams had remained his alone; he marched into the bathroom for his morning testimonials.

An hour later, he dropped off Willa at school. He was revolted by all the brown, black, and slanty-eyed children streaming into the building. America was becoming chokingly polyglot. What happened to the Arian purity that built our nation?

Later that day, somebody in an old Chrysler scraped against his Hummer on an exit ramp on I-66 near Fairfax. It left a long, white strip of paint and a sizeable indentation on the right side of his car. The driver stopped for a second, then sped ahead and Wayne wasn't able to read his license plate. There was a bumper sticker with a flag with green and red, from some country he didn't recognize.

When he got home, Wayne left a message for his old UVA chum, Arnie Heckleman at Allstate to report the accident. Then Wayne settled down with a stiff gin-and-tonic and his keyboard, contributing another post to *www.redhawk.com*.

> *The loathsome chimps are everywhere. The Asians can't drive. The Mexicans can't think, much less drive. The Middle-Eastern hash-smoking cabbies are repugnant. Who gave*

*everyone in America – hell, everyone in the
world, the right to produce more writhing
leechettes than they can afford? Who gave the
right to illegal aliens to proclaim their blither-
ing babies American citizens just because they
were born inside our borders, even if their parents are here illegally?
Why are drooling grandmothers hogging the left
lane???? Why doesn't Suzie hang up the phone
and put away her make-up when she drives?
What is going on on our highways?*

+ + + +

May 28

That weekend, Donna and the kids were home.
They got a babysitter on Friday night and went to
Olive Garden for dinner. Donna said as he spooned
some soup into his mouth, "You've been awfully
quiet lately."

He immediately thought she may have found
out his affair. He swallowed hard, shuttered and
stammered, "Work has been on my mind. Wilson
got all the sales people together on Monday and
said our numbers were down. My numbers are not
the best and not the worst. I think I'll be okay. You
know how tough it's been this year."

Wayne looked up from his plate. She was giving
him a hard, disapproving look. Could she read his
thoughts? A waitress dropped a full tray of food
near them. Wayne snickered and Donna scowled
at him. She wrapped her fork with pasta and said,
"Don't forget Eddie's soccer game tomorrow. You
said you'd take him. Willa and I are going to the
new *Harry Potter*."

That night, he and Donna made love, but it
seemed perfunctory to him. She didn't climax;

she didn't even seem aroused. Did she enjoy herself? He felt no hint of sexual excitement from her. When he closed his eyes, even being with Donna, he envisioned Cynthia. Why was sex so much more dynamic and urgent with Cynthia?

+ + + +

May 30

On a warm late May Sunday, Wayne played golf with Martin Kneeland, a friend from UVA. Martin had finished his law degree and worked for the Feds in the Labor Department downtown. Martin and his wife, Cheryl, lived near Wayne and had two boys. The elder son was Eddie's age and they were friends.

Martin had known Donna at UVA, too. Still, Wayne decided to confide in him. As Martin lined up an 8-foot putt on the 15th hole, Wayne said, "I've been seeing someone." As the words left his mouth, he was unsure why he'd chosen to confide in this friend his illicit couplings.

Chit, chit, chit, chit, chit, tttzzzzzzzzz. Chit, chit, chit, chit, chit, tttzzzzzzzzz. Drops of water from a nearby sprinkler borne on the wind dampened Wayne's shirt.

Martin looked up from his golf ball on the green and processed what Wayne had said. "Seeing someone? What do you mean? Are you having an affair?"

"Well, yes, I suppose I am. I met this woman several weeks ago and we've been seeing each other. Actually, we've seen quite a lot of each other," Wayne chuckled. He watched two small does wander from the woods to graze on grass by the fairway. He raised his iron and pointed it towards them as if aiming a gun. "Pow! Pow!" He bounced back in mock recoil.

Martin said, "I seem to remember you tried that type of behavior several years ago, with unhappy results. Weren't you sleeping with one of Donna's girlfriends? If you're sleeping around again, Donna will be livid!"

"She'll never find out. And if she does, she'll get over it," Wayne said, with all the conviction he could muster.

"Listen to what you're saying. You know you don't believe it yourself."

"She seems to have no interest in sex." Wayne protested. "She'd probably be happy someone else is satisfying me so she doesn't have to worry about it."

"Bullshit. You're treading on thin ice over a pond filled with piranhas, my friend."

"Remember Jason from UVA? I ran into him at the cleaners last week. We chatted in the parking lot for a few minutes and he was bragging about how many women he has had. He talks like he has more mistresses than Tiger Woods. What's the big deal? Why does he deserve more than me?"

Martin re-focused on his putt. He hit the ball which badly missed the hole, rolling to a stop 4 feet beyond. "Shit! Damn you! My concentration's gone to hell.

"So, what's she like?"

"Dark. Sexy... Great."

Martin shook his head. "Dammit, Wayne. How would you feel if Donna was sleeping around?"

"Good question. She doesn't have it in her, though."

+ + + +

Sitting in his bed at midnight, Wayne opened his laptop and lit a Marlboro. He logged onto *www.*

redhawk.com and began to rant.

Who saw the goddamn Redskins play the Cowboys Sunday? Pitiful! I long ago shut off the ceaseless, inane chatter from the mindless commentators, but the on-field antics are deplorable. Even when the Redskins were behind by 24 points, their jungle bunnies jumped for ecstatic joy whenever they made a rare good play. Their cornerback looked like he was going to fracture a rib as hard as he was beating his chest and flexing his muscles, whooping a war dance and glowering over the wide receiver he'd just sent into a concussive state. Looked like a fucking gorilla.

Blacks totally dominate football these days – basketball, too – and have turned the game into a glorified war dance. Are they taking the name Redskins a bit too seriously? Next thing you know they'll be taking scalps. May we please have some dignity and honor again in sports? These overpaid Sambos should all go back to Africa and do their celebratory bodily gyrations when they fell an elephant.

+ + + +

August 13

Late on a Friday night in mid-August, he returned home from an assignation with Cynthia to find a voice message from his mom, asking him to return her call. It was after midnight and he wondered if his mother knew Donna was out of town and sensed his misbehavior. Mothers somehow knew things.

He called her back the next morning. As they exchanged pleasantries, he feared his guilt echoed in his voice, but was pleased she seemed not to notice. She said, "Wayne, my uncle, Phil, in West

Virginia, is 94 years old. He's sold the mansion. He'll be moving into a nursing home sometime soon. The new owner doesn't want the furniture so Phil's got some things to give away. He wasn't sure when the new owner would be moving in. You're about the only family around, so I told him I'd ask you. He's probably got some nice things, some antiques. If you and Donna want any of his things, you'll have to go and see him. I have no idea what condition things are in."

"Thanks, Mom. We don't need anything but I'll keep it in mind."

+ + + +

August 27

By late August, three-and-a-half months had gone by since Wayne's first taste of Cynthia's forbidden fruits at the hotel in Baltimore. They had repeated their trysts every other Friday since April, except once in late July when Eddie was sick and Donna had to cancel her trip to New York.

Wayne shook off his flashback of a summer of licentiousness and deceit as Cynthia smiled at him. He thought of the lovemaking they'd done before his impromptu nap and breathed deeply again of her redolence. He took another look at her curvaceous backside and the rose tattoo and said under his breath, "This is too, too sweet."

She smiled a smile of sadness and resignation, and said, "I have something to tell you. Let's get dressed."

They took a walk to *The Beanery*. The night was steamy hot and moths danced around the streetlights. Lightning crackled from heavy, grey clouds over the Potomac River. He lit a Marlboro and took a few drags. Arriving at the coffee shop, he threw his burning cigarette into the street. They took a seat at a secluded booth near the front window where chilled air blew onto his legs from a floor vent. His right hand rested on the table. She started playing with the loose skin on the back of his hand. She said, "It's really been great what we've had together these few months. So it breaks my heart to say this. Tonight is the end for us. I won't be able to see you again. Ever."

He looked at her, disconsolate, wondering what he'd done wrong. "I..."

"Shhh. Please don't talk. My husband is coming back next week, on Thursday. His company, Xe, is bringing him back stateside, giving him a new job at the downtown office. They're a military defense contractor. He's been with them since he left the Marines after Desert Storm. He's the kind of guy who really shouldn't find out what we've been doing. If we continue to meet, he'd find out somehow, I'm certain."

Wayne took a deep breath and he gulped. He wanted to hug her hard. He took her left hand, held it by his cheek. His mind drew up a list of possible retorts. "Thanks for the memories." "It was good while it lasted." "Can't we find a way to continue?" But instead he said nothing. He got up, kissed her on the forehead, and without saying anything walked outside into a driving rainstorm, with drops splattering high from the concrete sidewalk. He had brought no wrap or umbrella and quickly became soaked. He walked past a Mercedes with diplomatic plates, parked in a marked handicapped space with the right front wheel on the curb. He looked around and saw nobody walking the sidewalk. He took his keychain from his pocket and ran one of his keys along the length of the car, putting a long scratch in the paint. Then he kicked the front quarter-panel hard enough to dent it and crack his big toenail.

He sat on the Metro train, livid and dripping. Whenever he looked up, invariably people were staring at him, and he sneered back. Continuing to vent his frustration as he returned to his empty home that night, he got right on *www.redhawk. com.*

> *Why do bleeding heart liberals think criminals will obey gun laws? Why are the Congress-leeches in the pocket of every warlord and corporate maggot in the Country?*
> *And where do the Jigaboos get the money for all their unlaced $200 basketball shoes?*

He took two drags from his Marlboro, played a funeral dirge on his harmonica, then continued typing.

> *"Diversity" and mass immigration are happy smokescreens for giving our nation to indolent, blood-sucking hoards from Second and Third Worlds. Diversity only strengthens the corporate blood-suckers of consumerism. For the rest of us, it's the road to poverty and mayhem.*
> *Forget the Chevy slogans: when the real American Revolution starts, count me in!*

+ + + +

August 30

On Monday, Wayne parked the Hummer at the expansive Metro lot and took the train into the city. He was already in a choleric mood from his terminated affair when a morbidly obese ebony woman sat next to him, her five curly-headed children in tow. Her folds of pulpy flesh strained the fabric of her Washington Wizards T-shirt and draped over his leg. The littlest girl had a hundred colored beads woven into her kinky hair. Wayne grumbled under his breath about the insane fecundity of Niggers. Who was going to pay for these kids when they became unwed mothers, starting their own indigent, fatherless homes? The woman berated her children from the moment she sat down. The children pestered each other mercilessly.

He was relieved to be exiting only two stops later at the Archives/Navy Memorial Station. He walked six blocks to his office on Eighth Avenue and could feel beads of sweat drip from his armpits by the time he arrived. He went straight to his cubicle without talking to anyone. He caught up with his email communications and made some phone calls. After their regular 2 p.m. sales meeting, Wilson, his boss, said, "Come to my office, Wayne."

Wayne wondered nervously what Wilson had on his mind. Private meetings following group meetings often portended strife. Sure, he'd had a couple of bad months. But there were several deals pending. He just needed to close a couple more sales. He burst into Wilson's office, yakking, "Boss, I think I'm just a couple of days from closing the Rez-Tech order."

"Sit down," Wilson ordered. The veins in Wilson's ruddy cheeks dilated, turning the skin a crimson color. His white shirt had a coffee stain on it and his tie was frayed and crooked. Wayne had always thought Wilson's complexion was particularly unappealing.

Wayne sat. He clenched his jaw. "I'm sure..."

"Shut up, Wayne." Wilson stared out the window and continued. "As you know, sales have been down in recent months. Corporate says we have to ax two salespeople. We're laying off Addison today because his numbers are the weakest. I don't think he'll ever really get it. I was having a difficult decision as to who else would be cut until Teri showed me the invoice for your corporate Master-

Card. It seems that you've been stocking up on a few household items on our dime. The $400 gas grill you bought at Home Depot jumped out like a red strobe-light. That made the decision easy. What were you thinking?"

Wilson was silent for a moment. Wayne couldn't tell if the question was meant rhetorically or if Wilson was waiting for an answer, which he didn't have.

"If I weren't firing you now, corporate would fire you and me both by the end of the week."

Goddamn, Wayne muttered under his breath. He wondered how many MasterCard invoices they'd looked over and if they were planning to come after him for months of unauthorized purchases. "Listen, Wilson," he protested.

Wilson interrupted, "You've got an hour to pack up your personal items from your desk. There's a cardboard box for you," pointing to a corner. "Personnel reminded me that by policy, I'm not to let you out of my sight until you leave the building. And I need your key and your corporate charge card right now. Don't make me call Security."

The room was quiet.

"Your key, Wayne. Do us both a favor and get out of here without saying another word. If you've been wrongly accused you can take it up with our corporate lawyer. But you and I both know you haven't been wrongly accused. The laptop computer is yours but we'll need to erase all your work related files. Let's get this done," said Wilson. "This is no easier for me than for you."

As the men marched out of Wilson's office towards Wayne's cubicle, Wilson's secretary and one of the other salesmen looked at Wayne sympathetically. Wayne removed the framed sales awards off the fabric walls and placed them in the box under Wilson's watchful eye. Wayne packed the photos of

Donna and the kids. Timmy, the company propeller-head, sat nearby with Wayne's laptop, erasing all company files. Wilson then escorted Wayne to the front door. Wilson held out his hand in a cordial farewell, but Wayne, laden with his large box, looked at him and said, "Go to hell, Wilson."

"Don't blame me for your dishonesty. You can go to hell alone."

Wayne walked to the Metro station and took the train back to the Vienna station. Other people stared at him on the train, but an unspoken rule on Metro was that practically nobody talked to anybody.

It rained heavily while Wayne was en-route. When he emerged at Vienna the parking lot was steaming. Rather than cooling things off, the rain had turned a hot August day into a sauna. He sweated profusely as he walked the hundred yards to where he'd parked the Hummer.

Fuck! The Hummer was gone. He dropped the box from chest level, cracking the glass on the framed photos and his ceramic Redskins coffee mug. Where the hell is the car? "Fucking shit! Goddamn fucking shit!" he screamed.

He grabbed his cell phone and dialed 9-1-1. He told the dispatcher that his car had been stolen, and within a few minutes, a cop was there to investigate. An hour had passed before he was on his way home in a cab. On the way he dialed Arnie Heckleman at Allstate. "Arnie, I have a bigger problem," Wayne said, and explained the situation. Arnie said he'd prepare the paperwork and call back the next day.

After he paid the cabbie, a dark-skinned man with a turban whom he couldn't understand, Wayne emerged from the cab and beheld his yard. A bedroom window was open on the second floor and his clothes were strewn across the shrubbery.

His black Harley Davidson V-Rod Muscle was on its side lying against a forsythia bush beside the driveway. The garage door was open but Donna's minivan was nowhere to be seen. He dropped the box hard enough to shatter more glass and ran to the garage. What the hell?

His heavy tool case was still there, but the golf clubs were gone, as was his Trek bicycle. He went to the front door, but it was locked and his key didn't work. He called Donna on the cell phone. As it rang, it occurred to him that she'd done this damage, and thought himself an idiot for taking so long to realize it. She didn't answer.

He sat on the front steps of his house, seething. The Mortons, an old couple from down the street, walked by with their dachshund on a leash. They looked at Wayne. He looked back at them. The dog barked. The Mortons stopped for a moment. Mrs. Morton, who always seemed to have a vacuous expression, looked like she wanted to say something but was unable to find words. They continued walking.

He gathered the clothes from the yard and put them in a couple of boxes he found in the garage. He lowered the garage door but didn't close it fully, preventing it from locking as his key no longer worked.

He called his golfing buddy Martin Kneeland. "Martin, I have a problem. Can you drive over?"

Wayne walked over to the fallen Harley and picked it up, leaning it on its side-stand. He straightened the mirrors. He looked at the sizeable dent in the faux gas tank. The muffler was also dented and the chrome was scratched. He shook his head and gritted his teeth.

Martin arrived a few minutes later in the BMW. They picked up Wayne's belongings and Martin drove them to his house as Wayne followed on the

Harley. As they arrived in Martin's driveway, Martin said sarcastically, "I think I may have suggested that Donna wouldn't be happy."

Wayne barked, "Did you tell her, you son of a bitch?"

"Not on your life, asshole. I haven't said a word. This one's on you."

Martin's wife, Cheryl, fixed dinner while Martin pumped the air mattress in the family room downstairs for Wayne to sleep on. Cheryl barely spoke at dinner, indicative to Wayne of her displeasure either with the behavior that precipitated his expulsion or over having her Acura SUV displaced by the Harley in the garage, or both. As they cleared the plates after dessert, Martin told Wayne, "You're my friend and I'll help you as much as I can. But don't overstay your welcome. This isn't a hotel."

At 8 p.m., Wayne tried calling Donna again. This time she answered, "Hello Wayne."

"Donna, where are you?"

"I'm home. I'm not *at* home, but I'm in town. The kids and I came back to town early because I had some things to attend to at the house."

"I noticed. Donna, my Hummer was stolen today."

"Really?"

"You don't sound surprised."

"Surprised? No, I'm not. I left your spare key on the hood."

"You bitch!"

"I'm not even going to honor that with a response. I know you've been sleeping around. One of my friends from college lives in Alexandria. She called me a few weeks ago to ask when we got divorced! When I asked her what she meant, she told me she saw you with another woman walking in her neighborhood. I hired the best private investigator around. Now I know everything. You better hope to God your Ms. Menendez' husband, Carlos, never finds out what you and she have been doing. You're a bastard. I never want to see you again."

"Let's talk this over," he insisted.

"There's nothing to talk about. You've committed an unpardonable offense. Our marriage is over. I hope you burn in hell." She hung up.

He wondered if she knew he'd been fired, too.

+ + + +

August 31

The next day, Wayne set up a working desk on Martin's ping-pong table. He called around and made some appointments to look at renting an apartment. He called Arnie Heckleman at Allstate again. Heckleman said their adjusters were determining a value for the Hummer and he'd call back when he could get a check cut. Wayne told Heckleman to call him on the cell phone rather the home phone when the check was ready. Heckleman said it would take a couple of days to arrange a rental car for Wayne to use.

Remembering that his recent call with his mother regarded furniture, Wayne called her. "Hi mom, it's Wayne."

"Hello sweetie. How is everything?"

"My Hummer was stolen yesterday. I've not had a very good week. Say, mom, when we talked a couple of weeks ago, you said Uncle Phil has some furniture to give away. Donna and I have been talking it over and we'd like to have a look. What's his number?" Beyond prevaricating about Donna, he made no mention of his firing. His mother gave him Phil's number and he hung up.

He gingerly called his uncle, having no idea what to expect from such an old man. The voice on the other end of the line answered cheerfully, "Professor McGranahan here!"

"Uncle Phil, my name is Wayne Quarles and I am your great-nephew. How are you today?"

"Well," the old man said with a gladsome tone, "I got out of bed this morning."

"My mom called me a couple of weeks ago and said you have some furniture you'd like to give away."

"Yes, that's correct."

"If it's okay with you, may I come the day after tomorrow and have a look?"

"Sure. You're welcome to stay a few days if you like. If you haven't been out of the city lately, it is lovely down here this time of year. The evenings are beginning to get cool."

"Where exactly do you live?"

"Union. Union, West Virginia."

Wayne decided to ride the Harley. He didn't know how much stuff he'd be retrieving, if any. He'd see what he wanted and what would fit whatever apartment he could find. Then he would return to Union the following week in a rented truck.

+ + + +

September 1

The next day, Wayne took a look at several apartment complexes and found one that had a vacancy and a secure, covered area for the Harley. Management said he couldn't move in until the following Monday. He signed a year lease and wrote a check for the first and last months' rent.

That evening, he told Martin and Cheryl about his plans to visit his uncle in West Virginia. They appeared relieved he was moving out of their family room. He spent much of the following morning, a Wednesday, packing away in boxes the clothes Donna had defenestrated. He took his shirts and suits to the dry-cleaner in Fairfax. He rode his V-Rod to the Harley shop in Tysons Corner to have a malfunctioning turn signal relay repaired. He sat for two hours in the showroom, smoking cigarettes, reading magazines, and watching a passel of tattooed men with sleeveless T-shirts and distended bellies and women with leather vests amble by. The Harley was only a year old but had been in the shop three times for repairs. Still, he loved the bike. It was long and low; the baddest bike in the product line, and he felt superior riding it. The repair was done on warranty. He charged a pair of saddlebags on MasterCard.

Back at Martin's house, Wayne printed directions he found on MapQuest. Union was in Monroe County, in southeastern West Virginia, only a few miles from the Virginia border. 461 miles, 4-1/2 hours. He packed one change of clothes, his rain jacket, and his laptop computer in the saddlebags. By the time he left the DC metro area, it was almost 4 p.m.

He took I-66 westward, watching traffic diminish with each mile. At Strasburg, he merged onto I-81 south, hopeful the largely rural highway would have even less traffic. Instead, he found the road populated by trucks from which he seemed unable to accelerate away. At the Augusta County line, it began raining hard. He stopped to put on his rain jacket under a bridge between Harrisonburg and Staunton. He thought about waiting out the storm, but feared that meant riding on unfamiliar roads after dark. With water streaming off all the trucks, his jeans got soaking wet and water flowed into his face under his half-shell helmet.

At Lexington, he turned westward on I-64. He stopped at a Shell station at the US-11 interchange to have a smoke. The rain had stopped, but not before it had leaked into his left saddlebag, dampening his packed clothes. He hoped the laptop would survive the deluge, cursing himself for not having wrapped it in a plastic bag. He was hungry and tired, but he decided to press on without dinner, buying and wolfing down a pack of Nabs instead. Motoring towards the West Virginia border, he estimated his arrival in Union just after sunset. He thought to call Uncle Phil with a progress report but didn't want to stop. He wondered about the memory acuity of his 94-year-old great uncle, whether Phil even remembered he was coming.

Wayne ascended Allegheny Mountain and then crossed the border into West Virginia, where a colorful sign said, "Welcome to West Virginia, Wild and Wonderful." The sun, by now low in the sky, peeked between the clouds and flowing green mountains. In spite of the anxiety of the previous three days, he felt himself feeling calmer and enjoying the ride and the scenery. Following the printed directions, he took the exit at Caldwell. He thought for a moment about stopping to remove his helmet, wondering whether West Virginia was an optional-helmet state. Not being sure of West Virginia's rules and not wanting to risk any hassles during the last short leg of the journey, he continued with his helmet on.

He turned south on State Route 63. He crossed a highway bridge over Howard Creek. He was surprised the bridge had a decking of wood, which was still slippery wet from the day's rain. He wondered derisively what manner of department of transportation still maintained wooden bridge decking on its highways. His brain filled with thoughts of decrepitude and backwardness he'd envisioned about West Virginia. He crossed under the tunnel of a railroad track and began ascending the winding two-lane road.

Finding himself finally away from traffic and feeling frisky, he wicked up the throttle. He was going about 80-mph when he rounded a right-hand bend and was temporarily blinded by a bright, setting sun. When his eyes re-focused, there were three deer sprinting across the road. "Shit!" He immediately stomped his right foot on the rear brake and reached his right index and middle finger for the lever of the more powerful front brake, but his rear tire had already begun to skid. BAM! The bike slammed to the pavement with his right ankle under it. Steel-scrapes and sparks. He gasped, wincing from pain in his ankle and ribcage, pounded by the impact. He and the Harley skidded across the oncoming lane and both arched off the pavement and over an embankment.

He barreled down the rocky slope face-first. He bashed his face against the rocks, gashing his left lower lip and chin, and fracturing his mandibular bone. His chest, left thigh and hip absorbed the remainder of the impact. The bike landed beside him, bounced and cartwheeled, and then landed again. Its crankcase cracked apart and oil spilled onto the rocks. The bike chugged for another few seconds and died.

He felt before he thought again. His jaw sent searing pain into his head. He had trouble breathing with intense pain in his chest, on his left side, where he landed on his pistol in a chest holster. His right ankle, left hip and thigh hurt like hell and he peed in his pants. His body was prone. His face and chest rested hard against a rock and his left arm was pinned behind him. His face was a rictus of agony. He tried to call out but his jaw shrieked in pain. It was almost dark. A car's headlights passed above him, but it didn't stop. Pain swept over him as if he'd been slammed by a dozen baseball bats. Several more headlights came and went. Panic. Nausea. Surely someone must have seen the crash. A rescue was on its way. Surely.

He tried to think, to plan what to do, but his brain wouldn't let him. His jaw felt as if it were gripped in Vise-grip pliers. He passed out.

Thunderbolts of pain, lightning pain, electric pain. Copperhead snakes slithering, scorpions across his cheek, lying atop Cynthia; Donna and kids appear. Donna screaming, shrieking. Cynthia devilishly red, cross medallion burning. Donna a pillar of salt, ghostly white. Lightning pain. Willa yelling Daddy, daddy, daddy, daddy...

A few minutes later, maybe hours, he didn't know, he heard the most despicable sound in God's creation, a mosquito buzzing by his ear. He reflexively slapped at the side of his face, causing intense pain in his fractured jawbone. He unclipped his helmet. He rolled from his stomach to his right side, away from his sore ribs but against a sharp rock in the small of his back. He couldn't get up. His jeans were ripped, then cold and wet with rain and urine. It was pitch dark. He could see the light of a distant house. He tried to yell again, but couldn't. His stomach churned and he vomited, with his voice loud as he wretched. Some of the spew rested on his tongue, but he couldn't expel it. He shivered. His mouth ached with vomit acids. Pain shot through his jaw into his head like spears and hallucinations swept through his mind's eye.

Soaring birds, hawks. Vultures. Perching atop him, pecking his eyes. Talons gripping, face bleeding, lightning pain. Acid pain lightning pain. People and people jumping from skyscrapers, burning. Faces melting, flames smoke. Guns, swords, percussion burning stench, lightning pain. Nazi firing squads. Yelling, spewing bile, acid bile.

He awoke again, wet with rain. He tried to remember the Lord's Prayer, but couldn't. "I walk through the valley of the shadow of death," he murmured, wondering why people found comfort in such a morbid phrase.

He saw a vision of Willa and Edmond riding on a school bus, looking back for him, as it drove over a cliff. He saw himself as a boy, learning to shoot a pistol for the first time, an image of his father from an old photo wearing an army uniform, strict and unyielding with him. He felt terror, embarrassment. He envisioned a dark, emaciated woman in a monk's robe and no eyeballs peering at him.

Hours later, he awoke again to the sound of rustling leaves. He shuddered in fear of an animal nearby. He heard the sound of breathing, as if human breaths. He looked above and a quarter-moon shone overhead. He saw several birds again, big, soaring overhead in the moonlight, reflecting light on their dark wings. Headlights came towards him and he tried to move but couldn't. He was overwhelmed with pain. His thoughts drifted away again and he implored himself to stay awake and keep his eyes open. "Focus!" he beseeched himself.

Drops of water inched across his face. He shivered uncontrollably and the skin on his arms bristled with goose flesh. He had trouble moving his chest and commanded himself to keep breathing. He fell unconscious again.

Part 2

September 2

Terry Yount worked for a highway department maintenance contractor, repairing and maintaining guardrails. He approached the scene of Wayne's crash around 6:40 a.m. the following morning, Thursday. When he saw the skid-mark and scratched pavement he knew instantly a crash had occurred. He parked his truck and looked over the embankment. He first saw the Harley, then the immobile body. Then he saw three deer, a doe and two fawns, nestled in the grass not fifteen feet from the victim. To him, it looked as if the deer were protecting the fallen man. He radioed his office dispatcher with the walkie-talkie. "Call rescue. There's an injured or dead man here," and he gave his location.

As he scampered down the embankment the deer fled. He reached the victim. He held his hand in front of the victim's nose and felt breathing. He shook Wayne gently by the shoulder. "Are you okay?"

Wayne opened his eyes. They were glazed, out of focus. Wayne roused, tried to think, to speak and say, "Help!" but his jaw screamed in pain. All Yount heard was a weak moan.

"Just rest. Help is on the way," Yount said, praying personnel would arrive before the man died. He removed Wayne's pistol from the holster and put it aside. He took off his coveralls and covered Wayne, not wanting to risk moving him. "What's your name, man?" he said, trying to keep Wayne conscious. Wayne said nothing back.

In 23 minutes, a team of three from White Sulphur Springs Emergency Medical Services arrived on the scene. Two others of Yount's maintenance crew arrived as well. The fire truck and wrecker were yet to arrive. One woman reached for Wayne's right arm and slipped a blood pressure cuff over it. "Can you hear me?"

Wayne tried to speak but winced in pain. He nodded. Strangers were flitting all around him. He had no idea where he was, but convinced himself he wasn't in hell. At least not yet.

The man slipped an oxygen mask over Wayne's face. Another woman jabbed his arm with an IV drip. "Don't move." The man slipped a brace on Wayne's neck. With a pair of scissors, he cut off Wayne's jean jacket. He removed Wayne's gun and cut the leather straps and removed his shoulder holster. He slit Wayne's blue T-shirt with the earth logo and the words 'Pave the earth' and looked at two significant hematomas, one on Wayne's shoulder and the other on his chest underneath where the holster was. He placed a backboard behind Wayne and lifted the sharp rock away from Wayne's back. "We're going to lay you on this board."

As a fire truck and a police car came into view, all three from the rescue squad, plus Yount and two more road workers, held Wayne's left side and slid him back onto the board, Velcroing the spider straps and righting the board to horizontal. Wayne yelled in pain with the pressure on his hip. A policeman and three firemen helped the six already there to lift his 208-pound bulk back up the embankment into the ambulance.

Yount had the presence of mind to put Wayne's saddlebags and pistol in the ambulance. He found Wayne's wallet in the poison oak patch nearby and put on his glove to retrieve it. He found a harmonica lying in the rocks. He gave everything to rescue squadsman Chris Witherspoon.

They were on the scene for 35 minutes before departure to the Greenbrier Valley Medical Center near the West Virginia State Fairground in Fairlea. A mile from the scene of the crash, Witherspoon radioed emergency room doctor Renu Ramkija.

"Doctor Ram, we have a multiple trauma victim from a motorcycle accident. White male, guessing 30 to 40 years old, 200 pounds. Accident must have happened last evening sometime. He's semi-conscious. Low blood pressure: 60 systolic and no discernable diastolic when we arrived. Heart rate 120. Responsive now to verbal stimuli and to pain, which he has plenty of! Trauma to face. Swollen around left eye. Deep laceration on left cheek. Crepitus to the left ribs. Significant ecchymosis in the area. Decreased breath on the left side. Left thigh deformity, probably broken pelvis or femur or both. Open fracture of the right ankle. Resuscitated with two IVs. Blood pressure 90-over-60 now, heart rate down to 100. Fully packaged. ETA, fifteen minutes."

Ramkija and her team were waiting when the ambulance arrived, siren wailing.

Upon Wayne's arrival, Ramkija's team got right to work, with two nurses, an X-ray tech, lab tech, and respiratory specialist swarming over him. Ramkija placed her stethoscope on his chest and listened, hearing an absense of breath sounds over his left lung. One nurse placed a new IV in his right arm. The other nurse removed the blood pressure cuff he'd worn during the ambulance ride and placed another on his left arm.

Ramkija, a tiny, dark woman in her eighth year at Lewisburg, said to Witherspoon in an accented voice, "Do we know his name?"

"Yes, Wayne Quarles. The maintenance worker who found him looked through his belongings while he waited for the rescue squad to arrive."

She said to Wayne, "Wayne, do you hear me?" He nodded. "We're going to give you a good looking over and see what you've done to yourself."

The X-ray tech took a large film and placed it in a tray under the backboard. He positioned the X-ray machine above his neck and head and took that shot. He repeated this for his chest and abdominal area. He took additional shots of his pelvis, upper legs, and right ankle.

As he left to develop the film, Ramkija said, "I think you have punctured a lung. As soon as we see these X-rays, if I'm right, we'll need to re-inflate your lung."

Wayne's eyelids collapsed and he hallucinated.

Firing range. Wilson shooting. Other guys shooting. Wilson shooting. Wayne at targets, Wilson shooting him, laughing. Blood spurting, bullet holes. Everybody shooting Wayne, laughing, laughing.

Four minutes later, the X-ray tech returned and said, "He has a white-out on the left side over the lung, under two broken ribs. Massive pneumothorax. He also has a broken jaw on the left, a subtrochanteric fracture of the femur, and an unstable trimalleolar fracture of his right ankle."

"Wayne, wake up," said Ramkija gently, nudging him on his right shoulder. "I was right. I'll need to stick you." Ramkija took out a hypodermic and shot Wayne multiple times beneath his rib-cage on the left side. "I'm shooting you with Lidocaine to numb the skin." It hurt like hornet stings from hell. Without telling him what was next, she shoved a sharpened chest tube the diameter of a kindergartener's pencil between two unbroken ribs into his chest cavity, using all the force her small body could muster. The pain he'd endured overnight was excruciating, but this was an order of magnitude worse than any pain he'd ever felt, like the burn of an immense waffle iron. He wanted to scream, but couldn't. Through his pain, he heard a sucking noise emanating from the tube. Blood and air squirted through it.

The medical team let him rest for a few minutes. When Ramkija returned she said, "Wayne, you're stable now. Your hip and ankle are broken and we've got to fix them. Our orthopedic surgeon, Dr. Meier, is on his way back from Beckley. When he arrives, we'll prep you for surgery. Your jaw is also broken. We're going to strap it shut."

Five hours later Wayne was in surgery. First, Dr. Meier placed a hollow cylinder into Wayne's shattered tibia and screwed it into the bone surrounding it. Afterwards, maxillofacial surgeon Dr. Keith Pearsall worked on Wayne's jaw. Pearsall joined together the mandibular bone fragments with screws and a titanium plate, wired his jaws together with dental braces and sutured the jagged laceration that extended from his lip to under his jaw. Ominously, Pearsall was unable to find or repair the remnants of the facial motor nerve that passes through the lacerated region.

+ + + +

The previous midnight, Philip McGranahan had awoken where he'd fallen asleep in his living room chair. He got up groggily and went to his bedroom where he put on his pajamas. He brushed his teeth and went upstairs to bed, using the motorized ascender which he only used when he was sick or tired. He gave no thought to his missing great-nephew.

By the time the ambulance containing the broken body of Wayne Derek Quarles screeched to a stop at the emergency room, Phil was brushing his teeth and combing his thin hair. Phil McGranahan was uncommonly lucid for a nonagenarian. He dressed, then walked downstairs into the kitchen and fixed some toast and coffee for breakfast. While eating, he remembered that Wayne had said he was coming the evening before.

Phil looked throughout the house, thinking Wayne may have arrived and let himself in after he'd gone to sleep. The doors were never locked. He climbed the stairs to see if Wayne was in one of the guest bedrooms. Not finding him in the house, he rummaged through his roll-top desk looking for the snippet of paper he'd written Wayne's number on. He dialed it. He got a recorded message, saying, "You have reached the Quarles residence. Nobody is here to take your call. Please leave a message."

McGranahan said, "This is Phil McGranahan in West Virginia. If my memory serves me, Wayne was due here last night, but he's not around. I was calling to check on him. Please return my call," and he left his number.

He looked for Wayne's mom, Betsy's, phone number. But he couldn't find it. He couldn't remember Betsy's remarried name. As he sipped his coffee and pondered his next step, his phone rang. "Hello, this is Phil McGranahan."

"Mr. McGranahan, this is Sheila. I'm an orderly at Greenbrier Hospital. We have a patient in our emergency room named Wayne Quarles. He has your name and phone number on a sheet of paper in his pocket. Do you know him?"

Phil identified Wayne and offered to come over. Sheila said, "Wayne is under anesthesia right now and there is no reason for you to be here. Why don't we call you when we have some news?"

"What happened to him?"

"He crashed his motorcycle near Caldwell sometime last night. We think he'll survive but he's severely injured. If you were in the immediate family, we'd ask you to come over. Why don't you stand by and we'll let you know."

At 4:30 p.m., Dr. Ramkija was into her 14th hour on the shift, when she called Phil McGranahan. She and her husband lived in an old farmhouse near Union. Her husband was an international trade consultant, and he and Phil were members of the Union Rotary Club.

"Dr. McGranahan, this is Renu Ramkija at the hospital. How are you today?"

"Well, I got out of bed this morning. I understand my nephew Wayne Quarles is your guest. What's his condition?"

"He is stable, but heavily sedated. Why don't you come over around 11 a.m. tomorrow and we can talk about him. Is he married? I'd like to call his wife."

"Yes, he's married. I left a message on his home phone but haven't heard from his wife."

"If she calls you, have her call me at 304-555-3921. If we can't reach her, we'll need someone to sign some papers regarding next of kin and payment. Ultimately we'll need to release him to someone who will be responsible for him."

"Until we can contact his wife and make arrangements to get him home, I suppose that'll be me," Phil said with resignation.

"I'll see you in the morning."

Phil called his friend Truman Hankins. Truman was 71, the retired president of First Bank in Union. Although Phil still had an old car, Truman acted as Phil's chauffer for most of Phil's trips. They were members of the Union Rotary club and Truman gave Phil a lift each week to the meeting at the Kalico Kitchen. They also typically went together each Sunday to the Monroe Methodist Church just south of Union. "What's up, Dr. Phil?" For years Truman just called him Phil but when Phil Mc-Graw made "Dr. Phil" famous on TV, he started using that moniker teasingly instead.

"I have a great-nephew from the DC area who was on his way to visit last evening. Apparently he only made it as far as Caldwell. Right now he's in the hospital in Lewisburg. Would you please give me a lift there tomorrow morning?"

+ + + +

At 5 p.m., Dr. Ramkija walked to Wayne's bedside where he had returned from orthopedic surgery. She said, "Wayne, do you know who I am?"

He shook his head, no.

"Here is a piece of paper. Please write your name on it."

Wayne Quarles

"Where do you live?"

Vienna

"Do you know where you are?" Dr. Ramkija asked.

He shook his head.

"Are you married?"

He nodded his head affirmatively. He thought for a moment, then changed his mind, writing on his sheet, No wife no home.

+ + + +

September 3

When Dr. Renu Ramkija met Professor Phil Mc-Granahan and Truman Hankins at the entrance to Wayne's room the next morning, Friday, her face was grim with resignation. "He's in bad shape, Phil. He fractured his jaw and broke two ribs. He has been bleeding internally. He broke his left hip and right ankle. Dr. Meier operated on his hip and ankle. The ankle wound was open and dirty, so we're treating him with antibiotics to prevent infection. Our maxillofacial surgeon operated on his jaw and has wired it shut.

"Many of his injuries were preventable and would have been less severe if he had been wearing a better helmet and an armored suit. This is a popular area for motorcyclists and we see too many crashes. I treated a man from Pennsylvania a month ago who told me he spent $19,000 for his motorcycle, but somehow $500 was too much for a good protective suit. He said he had always thought protective gear infringed on his freedom. I didn't see his final invoice, but I'm guessing his medical bills approached a hundred-thousand dollars. By the time we release him, Wayne's will probably be higher than that.

"Our orderly called Wayne's house in Vienna yesterday but got no answer. One of our nurses called several more times but we finally left a message. He'll survive, but he'll need constant care for awhile when he gets home."

"My intuition tells me something's wrong at his home," said McGranahan. "I have a feeling he'll be my guest. How long do you think he'll be here?"

"Seven to ten days is my guess; perhaps longer if the ankle becomes infected. When he wakes, I'll call you and you can come back and see him."

"Thank you, Doctor, for everything you're doing," said Phil McGranahan.

Dr. Ramkija escorted Phil to the hospital billing

office. The billing clerk told Phil that Wayne was carrying an insurance card in his wallet when he crashed. She learned he had recently been fired from his job but his former employer had paid the insurance premium for the month of September before they let him go and had neglected to cancel it. In a rare stroke of luck, all of the expenses associated with Wayne's accident were covered.

+ + + +

September 4

On Saturday morning around 10:30, Phil was working in his greenhouse when he got a call on the wireless phone. "Hello. Phil McGranahan here."

The woman on the line said, "I'm Donna Quarles. You left a message on my answering machine a couple of days ago."

"Donna, I don't know if Wayne has ever spoken about me, but I am his great-uncle, Betsy's father's oldest brother. Wayne was on his way here to visit with me on Thursday. He had a serious accident."

"Is he...?"

"He's still in the hospital in Lewisburg. He has multiple broken bones but is conscious but groggy. His doctor told me she'd call me today with a status report."

"Tell him..." Silence. "I don't care what you tell him. He's not part of my life any more."

"I'm not aware of any other family he has."

"I am sorry to be so insensitive, Uncle Phil. But I want nothing to do with him ever again. I would appreciate it if you would respect my privacy and not ask any more about our situation."

"Fair enough. I don't know what's gone on between you and Wayne and it's none of my business. But before you go, would you please call Wayne's mother?"

"I'll try, but I think she's gone out of the country on a mission trip with her husband. Wayne might know where they are, but I don't."

"It sounds like it will fall to me to take care of him," Phil said with acquiescence.

"Again, I'm sorry to burden you with Wayne and his problems. But I am in no emotional position to help him."

"Well, nobody goes uncared for in Union, West Virginia, family or not. Goodbye, Donna."

+ + + +

September 6

On Monday just before 2 p.m., Professor Phil McGranahan's phone rang again. Dr. Ramkija said, "Wayne is alert today. If you'd like to come by before 4 p.m., you can see him."

McGranahan phoned Mildred Webb who worked as his home health technician and asked her to come along. She had worked for him since his wife died, 25 years earlier, coming to his house every Wednesday morning. Initially, she worked solely looking after his health, taking his blood pressure, pulse and temperature. But over the years, she had, without being asked, begun doing housekeeping chores. In recent years, with each visit, she always straightened up things a bit and washed some of his clothes. She also did his grocery shopping, including fresh fruit and vegetables from the roadside markets in season. She was 59 years old, with chocolate skin and short, curly salt-and-pepper hair. Then he called Truman Hankins. Within an hour the three of them were making the 18-mile trip to Lewisburg.

McGranahan and Webb were standing inside

the door to Wayne's room when Dr. Ramkija appeared with another doctor wearing the nametag, "Dr. Allen Smart." They exchanged pleasantries. Dr. Ramkija said, "I am the emergency room doctor who worked with Wayne when he arrived. Dr. Smart is the attending physician who took over when Wayne left the emergency room. I have followed his progress because I know he's a family member of yours, Phil."

"Thank you, Dr. Ram," Phil said.

Smart said to Phil and Mildred, "You are looking at a broken man. He'll survive this, no doubt about that now. But there will be times when he'll wish he hadn't." He directed his conversation to Mildred and continued, "His broken jaw will be wired shut for several weeks. He'll need to write to you what he needs. He won't be eating any solid food for at least six weeks. He'll need to live on liquid food: high-nutrition with protein supplements. In a few weeks, we can transition him to pureed food. He broke two ribs, and had pulmonary contusions. He also broke his left upper femur and his right ankle. He has new hardware in there, but the hard cast on his hip has already been removed, partially because he was in agony over the poison oak rashes under it. He now has a soft cast. We remove it twice each day to put some salve on the rash and then we replace it again. He'll need to be on a blood thinner to prevent deep vein thrombosis. He won't be able to swallow a pill, so you'll need to administer it with a shot to his abdomen every day."

Webb shook her head knowledgeably. "Yes, sir."

Smart continued, "He'll be in a lot of pain when he moves, but you need to make sure he moves around every day regardless. Keep him motivated and keep him from becoming lethargic and despondent. If he stays in bed, he may develop pneumonia. He needs to keep his lungs clear. Watch for fever. And of course, no smoking, no matter how much he begs. The EMTs found a pack of cigarettes in his jacket so there's a good bet he'll be asking for it. He'll be doing most of his moving around by wheelchair for one or two months more while his leg and ankle heal, but as soon as he can stand crutches, get him on them."

McGranahan said, "Mrs. Webb and I have already talked about this as a possibility. I made arrangements to rent a bed. As soon as you release him, we'll have it set up in the library on the first floor at the house. So we're ready to bring him there whenever you release him."

Smart said, "I've got to make my rounds. You're welcome to stay for a few minutes and talk with him." He looked at Mildred and said, "He will need lots of care. Feed him as much as he wants as his weight has dropped already and will drop more. We'll release him when we're sure he has no infection in his ankle and when he can make his way to the bathroom on his own. He'll need to go to the rehab clinic in Union twice a week for physical therapy. And he'll need to come back here so we can analyze his blood."

Dr. Ram said, "And get him into the waters at The Old Sweet as soon as you can." Both doctors departed.

Wayne had been listening and watching this meeting with a curious detachment, as if it were about someone else besides himself. Still, in his helpless state, his trepidation level was high about what might happen to him next.

"Wayne, I'm Phil McGranahan, your uncle."

Wayne looked at his uncle, a man he had seen only briefly two decades ago. He was a short, alert man, with mottled blue eyes and a rim of white hair around the base of his head. He had unsightly skin splotches on his bald head and the back of his hands. He had bushy eyebrows, the right longer and lower than the left. He wore no eyeglasses.

"This is Mildred Webb. It looks like we're your family for awhile. We'll be back in a few days to visit again."

Wayne nodded.

+ + + +

September 10

Four days later, eight days after his crash and three days after Labor Day, Wayne Quarles was released from the hospital. He was taken by ambulance service to the home of Phil McGranahan, just north of the main business district in Union, West Virginia. Wayne emerged from the ambulance and was placed in a wheelchair. Wayne looked at the house. It was stately and venerable, with two stories. The crimson bricks and white columns reminded him of Monticello, which he had visited at his mother's insistence when they did a campus tour when he was considering enrollment at UVA. It had white painted shutters on the windows and four tall white columns holding the portico over the front entrance. There was a fan-shaped window over the veranda. There were four rectangular brick chimneys, two on each of the two sides. An out-building topped with a white, pyramidal cupola, sat behind it. It was surely over a hundred years old, he thought.

The ambulance men rolled Wayne up the wheelchair ramp Phil had had built years earlier in anticipation of his own incapacity. Phil was glad that although he was yet to need it himself, it was here for his great-nephew. Phil met them at

the door and exchanged pleasantries. They rolled
Wayne into the library. Wayne lifted himself from
the wheelchair onto the bed and made himself as
comfortable as possible. They left his saddlebags,
still containing a damp change of clothes and his
laptop computer. They placed a Ziploc plastic bag
containing his wallet, checkbook, gun (emptied of
bullets) and cigarette lighter beside the bed.

Phil said to Wayne, "Can I get you anything?"

Wayne held up his index finger, touched it to
his lips, and said, "Wah." His great uncle brought
him a glass of water and a straw.

"It looks like you're going to be here for awhile.
I suspect we won't be having a conversation about
furniture any time soon," Phil said fatefully.

Had Wayne's mouth worked, an expletive would
have emerged. He cringed at his wretched condition and wondered by what cruel fate he would be
so broken and confined to the lair of this ancient
man.

"I thought we'd spend some time getting acquainted," Phil said. "But it looks like you'll be
hearing a lot more about me than I'll be hearing
about you for awhile. By the way, I won't be moving from this house for several more months. The
new owners are overseas. They won't be moving in
until sometime next year."

It occurred to Wayne that his uncle was settling
in for a conversation that was going to be decidedly
one-sided.

"The house was built in 1845, before the Civil
War, when Monroe County was still part of Virginia.
It is called, *Serenus*, which is Latin for serenity. I
was born in this house in 1915. My mother died in
the flu epidemic of 1918. I went to school here and
graduated from Union High School in 1933. I got a
degree in biology at Marshall University, Marshall
College in those days, in Huntington. I was able

to catch the bus right at the end of our driveway, which is on US-219. I would ride to White Sulphur Springs where I would catch the train, the C&O, to Huntington. It was a beautiful trip then and it still is today.

"I always did well in school. After I got my degree, I went to Ole Miss and got a masters degree and a doctorate, in biology. My expertise was in toxicology, how living organisms deal with poisons in their environment. I did much of the research cited in Rachel Carson's *Silent Spring*, the touchstone of the environmental movement of the 1960s.

"Only a few months before I was to complete my dissertation, I was one of the older men drafted into the Army. I marched with our troops across France chasing the German retreat. I was captured with six other soldiers in Alsace-Lorraine by the enemy in the Battle of the Bulge three days after Christmas in 1944. I'm sure we would all have been executed by the end of the day. But a bomb blast that killed a dozen Germans and three of my comrades distracted the Krauts long enough for me and two others to escape. We hid in the snow in a forest for two days before British troops found us. Three of my toes were frostbitten and hurt me to this day. I never knew if any of the other guys survived the war.

"After that, I returned to Ole Miss and finished my doctorate. Then I taught at the University of Illinois in Champaign-Urbana. I worked there for my entire career until I retired at age 65, almost 30 years ago.

"I was married way back in 1940. My wife and I had two children who I suppose would be your second cousins. My wife died 25 years ago here in Union. The last I heard from her, our daughter lived in Amsterdam but we are estranged. Our son was one of the first casualties in Viet Nam, even before it was a real war. He had never married. I have no living heirs.

"How about yourself?"

Sales, Wayne wrote on the piece of paper his uncle had given him.

"Oh, sorry! I'll let you get some rest. We can talk more tomorrow."

Wayne napped for a couple of hours. When he awoke, he struggled into his wheelchair and wheeled himself into the bathroom, where he stood and urinated. On his return to bed, he took in his surroundings. He looked through his possessions and realized everything was accounted for except his bullets and his cigarettes. To his astonishment, he found every penny of the $59.72 cash he'd had when he crashed.

Phil, knowing Wayne would not be able to use an upstairs bedroom, situated him in the library on the ground floor, on the southwest corner of the house. The early afternoon sun streamed into both windows and illuminated a rug that covered the entire room to within a foot from each wall. It had a colorful floral pattern in it. The walls were made of a dark hardwood and the wainscoting and stairway railings he saw outside his doorway were intricate and appealing. It smelled musty but in a pleasant, timeless way.

Each wall in his room was lined with book-shelves. The books had titles such as,

Principles of Ecotoxicology
The Structure of Scientific Revolutions
Blind Watchers of the Sky
The Selfish Gene
The South Was Right
Guns, Germs, and Steel
The Party's Over
The Two Cultures
Global Tectonics

The Evolution of Species
The Real Lincoln
The Collapse of Complex Societies
Principles of Biochemistry
The Long Emergency

He thought about the books in his own home and in his friends' homes. He had never seen a collection of such academically strenuous works in a private library.

The ceiling had an ornate plaster fresco. A crystal chandelier hung in the center of the room. A hardwood executive desk sat across the room from his bed. On it was a large stuffed bird perched on a two-inch diameter tree branch. It had a rich brown back, a reddish brown head, and a curved grey beak. Its breast was white with brown splotches. It had a dramatic auburn-red tail. It had piercing glass eyes that gave him the shivers when he looked at them. He guessed it was a bird of prey, but he had no knowledge to identify it.

There were four portraits in the room, all with elaborate frames and individual spotlights. All appeared to be Confederate military men. Two were instantly recognizable to Wayne from his childhood interest in history and the Civil War. The one with the distinguished grey beard was General Robert E. Lee. The one with the blue-grey eyes, the full, dark beard and the receding hairline was Thomas J. "Stonewall" Jackson. The third had a long, dark goatee and an intense, disturbing stare. The last had a kindly face of freckles, blue eyes, and reddish hair. Wayne was sure at some point Phil would tell him about them.

He picked up the voluminous book, *Stonewall Jackson: The Man, the Soldier, the Legend*, and began reading it.

Other than the ticking of the great clock in the entranceway, the house was quiet, but he could hear birds singing outside and the chirping of cicadas which reminded him of the noise coming from a rattlesnake he'd once seen at a zoo.

+ + + +

After noon, Mrs. Webb came by to attend to Wayne. "How are we today? You and I didn't have much of an opportunity to get acquainted the other day at the hospital. My name is Mildred Webb. I am a home health technician. Think of me as part nurse, part maid. My husband and I live only a half-mile away in Union."

Sensing his disinterest in her, she said in a businesslike tone, "You and I need to work out a system so you can tell me what you need. I brought you this little bell that you can ring when you need me."

He held up his index finger and placed it to his lip. He wrote the word, water, on the paper. He held his index finger and his middle finger and placed both on his lip. He wrote the word, food, on the paper. He pinched his nose and wrote the word, shit, on the paper. He tried to smile at his attempt at humor, but his jaw would not move.

She looked at him with disapproval, resenting his vulgarity. "Yes, Wayne. Now I need to give you your shot."

It occurred to Wayne as the needle plunged into his gut that there was no painless way to give a shot, but somehow he had the impression she made this one hurt more than necessary.

Mildred fixed some food for him and refilled his water pitcher. She removed his soft-cast and handed him some salve to rub on his hip. Then she replaced the cast and asked him if he needed anything else. He brushed her off dismissively. She left for home.

+ + + +

That night, he slept fitfully, alternatively dreaming and lying awake. He looked at the figures in the portraits on the wall, illuminated only by the red light of a digital clock. All seemed avuncular and kindly in a detached way, except the one with the dark goatee. It was sinister. Malevolent.

Wayne imagined a forest fire, animals scurrying away, trees crashing. He trampled his way through the burning embers, which scalded his feet.

Trees like burning crosses. Burning, like crucifixions; Christ-like. The Mortons, the couple from home, Nailed to crosses. Wilson, Nailed to cross. Fire, leaping from Wilson's eyes. His body, ablaze, dropping to the ground in a burst of flames.

Wayne shook his face awake. He looked at the ominous face in the portrait. Its eyes vanished into its head. Red swastikas took their place. The face in the portrait turned to Wayne and hissed, Darth Vader-like. Wayne's jaw ached and sweat poured from his forehead.

Get a grip! he thought to himself. He wondered whether his nightmares were an unfortunate aspect of his pain medication or whether they would haunt him permanently. Was this punishment from a lifetime of transgressions? He had utterly rejected religion and the notion of a supreme being as a teenager, but he remembered the thoughts and fables of his grandmother, speaking to him as a youth. "Everything has a season and a reason." "God never gives us more pain that we can endure." His mind flooded with regret and recrimination. Was God finally punishing his malevolence or was he merely a victim of his own selfishness and stupidity?

+ + + +

September 11

The next day when Mildred arrived, she had a stack of neatly folded clothes. "How are we today? I bought you two t-shirts, two button-down shirts, two pairs of slacks, and some underwear from the second-hand store. I bought you four pairs of socks and a pair of sneakers at the Dollar General."

He sneered. He thought of the Armani shirts he'd left at the dry-cleaners in Fairfax and wondered what the proprietors did with clothing that had been seemingly abandoned. He was revolted by the thought of wearing somebody else's clothes. As Mildred placed them in a drawer in the expansive, built-in hardwood cabinet, he touched two fingers to his lips, "food."

She brought some liquid food in a paper cup which he drank through a straw. She was in the kitchen when he dropped his cup, spilling the contents, but he made no effort to clean it up, leaving it for her when she returned.

He motioned for a piece of paper, pls cover picture. He showed it to Mildred and pointed at the portrait.

"What's the problem, Wayne? Has this man gotten under your skin?" she asked mockingly, chuckling to herself. He nodded, embarrassed by showing his timidity to an inferior person, but willing to accept it. She found a bath towel and pinned it with clothespins to the picture frame.

+ + + +

September 14

For a few hours each day, Wayne was able to sit upright. Looking out the window, he noticed the onset of autumn colors, the change of the leaves on the maple tree outside. There was a grassy lawn, as long as a football field, bordered by hardwood trees to the south. At the end was a white picket fence and on the other side, a two-lane highway. Beyond the highway was another fence surrounding a pasture. On a high point in the pasture was what seemed to be a monument, a pedestal atop which was a figure of a standing man. It was too far away for Wayne to see in detail, but he thought the man held a rifle before him. Wayne wondered why a statue would be in the middle of a cow-pasture.

+ + + +

That night, illuminated only by the dim red light of a digital clock, the sinister portrait turned on him again. The clothespins were still attached to the frame, but the towel had mysteriously fallen to the floor. The face grew puffy, marked by scars and welts. Blood dripped. Wayne focused on the baleful man's eyes. The face sneered, malevolently.

Wayne fell into phantasms.

Black man — Anderson, from the gym. Naked, endowed. Angry white men. Bats. Blood. Anderson beaten and whipped.

Nooses from Trees. Anderson. Napalm. Napalm rain. Mildred — Noose, Blood and bats. Rats. Naked emaciated women — brick ovens and smoke. Screaming. Rats. Vultures. Willa and Eddie crossing street hit by car, mashed. Black kids laughing. Mildred noose, crying. Wayne Noose, eyes popping.

The grandfather clock in the hallway struck the Westminster chime. Wayne gasped awake, choking on his own spittle. His ribs and jaw cried with pain. He cursed his pain medications, cursed his pain, and cursed himself.

+ + + +

September 15

The next day, 14 days after Wayne's accident, Truman stopped by for a visit, graciously thinking Wayne might like to see another face besides Phil's and Mildred's. Truman wheeled Wayne outside where they sat with Phil for an hour on the painted wood plank front porch. An intricately carved sign tacked to the house said, *Serenus*, with the word in an ornate script font. Several hummingbirds darted to and fro, sometimes hovering at the three pink feeders hanging from the porch ceiling. Goldfinches and a little grey bird he couldn't identify stopped to get sunflower seeds at a feeder in the yard. Crows cawed from the trees. Squirrels ran across the yard, often stopping and standing humanlike on their hind feet.

Wayne turned to Phil and pointed at the monument across the street and wrote on his pad of paper, "statue?"

Phil said, "That is a monument to the Confederate soldiers of Monroe County. The image at the top of that statue is my great grandfather, Andrew Jackson McGranahan. Andy. I suppose he would be your great-great-great-great-grandfather. Would you like to hear his story?"

His interest in history reviving and his boredom increasing, Wayne nodded.

"Normally I tell people the short version. But since you aren't going anywhere, I'll give you the long version. Much of this was told to me by my grandfather, Robert Craig McGranahan, who I must say was prone to embellishing his stories. The rest is from Andy's memoirs. You'll have to forgive me, as I suppose I am prone to embellishment, too. This will take several sittings, I'm sure."

Truman said, "I'm not sure I've heard the story myself. Mind if I stay and listen?"

"Not at all. But let's go into the living room. I'm getting chilled."

"I'll make some tea," Truman offered.

+ + + +

Moments later, the three men gathered in the library, near Wayne's bed. Phil sat in his favorite chair, an ornate upholstered high-back chair with carved armrests. Truman sat on the sofa. Wayne moved from his wheelchair to the other end of the sofa. Truman poured a cup of tea for Phil, then himself.

Phil began his story, speaking gently, almost at a whisper. "Andy's heritage began on the windswept and soggy grasslands of the Isle of Skye off the West Coast of Scotland, where in the spring of 1777, his great-grandfather, James Bruce Mc-

Granahan at the age of 19 married Annie Hazel McCoy, aged 14.

"James lived in the croft of Boreraig on the shore of Loch Dunvegan. Like most in the village of 45 people, James was illiterate, but had a talent for music and mastered the fiddle by age eleven. On a trip to nearby Dunvegan at the mouth of the Loch to trade pelts and fish in November, 1776, he met Annie who was laboring in the kitchen of the sole guest house. He returned in February, braving a fierce, frigid winter storm to Dunvegan to marry her.

"Their first child, Mary Margaret McGranahan, was born with the backdrop of a double rainbow in March, 1778. Annie squatted on the dirt floor of their thatch-roofed, stone hut, and the baby was caught by the village midwife. In January, 1780, their second child, Ian Robert arrived as a rare, beautiful snowfall blanketed the fields.

"James had heard rumors as visitors from other crofts told of evictions by absentee landlords. One afternoon in October, 1781, as he walked the soggy fields above the village, he spotted black smoke rising from the direction of the village. He crested the rise and saw flames leaping from the roofs of most of the homes. He sprinted back and watched in horror as seven armed sheriffs, employees of the landlord he'd never seen, set fire to the remaining structures, mounted their horses, and galloped away.

"James found Annie kneeling on the ground, wailing, with her child and infant in her arms. Behind, their home was ablaze and their cow and all their chickens were knifed to death. Screams from neighboring women and children filled the air and blood ran in rivulets into the village stream. Two men, eight women, and six children had been murdered along with every kept animal. A frigid wind blew from the dark northwest ocean and a storm of immense proportions developed. Rain fell in torrents, but too late to extinguish the fires before they'd done their dastardly damage.

"James and Annie were soon soaked to the skin. They attempted to prop the burnt remnants of their kitchen table above them and their children as they lay in a corner of their roofless cottage. The temperature dropped steadily through the night and ice formed on the scorched timbers."

The clock in the hallway chimed the hour. Phil took a sip from his tea and continued.

"By morning, toddler Meggie and infant Ian were dead from exposure. A mounted representative of the landlord arrived, barking eviction orders.

"By noon, the 36 surviving villagers marched beyond sight of the wrecked village, which none of them would ever see again. Walking to the south, they came in sight of the mighty Cuillin Hills to the west. They joined with 140 other crofters who had also been evicted from neighboring villages the night before. Annie was re-united with her sister Kate, only 12. Kate told Annie that their parents and two brothers had died the day before. They shared what little food they carried. They were grateful to find shelter in a barn and slept on the floor amidst excrement and livestock.

"The next day, the group plodded to the east side of the island to the steep, rugged boat landing at Kylerhea, facing Gleneig Bay, the narrowest strait separating Skye from the Scottish mainland. There, a small craft capable of carrying ten people, two rowers and eight passengers, began the laborious, three-day process of ferrying 140 people across, forty minutes or so per round trip, depending upon the strength of the tidal currents and wind.

"Once on the Scottish mainland, the group was

informed that no land was available for them anywhere within the Highlands, and they would need
to migrate south. They hastily picked three leaders and began walking southward. They passed
Fort William, then Glencoe, Crianlarigh, and Loch
Lomond. They foraged for food and relied on the
kindness of strangers but were generally famished. They finally arrived at the teeming city of
Glasgow.

"Thousands of Highlanders were flooding the
city, victims of the evictions which came to be called
the Highland Clearances. Because there were so
many illiterate, penniless newcomers, there were
no options for work or lodging. The McGranahans,
along with three other families from Skye, continued southward to the city of Ayr on the Firth of
Clyde.

"Efforts to begin their lives anew were fraught
with anguish. James worked at the dock and made
extra money in boxing matches, but was defeated
as often as not, and routinely came home drunk,
battered, and demoralized. A pregnancy in 1784
produced a stillborn boy.

"One evening, James told Annie that he had
spoken with a sailor who spoke of new opportunities and the chance for land ownership in Ulster,
the northernmost county of Ireland. Within weeks,
they booked passage on one of Mr. Kennedy's
ships, paying for their fares by working for Mr.
Kennedy beforehand and during the voyage. They
passed by Magilligan Point and entered the Lough
Foyle. They landed in Derry in June, 1787, and
began the 60-mile walk southward to the village
of Enniskillen where James had heard of employ-
ment opportunities in the blacksmith shops on the
shore of Lower Lough Erne.

"Ireland was more verdant than Scotland and
the McGranahans, with their new outlook, made

friends and assimilated into the community. Thomas Robert McGranahan, their youngest child was born in 1790. Life attained a peacefulness and contentment not known since before their eviction from Skye.

"In 1810, Thomas, now a tall, blue-eyed man, married Katherine Elaine Lindsay of nearby Ballinamallard, also from a Highland refugee family. Thomas did not follow his father into metalwork, but became a dairy farmhand. The couple moved to Ballinamallard and Thomas joined his father-in-law in farming.

"Their first child, Heather Marie McGranahan, was born in 1812, but she was slow and didn't utter her first word until she was three years old. Their second child, Katie Maxine, was born in 1815. They barely survived the year 1816, when the summer never turned warm and the crops failed. Their third child, Thomas Robert Jr. was born in 1817.

"By 1821, with their children aged 9, 6, and 4, Thomas and Katherine yearned for their own land, but the population of Ulster had overrun the ability of the land to provide for all. One of Katherine's brothers, Mick, was a seaman. He returned from America and told them of rich agricultural land in a new state called Ohio. Within weeks, they said goodbye to their parents, whom they expected they would never see again, and booked passage on a wagon which carried them north to Derry along the same road his parents had traveled 34 years earlier.

"Their ship, carrying 60 passengers and 12 crew including Mick, left the docks of Derry on October 2, 1821, destined for Philadelphia. But tragedy struck only three days later when Thomas became sick with fever and nausea. A storm rocked the boat and sheets of rain slickened the deck. Thomas retched and shook convulsively for 40 hours and then passed away. The crew threw his body overboard into the slate-grey, icy North Atlantic on October 9, 1821.

"Five mournful weeks later, Andy's grandmother, Katherine McGranahan and her three children, Heather, Katie, and Thomas 'Tommy' Jr., reached America. They found a home where the landlady cared for the children while Katherine found work, cooking at a hospital on Market Street."

Phil became quiet. The old man nodded off in his chair. Truman and Wayne looked at each other sympathetically and Truman chuckled quietly. Phil snored a few breaths, sleeping for a couple of minutes. He snapped awake and continued his story right where he left off, as if nothing had happened.

"Katherine, now a young widow, quickly abandoned the dream of land she had shared with Thomas. But just six months after her arrival her dream was revived when she met Stefan Holtz, a German immigrant, in May, 1822. They married two months later. Stefan had been endowed by his parents with the princely sum of $6000, and he soon booked passage on a stagecoach to Harrisburg, Pennsylvania, and then to Strasburg, in the middle Shenandoah Valley of Virginia. They headed for Strasburg because Stefan had a cousin there.

"Strasburg was an orderly, well-established town, heavily influenced by a substantial German influx over the previous 70 years. Stefan got a job in the thriving pottery mill, and the family lived in Strasburg for three years. However, the good agricultural land was already claimed and population pressures were increasing. So in 1825, upon advice from a friend who sold Stefan's employer's pottery, they moved to the mountain village of Centerville

– today known as Greenville – in Monroe County, and bought twelve acres of land. The older daughters, Heather and Katie, never married. But son Tommy did. He met Victoria Lynn Phelps at a festival in nearby Union, the county seat of Monroe County, in 1837. Vicky was from Zenith, on the northwestern slope of Peters Mountain. Tommy was 20 and Vicky was 16 when they were married at the white-framed Methodist Church in Zenith, Virginia, in July, 1838.

"In late November, 1838, just four months after the wedding, Thomas Robert McGranahan III was born. In November, 1840, Vicky gave birth again, this time to twins, Andrew Jackson McGranahan and Teresa Dawn McGranahan. Andrew is my great-great grandfather, and your great-great-great-great grandfather."

Phil looked at Wayne and said, "You look tired. I'll continue with my story on another day."

Truman bid the men adieu, but before he walked out the front door he said to Phil, "Let me know when you continue telling your story. It's fascinating."

+ + + +

September 16

The next day, as Wayne was napping in the afternoon, he was awoken by music. It was a flute, sweet and clear, coming from elsewhere in the house. He closed his eyes again and immersed himself in it. It was a classical piece he'd heard before, but he had no background in classical music and couldn't identify it. If he'd been a contestant in a game show, he would have guessed it was Mozart or Beethoven.

As the music washed over him, his life's vicissitudes replayed in his mind's eye. He smelled Cynthia's perfume and envisioned the curvature of her back and her rose tattoo. He recalled his wedding anniversary was yesterday. He had a vision of Donna, wearing a long white dress, surrounded by beautiful women in pink, particularly the one with whom he'd fornicated. He envisioned the smoke of an airplane crash in the backdrop.

He saw himself at the Metro lot looking hopelessly for his Hummer. He saw his erstwhile boss, Wilson, trying to look disinterested as he packed his belongings from his cubicle. He saw a vision of himself, lying hurt on his back on a pile of rocks, in the earliest morning light, blood trickling from his forehead into his eyes. He envisioned birds of prey circling overhead.

A tsunami of regret, remorse, and despair swept him. He became anguished and nauseous, overwhelmed with self-pity. He craved tobacco and wondered if there was any in the house. He felt alien within his own body, as if the poisons in his bloodstream and his traumatized nervous system were overwhelming his ability to control himself. He cursed himself for the stupidity and recklessness that resulted in his abject condition. He listened to the sweet flute and began to weep.

He had a vision of his daughter, Willa, hugging him with her little arms and kissing him goodbye as he left for work. "I love you, daddy." His weeping broke to an uncontrollable, unabashed wail. Tears dripped from his eyes to the pillow below.

+ + + +

September 17

When Mildred returned the following day, she said, "Good morning, Mr. Wayne! How are we today?"

Wayne wondered if she intended to always refer to the two of them together, as "we". The "I" part of "we" hurt like hell and was bored. He didn't care how the "you" part of "we" was. Her cheerfulness grated on him and he resented her.

She said, "Do you remember Doctor Ramkija suggesting that you take the healing waters at Old Sweet Springs? Truman is taking us there today."

Mildred mixed some of the nutrition drink for Wayne and helped change his clothes. She handed him a second-hand T-shirt with a tie-dye pattern. He felt silly wearing somebody else's clothes, as if he were impersonating a Woodstock-era hippy.

At noon, Truman arrived and pushed Wayne in the wheelchair down the ramp to his car as Phil waved from the porch. The pain in his hip was intense whenever he moved it but it was still satisfying to be mobile and outdoors again!

Wayne settled into the passenger seat of Truman's car and Mildred sat in the back. Truman drove downtown, turned left on SR-3, and drove eastward towards the Sweet Springs Resort. Wayne wrote on a sheet of paper, "Why sweet water?"

Truman said, "Let me tell you the history. Two hundred years ago, European Americans began to settle in the region west of the Blue Ridge Mountains in significant numbers. The Blue Ridge range is the easternmost sub-range here in the mid-Appalachians. From the late 1700s until the start of the Civil War, wealthier residents of the low-lying areas of the Eastern Seaboard began to come to the mountains to take the waters.

"The Appalachian Mountains are blessed with thousands of natural springs. Some of them are hot springs. Many have a natural effervescence and are imbued with various minerals. Combinations of these attributes were considered healthy, both for bathing and drinking.

"Throughout most of our nation's history, until the early 20th Century, there were virtually no municipal water or sewer systems, even in the larger cities. People didn't understand the concepts of how diseases spread. People did know it was more pleasant in the mountains and maybe safer from some of the illnesses. Many of the major coastal cities were adjacent to swamps that would send huge, swarming clouds of mosquitoes into the air each summer. Without air conditioning, many of these cities were unbearable. The poorer people were stuck and many died of diseases that are now preventable, but the people with means traveled to the mountains where the air was fresher and cooler, and diseases were less prevalent.

"Soon a resort culture emerged. There were many commercial enterprises in Virginia and West Virginia. Many gained reputations for the healing qualities of the water. Our bodies contain up to 90 percent water, so while there have always been and continue to be skeptics, many people still believe these waters can heal. I'm guessing you are skeptical yourself. Newcomers often are. Dr. Ramkija apparently believes in the healing power of the water or she wouldn't have asked us to bring you here.

"As municipal water systems and modern medicine emerged in the 20th Century, most of the resorts declined and eventually closed altogether. Two in particular managed to weather the vicissitudes of the marketplace. One is The Greenbrier, just north of here in White Sulphur Springs, near where you crashed. The other is The Homestead, over in Virginia. Both have faced financial struggles but have managed to stay afloat. Their clientele includes the wealthiest, most influential people on earth."

As they approached Gap Mills, Mildred said, "Truman, would you mind stopping here at the store? I always like to buy cheese from the Mennonites."

Truman stopped the car and Mildred walked into the tiny roadside Cheese and More Store. Wayne watched two women dressed in identical, ankle-length blue dresses and matching bonnets emerge from the store. To Wayne, these women looked like strays from the year 1820.

Truman continued his story. "Sweet Springs saw its first paying guests in 1792, which makes it the oldest spa within a five or six county area. Within a few decades, Thomas Jefferson was commissioned to design a new complex. He envisioned a resort consisting of a ring of buildings surrounding the springs. Several buildings were constructed around 1833, seven years after Jefferson died, so it is not well known how closely his plans were followed. My guess is that a Jefferson protégé took Jefferson's plans and updated them but his influence is clearly evident. Several of these buildings are still on site and all are on the National Register of Historic Places. The grand Jefferson Hotel is still standing. You'll be surprised when you see it how huge it is.

"One of the springs on site issues water that contains carbonic acid which makes it particularly brisk and refreshing. You'll see. Others produce some of the most delicious drinking water you'll ever taste. We save our milk containers and bring them each time we visit to come home with some of their water."

Mildred emerged from the store and they continued in a northeasterly direction, with the long, level ridgeline of Peters Mountain looming alongside, parallel to the road, on the right. The reds and yellows of leaf change were more advanced on the trees towards the top of the mountain, where temperatures were typically lower than in the valley. They passed an almost imperceptible rise where a roadside interpretive sign marked the Eastern Continental Divide, separating the Atlantic Ocean watersheds from the Gulf of Mexico watersheds. Bright, puffy white clouds hung over the crest of the mountain. White wraps of hay stood in rows in the pasture looking like giant marshmallows. One large white frame house had a flagpole outside, with a United States flag atop a Confederate States flag. Black cows grazed on pastures that gave way to forests as the terrain swept upwards.

Mildred pointed at a large grey bird as it took flight from the creek. "That's a great blue heron. One of my neighbors used to have a goldfish pond in her front yard. A great blue ate all her fish. They're brazen!"

Truman continued, "When the Great Depression struck, the resort couldn't make ends meet and it closed. It changed hands a couple of times until the state of West Virginia bought it in 1945. They used it for several years as a tuberculosis sanatorium and later a home for the aged. It went back into private hands in the 1980s but nobody did anything with it, at least anything constructive. Buildings were beginning to deteriorate and it looked like it would be lost to time and decay.

"Just a few years ago, the Fosters, a wealthy couple from the Atlanta area bought it and have brought it back to life. They have plans to completely refurbish the resort, offering golf, horseback riding, hiking, and bicycling. The first order of business was to restore the pool. The whole community is ecstatic with what they're doing."

Wayne looked out his window and saw the side of a large, three-story brick building. As Truman drove to the front, he saw a huge façade, with four grand porticos each with four gleaming white columns. Wayne's mouth wanted to say, wow, but the wires prevented it.

Truman parked in the handicapped parking area in front of the bathhouse. "The bathhouse was originally constructed in the 1830s. There was a tower at each front corner. The prior owner tore much of them down, but the new owner had them rebuilt according to the original plans and old photos. It's impressive, isn't it?" He looked to Wayne for acknowledgement. Wayne nodded.

An attendant, a large man wearing a white uniform emerged. He helped Wayne into his wheelchair and wheeled him down the ramp to the bath house and into the men's dressing room. Wayne put on a bathing suit Truman had loaned him.

The pool was perhaps 30-feet by 40-feet in size, 5-feet to 9-feet deep. It was open to the air, but surrounded by a brick building, clearly quite old. There were passageways and dressing rooms on the circumference, separated from the poolside by ornate brick archways. Small birds he thought were swallows darted in and out. The water was crystal clear, making the pool look much shallower than it really was.

Management had equipped the pool with a lift because of the many infirm people who came to the pool for therapeutic reasons. Wayne was fitted with a buoyancy strap and used the special chair to lower people who used wheelchairs into the pool. Bubbles filtered through the gravel floor of the pool and he felt a light tingling all over his body. He felt a buoyancy he'd never felt before in a pool. The water was cool, bordering on cold, but completely refreshing. As the bubbles hit the surface of the water, it sparkled in his nose and reminded him of when, as a child, he let the bubbles of a Coca-Cola tickle his nose.

The buoyancy of the water, along with the strap, allowed him to float on the water effortlessly. He closed his eyes and soaked in the warm rays of the sun. He felt a contentment he hadn't felt for months, perhaps ever. He felt as if the constant pain he was enduring was somehow placed on hold. He was daydreaming of songbirds singing in a woodland dell when Truman interrupted his reverie and said it was time to depart.

+ + + +

September 18

The next morning, Phil wandered into the library and said to Wayne, "I trust the Sweet Spring water did you well."

Wayne nodded. He pointed at his poison oak rash with one hand and gave a thumbs-up sign with the other.

"I thought I'd tell you more about Andy, my grandfather."

Wayne shook his head and wrote, flute?

"Yes, wasn't it lovely? Sarah Noflin is from Lewisburg. She's quite remarkable. Lewisburg has attracted many artists, musicians, and other creative people. It's a town of only 4000 people, but there are three major performing arts venues and six art galleries. Sarah comes from a family of musicians. Most are traditional Appalachian musicians, but Sarah gravitated to classical. She studied at the Longy School of Music in Boston and played in the symphony there. She has played all over the world. But she came home to Lewisburg a few years ago.

"Twice each month since my Flora and I moved here, I have been hosting what I've come to call Chautauqua Thursdays. Chautauqua events were educational sessions for adults that were popular around the country in the late 19th and early 20th Centuries. They brought entertainment and culture to small communities that otherwise wouldn't have access to teachers, musicians, and speakers. I remember my dad talking about them and decided to revive the tradition here in Union.

"On the second Thursday of each month, we host a musician or some other live performer. On the fourth Thursday, we have lectures or book reading. Some of the lectures I do myself while guests do others. We typically have six or eight people attending, but we've had as few as three and as many as 15. I hope you'll be joining us for some in the coming weeks. You'll find them fun and interesting."

Portraits?

"Yes, I see the portraits have gotten your attention. This one, I'm sure you recognize, is General Robert E. Lee. Next is Andy, my great-grandfather, the man whose life story I started to tell you about. The one you've covered with a towel is Nathan Bedford Forrest." Phil peeked under the towel to see if Forrest was still there. If he was surprised that Forrest's portrait had been covered, he didn't say anything to Wayne. "I'll tell you about him, too. That one is Thomas J. Jackson. Old Stonewall. Stonewall was from Weston, in Lewis County, not too far from here. Like Monroe County, Lewis County was in Virginia in those days but it is in West Virginia now."

Bird? Wayne wrote, and pointed at the stuffed animal on the desk.

"That's a red-tailed hawk. My father was a falconer. This was his last bird, named Ruby. I'll tell you more about her and how she got there later. Let me return to my story about Andy."

Truman? Wayne wrote.

"You're thoughtful to ask about him. I'll see him tomorrow and I can catch him up."

+ + + +

Phil fixed himself another cup of tea. The men went into the library where Phil sat in his favorite chair. "When I left off, Vicky McGranahan had given birth to twins, Andy and Teresa. Tommy and Vicky bought a farm on Laurel Creek Road, a dirt track near Centerville. Tommy got a job at the grist mill in Centerville and joined Vicky working the farm in the afternoon.

"Andy and Teresa, although fraternal twins, looked amazingly alike. Both were covered with freckles and had pale-blue eyes like their mother's, auburn hair like their father's.

"While older brother Tom was withdrawn to the point of being reclusive, Andy and Teresa were precocious and inseparable. Teresa was gregarious while Andy was circumspect, unlikely to speak unless spoken to.

"Andy and Teresa often walked the hillside behind the cabin with their dog, Bridger, named because Stefan had found him under the covered bridge over Laurel Creek the year before they were born. Andy was fascinated with tools and loved to watch his father carve toys and wooden bowls. Teresa loved animals and bonded instantly with Bridger and with Cricket, the family's horse. When the twins would ride horseback with their mom, Teresa rode in front of Vicky and Andy sat behind. They often rode to the general store or to see Tommy at the gristmill in Centerville, just a half-mile away. A second mill was nearby, where gunpowder was made from saltpeter from the John Maddy cave.

"At age six, the twins started school in Centerville's one-room schoolhouse. Andy struggled with penmanship, but quickly mastered his lessons in arithmetic and amazed his teachers and classmates with his ability to do long multiplication accurately in his head.

"Andy was the first in class to teach himself to read, so motivated was he to learn the history of Virginia. He loved the tales of George Washington. He was rapt over the story of the honesty Washington displayed after he chopped his cherry tree. But he was particularly enthralled by Thomas Jefferson, a redhead like himself, and Jefferson's amazing ingenuity with mechanical devices. He was innately proud of his heritage and loved being a Virginian, as he concluded it was the most beautiful and important state of all.

"With each trip to the gristmill, Andy became more enthralled with the myriad of mechanical devices within it. Teresa had an innate sense for healing. By the time she was eight, she had already learned a lot about healing from a neighbor who practiced apothecary arts. When their horse, Cricket sliced her fetlock on a barb, Teresa found some slippery elm along the creek below the house and from the inner bark she made a healing poultice, which she applied to the wound. She also stored many of the slippery elm leaves, knowing they would be useful for digestive ailments.

"By age ten when Teresa finished fourth grade, she was already being sought as a healer, both for animals and people. She collected herbs from the forests and made remedies for colds, fever, snakebites, and lacerations. Animals of all types seemed to gravitate to her. Whenever she and Andy went in separate directions, Bridger went with her. She also took an interest in care of the chickens that Vicky raised and soon took over most of the work herself.

"One Saturday in 1850, when Andy was 10 years old he had a long conversation with Josiah Raney, the cobbler who rented the top floor of the mill. Like many craftsmen, Raney often worked alone and was always appreciative of companionship. Andy loved the smell of leather, the strips of material draped over wooden dowels, and the finely crafted hand tools.

"In the fall of 1851, Vicky took ill, with a fever and dysentery. Teresa sat by her bedside for four days, administering an elixir she made from an infusion of boneset – a flower from the daisy family – and rubbing her chest with healing poultices of wintergreen. But Vicky couldn't be saved and she passed away. The twins were eleven, and Teresa vowed to devote the rest of her life to learning more about medicine.

"A few months later, Bridger wandered into the woods and never returned. Soon, a neighbor offered the McGranahans two new puppies. They named the female Sasha, and the male Orion. Littermates, they were short in stature with wolf-like faces. Both had long, cottony black hair with tan faces, Sasha's lighter in color than Orion's. Sasha quickly became Andy's dog while Orion became Teresa's.

"After his wife's death, Tommy did his best to look after the children's emotional needs, even as his own suffered. Mr. Stanley, the owner of the gristmill, had gotten the cancer the following year, so Tommy's responsibilities and work hours increased. But in September, 1852, disaster struck again. Tommy was working with a winch to lift hay to the loft for winter and a bale fell, striking him and crushing two vertebrae in his back. Although he was still able to walk short distances, he never had another pain-free day in his life and spent most of his waking hours in a chair. Fortunately, Andy's and Teresa's grandfather Stefan, had invested his money wisely. He had bought several pieces of land in the area, and he leased timber and grazing rights to neighbors. So there was income and the family was well-provided for. The community was tightly knit and nobody went hungry.

"Andy shared his father's interest in history. After his accident, Tommy began to collect and read more and more history books. Father and son spent many evenings sitting by the fireplace, trading stories of the Scots, the Irish, the settlers, and the founding fathers of their great nation. But stories of Patrick Henry, Daniel Boone, Alexander Spotswood, and other great Virginians were their sources of greatest pride.

"In 1852, Andy was 12 years old and was in his last year of school, sixth grade. Andy asked his father to negotiate an apprenticeship with Mr. Raney. For the next three years, Andy walked to Centerville each morning and worked until mid-afternoon learning the shoemaking trade.

"Like most youngsters, Andy went barefoot during the warm months of each year. Mr. Raney decided the first thing he would have Andy do was to make a pair of shoes for himself. Andy watched each day as Mr. Raney would measure the feet of customers for a custom fit. He practiced with the tools Mr. Raney had accumulated. Andy was a careful learner and was attentive to the thickness and flexibility of the leather.

"Every few months, Mr. Rainey would travel to Narrows to shop for leather at the tannery. On one trip, in April, 1856, Andy went along. Andy and Mr. Raney rode his wagon on the dirt Union–Peterstown Pike with Peters Mountain looming to their left. Once through Peterstown and Rich Creek, they entered the Narrows of the mighty New River. Mr. Raney and Andy took their wagon by ferry across the River. Until 1861, this was as far away from home as Andy ever ventured.

"Andy's interest in shoemaking had already led him to build a workshop behind the family cabin. After a two-year apprenticeship, he left Mr. Raney to work for himself. He had made his first pair of shoes for himself, but Mrs. Stanley, widow of the late gristmill owner, was so impressed that she commissioned Andy to make a pair for her. Andy always maintained a good relationship with Mr. Raney and there was ample work for both craftsmen.

"Salt Sulphur Springs, just six miles from Centerville and three miles south of Union, was a grand resort, with hotel accommodations for several hundred people. Its famous and elegant Erskine House contained 72 rooms. Three springs, the Iodine, Salt Sulphur, and Sweet, were said to have curative powers for diseases of the brain, including migraines and headaches, and palsy resulting from congestion or chronic inflammation. The waters also cured neuralgia. Because of the water's reputation and the pristine mountain air, the 'Salt,' as neighbors called it, brought visitors from throughout Virginia and the Carolinas, particularly from lowland areas where heat, filth, and insects were summer maladies. The Salt became a major source of outside revenue for all the support industries of the region, including food production, apparel, and alcoholic beverages. The McGranahan family became part of the economic system. Andy's reputation for quality shoemaking quickly spread to the resort.

"Andy was fascinated with technology and was thrilled to live in such an advanced, modern age. He loved to talk with guests at the Salt who had ridden on the new railroads. The Virginia and Tennessee Railroad was being built along the Great

Valley of Virginia, just two days horseback ride away to the east and south. He often visited with Sam, who operated the Salt's telegraph, a machine that sent messages to cities as distant as Richmond and Washington through a simple wire. He loved to watch the clicking machine and see Sam's hand chatter on it as actively as the beak of a flicker. He and Sam chuckled at the prospect that someday a person's voice might be transferred over a wire.

"By age fifteen, twin sister Teresa was taking care of 45 chickens. Each morning, she would open the coop and the chickens would feed on the insects in the garden and wander into the woods in search of grubs and grasses. Chickens, being naturally social, would instinctively return to the coop each evening. Teresa's chickens produced about twelve dozen eggs each week. Each Tuesday she sold the eggs, plus three or four live chickens to the restaurant manager at the Salt. She also worked the family vegetable garden and always kept the windowsills filled with fresh flowers in season.

"Teresa collected ginseng and herbs from the forests and made healing tinctures and poultices. She made friends with the pharmacist at the resort, a Jew named Mordeci Mishkin and his wife, Rivka, and their young son Hyman. The Mishkins had moved to the resort from Newport, Rhode Island, in the 1840s. Mr. Mishkin, whom everyone simply called 'The Jew', had been a personal physician for a wealthy slave importer named Spangler. But when Spangler's wife had died from what Spangler deemed an improper prescription, the Mishkins were fired. They had once visited the Salt Sulphur Springs in the entourage of the Spanglers, and decided to return there. The Jew set up an apothecary and Rivka became a midwife. The Jew often bought herbs that Teresa collected. He loved to talk about pharmaceuticals and medicine with the young lady and taught her about diseases of the digestive and pulmonary systems. He also was an amateur astronomer and spent many hours on new moon nights staring at the sky with his Alvan Clark refracting telescope that he had carried with him from Rhode Island. Andy learned of the Jew's fascination with the sky and joined him on many evenings to stargaze. Andy was particularly fascinated by Saturn and its rings and the moons of Jupiter."

Phil took a sip of tea and said, "This is a fascination I share. I think about Andy whenever I see Jupiter on a dark night.

"Older brother Tom became quarrelsome and argumentative. He often spent several days at a time alone in the woods. But he did provide the family with fresh game, rabbits, squirrels, and occasionally a boar, bear, or deer.

"One beautiful Monday in May, 1856, with colorful blossoms on cherry and apple trees, as I imagine, Andy rode Cricket to the mill at Centerville, to buy flour and take measurements of a customer's feet for a new pair of shoes. As Cricket trotted past the Huff cabin, Andy looked to the garden and saw a young woman with a hoe in her hand, tending a row in her garden. The Huffs were a childless middle-aged couple, gruff and standoffish. The girl in the garden was thin and dark-skinned, with hair darker than a raven's wing. She was wearing a simple gingham dress and a plain bonnet. She had a necklace of a plain leather strap with a pendant of an Indian arrowhead. It was as white as the pearls in the earrings the rich ladies at the White Sulphur Springs Hotel wore. When she turned to look at him, he saw the darkest eyes he'd ever seen, almost as if her pupils and irises had melded into one. She smiled shyly, just as Cricket ran under the overhanging branch of the big maple tree, which smacked him in the chest, knocking him off and sending him sprawling to the dirt. When Andy picked himself off the ground and replaced his hat, the girl was gone.

"The following Sunday, Andy and Teresa took their dad with them to a revival at a church in Rock Camp, a few miles from their regular church in Centerville. The church had seating for 40 people, but there were easily one hundred in attendance, many of them standing in the aisle or along the back. Andy was so preoccupied with his dad that he didn't take notice of the other worshippers. But as he sat down, he saw in a row ahead a wave of ebony hair flowing below a red bonnet. She turned for a moment, and he saw her eyes again. It was her! To her left was Mrs. Huff, her head under a huge hat of flowers and feathers. To her right was a tall teenage boy with equally dark hair. And beyond him was Mr. Huff, with his bald pate ringed by wisps of reddish-blond hair.

"Andy felt his chest tighten and his pulse quicken and he paid no attention to the interminably long service. After it was over, he helped his father to the wagon. He told Tommy and Teresa that he'd forgotten something inside. He ran to the dark girl and said, 'I'm Andy McGranahan. I...'

"Before he could speak another word, she shot back sarcastically, 'It's nice to meet you. You are quite the horseback rider!' Seeing his embarrassment, she smiled shyly again and said, 'I must go. Maybe I'll see you again.'

"For the next few weeks, Andy looked for every excuse to make trips to the mill, but the girl was not to be seen. He asked Mr. Raney, if he knew the Huffs and about the girl. He replied, 'The girl and her brother are staying with the Huffs. That's all I know.'

"Then one day in June, as he rode past, she was standing by the picket fence as if waiting for him. He brought Cricket to a stop and she said, 'Hello, Andy McGranahan. It's nice to see you again.'

"He was flabbergasted. She had remembered his name, but he'd never even heard hers. He looked at her hauntingly warm eyes, mesmerized. She spoke again, 'If you'd like to come to my church again this Sunday, we're having a picnic afterwards.' And she walked away.

"He yelled, 'What is your name?' She turned, coyly put her index finger to her lips, and kept walking.

"That Sunday, Tommy wasn't feeling well, but Andy and Teresa took the wagon to the church in Rock Camp again. The ebony-haired girl sat a few pews ahead again, and Andy sat transfixed during the service. 'The heart is deceitful above all things and beyond cure. Who can understand it? Jeremiah 17:9' shouted the preacher, but Andy heard none of it.

"Outside afterward, a feast emerged, with piles of ham, turkey, sweet potatoes, fried okra, baked beans, and yeast biscuits. There were pies of apple, blueberry, and peach. Andy and Teresa sat together and spoke with the family of a man Andy knew from the mill.

"Soon, a band with banjo, fiddle, and a piper began to play jigs and reels. As Andy swung to and fro in the line dance, he swung by partner after partner, but as he took the hands of the dark-haired girl with the white arrowhead necklace, his heart fluttered, and he went silly. On the fourth dance, as the music stopped, she was still in his hands. Her hand was thin and her grip was firm. She leaned to him and whispered, 'Come to my house at five o'clock tomorrow afternoon,' and then she walked away.

"The next day, he rode Cricket to the mill and delivered a pair of shoes for the miller's brother. On his way back, he stopped at the Huff cabin. There she sat, rocking on the porch. She said, 'Let's go for a ride.' So he extended his right hand and took hers, pulling her astride Cricket behind him. They left the road and rode through the pasture east of the house. He felt her legs astride his hips and her left hand around his waist. He was smitten and knew immediately he would marry this nameless, dark and beautiful lass.

"They stopped at the top of the Walnut Knob, where Andy tied Cricket to an oak tree. He removed the saddle and placed the saddle blanket where a grand view opened to the grand expanse of Peters Mountain, stretching left to right against the southern horizon, broken only at the gap of the New River in the Narrows. To the west lay the rugged valley of the New River, the river itself unseen behind waves of hills. A giant cloud towered over the western horizon and sent silent shards of lightning against its surface, all backlit by the afternoon sun.

"He and she sat near one another, not touching, staring at the western sky. She said, 'What a beautiful place this is!' He tried to speak, but no words came. After a long silence, she spoke, wistfully, without looking at him, 'My name is Alison; Alison Larkin Littletree. Everyone calls me Allie. My father was a Cherokee. He lived in what is now the state of Georgia. He married a woman named Alise, an Irishwoman. My brother, Wes, was born in 1838, the year father's people were evicted from Georgia, where they had lived in peaceful, civilized settlements like their European neighbors. They were forced to march westward to new, horrible lands across the Mississippi River. Pa understood mountain life, and when the army came to evict our people, he, Ma and Wes escaped to the rugged Cherohola Mountains. I was born in 1842 in a lean-to in a ravine where my family lived like Pa's forefathers.'"

Phil said wistfully, "I can only imagine how rapt Andy must have been listening to her story."

Wayne nodded in agreement.

"Allie continued, 'We moved and set up a new camp every spring. When I was four years old, Ma and Pa died of disease. An old widow woman lived in a cabin near us and was the only person who knew about us. She took in Wes and me, but within a year took us to an orphanage. My mother had an aunt and uncle named Fenwick. Mrs. Fenwick, who lived in Bristol, Tennessee, spent many years searching for us. When she found us in the orphanage, she made arrangements to have us moved to Bristol to live with her. We lived there until a few months ago when she died. She had arranged for us to be sent here, to live with her sister, Mrs. Huff, our great aunt. The Huffs are fine people, stern and religious, but they don't want me and Wes with them.'

"Andy spoke about his family and the stories he'd been told by his grandmother, Katherine, during the expulsions of her ancestors from Scotland and Ireland. He told her of the Highland Clearances and the death of his grandfather, Thomas Sr., at sea. They talked and talked, laughed and cried together, oblivious to the storm clouds building around them. She said, 'It is so wonderful that we now live in peace, with abundance and security all around us.'

"Finally, he said, 'I must go. Teresa and Papa will be worried about me.'

"She said, 'Please kiss me.' She took her hand behind his neck and pulled him to her. They kissed long and soft and wet. Andy blushed. Allie said,

'Life can bring us anything. Since my parents died, I have been waiting, wanting to be happy again.' As they hugged, bolts of lighting swept the sky. Drops of rain fell sparsely, then more heavily, hastening an end to their embrace. They tacked Cricket and rode down the hill. Andy lowered Allie to the ground a short distance from her house and he galloped home.

"Each Monday for the next several weeks, this rendezvous repeated itself, as their affections for each other grew stronger. Andy took Allie to many of the beautiful mountaintops and meadows for these assignations, all hidden as much as possible from prurient eyes.

"Invariably, their increasing togetherness attracted attention. One Monday as Andy arrived, he was met by both Alison and Mr. Huff. Mr. Huff was purposeful but not brusque. 'Andy,' he said, 'If what I've been hearing about you and Allie is true, I think it best that you set a wedding date. Come to the house when you decide.' He walked inside.

"Allie and Andy stood looking at each other, flummoxed. She grinned and he started to chuckle. Soon both were in spasms of laughter. When they finally settled down, Andy said, 'Let's get married on the night of the harvest moon!' Allie agreed.

"Andy returned home that evening and told Tommy and Teresa about his engagement. Tommy was ecstatic. Andy had worried that Teresa would be hurt, as they'd been lifelong companions. Yet she was strangely quiet. An hour later, they walked to the springhouse together to get some water and Teresa said, 'Andy, I've been seeing Wes Littletree. We've been talking about getting married, too.' Andy, having been for weeks in a state of lustful obliviousness, had failed to notice that his twin sister had been pursuing her own marital ambitions with his intended's brother.

"On the evening of October 14, 1856, in the Baptist Church in Rock Camp, Virginia, Andrew Jackson McGranahan married Alison Larkin Littletree while Weston Maurice Littletree married Teresa Dawn McGranahan. All four went by carriage to the Salt Sulphur Springs for the first night of their honeymoon, a gift from Mr. Warren, owner of the Salt. Fifty friends of the family followed the carriage and joined the reception, which lasted until midnight. Mr. Warren gave each couple a grand three-tiered wedding cake and several bottles of champagne. Revelers rode home under a gorgeous full moon.

"The next day, the happy couples went north through Union, then east to the grand hotel at Sweet Springs, for the second night. They stayed in the easternmost brick cottage and bathed in the Bath House, with its two rectangular towers, topped with brick parapets. They had never before experienced such opulence, and they danced in the grand ballroom well into the night.

"Upon their return, each couple began construction of a cabin for themselves. As an inheritance, step-grandfather, Stefan, had deeded the twins adjoining land, of 28 and 34 acres, conveyed at their marriages. The properties were east of Centerville and across Indian Creek and the Union–Peterstown Pike, one on each fork of Humphreys Run. Andy and Allie's foundation was set on the east fork of the draw, about a mile above the junction near the most productive spring and the largest land for a garden. Wes and Teresa were on the south fork, about a half-mile above the junction, where there was good forage for the chickens and a south-facing slope for an orchard. The junction was still a half-mile above a ford of Indian Creek.

"Wes had participated in several house raisings before, so they decided that Wes' and Teresa's house would go up first. Wes and Andy worked for several weeks cutting trees and notching logs while Harish Grover, the area's best stonemason, worked to build the chimney using stones from Indian Creek. Fifteen men, including Archibald Ganoe and Bartley McNeer, Andy's friends from the mill, assembled just after noon on the second Friday in November and by dark, the foundation had been excavated and leveled and the foundation logs had been set. Forty men were at the construction site by the next daybreak and by dinnertime on Saturday, the house was essentially complete. On Sunday after church, eight men returned and finished placing the doors and windows while the women and children chinked the logs with mud.

"By the time the entire process was repeated at Andy and Allie's house in December, the first snow had fallen. As they moved Andy's belongings from his house and Allie's things from the Huff's, it was already time to hang a Christmas wreath on the door.

"Life soon settled into a routine for the happy newlyweds. At age 18, Wes was a muscular 5'11" tall, 170 pounds, and an expert marksman. He was equally adept with rifles, archery, and tomahawks. He began to travel to local shooting competitions where he won numerous awards and some prize money. He built a small forge along Indian Creek and made ceremonial knives, shields, and swords. He also bought a fiddle. One of the musicians who played each summer at The Salt showed him how to play.

"Teresa was 16, 5'4" tall, and 99 pounds. She continued to raise chickens and sold eggs and chickens to friends, to the general store in Centerville, and to the Salt. She collected herbs for her own use and for sale to neighbors and to the Jew's apothecary at the Salt. She had a beautiful voice and loved to sing while Wes played his fiddle.

"Andy, also 16, was 5'7" tall and 135 pounds. He rode Cricket down the hollow every day to work in the cobbler shop with Tommy.

"Allie was 14 years old, also 5'7" tall. She loved being the same height as her husband, as when they approached one another their noses touched. She weighed 110 pounds. She raised a flock of geese and worked on the garden each day. She made clothes for the family and for sale. She had an affinity for the deep forests. She often walked alone and hunted for ginseng and wild mushrooms.

"By springtime, Allie was pregnant. On a Sunday night in July, 1857, Andy rode to the Salt to fetch the midwife, Rivka Mishkin, as Allie was having labor pains. Their first child, Robert Isaac, was born the next morning at 8:20 a.m., a red-headed boy with freckles, just like his dad. A second child, a girl, was stillborn in 1860. Their third child, Alicia Jewell, was born late in the evening on April 10, 1861. This was the happiest time Andy and Allie would ever know.

"I'm getting weary just now. I'll need to continue later on."

Wayne wrote, "Great story." He wondered what was real and what was embellished. He was becoming fond of his ancient uncle and admiring his storytelling skills.

+ + + +

September 19

The next morning, Sunday, Mildred burst into Wayne's room with her now-typical, "How are we this morning?"

Wayne shrugged and thought to himself, this is the way it is going to be. Might as well accept it.

She continued, "It's a gorgeous morning! The leaves on the sugar maple at the end of the driveway are turning red and the sky has that special fall crispness. I love this time of year!"

She had an innate cheerfulness that befuddled him. The black people he knew in the DC area were always so militant, but she seemed so happy and contented. He wondered how a race that had seen so much strife could still have people filled with such sangfroid.

She cooked pureed carrots and mashed potatoes for Wayne. "The hummingbirds are buzzing all around. I think they're getting ready for their migration. It has always amazed me they can migrate all the way to the tropics. I read once that when they fly over the Gulf of Mexico, they travel over 450 miles, often with storms and headwinds, without ever taking a break. They have nowhere to land! It's hard for me to imagine. The people who work the fishing boats and the oil rigs see the birds as they perch on the boat and rig railings, presumably just to catch their breath. Can you imagine that? I imagine a tiny little bird sitting on a boat's rigging, heartbeat going a mile a minute, ready to fly again for hundreds of more miles. It really says something about determination. My Sherwood and I always set several feeders with sugar water in them. Their resolve and perseverance inspire me and I love watching them."

Wayne wanted to say how much he'd enjoyed watching them as he sat on the front porch earlier. She must have been reading his mind.

"The sun is warming the front porch, Wayne. Would we like to sit outside for awhile today?"

Wayne looked out the window and nodded. He pushed her away as she tried to help him into his wheelchair. He rolled himself outside with Mildred following. As they arrived, they found a paper sack on the porch. Wayne was immediately on guard, fearful and suspicious of what may be in it. For the first time since his accident, he thought about his gun. Mildred walked right over unhesitatingly and picked it up. She looked inside and said, "Here are some nice home-grown tomatoes, peppers, potatoes, and beans. This has been a great summer for all the gardens around. Somebody must have had some extra veggies. I wonder who it was."

Wayne was discomfited that he'd been so suspicious.

When Mildred returned to the porch, she sat nearby and began reading a book she'd brought. Wayne watched the hummingbirds and tried to smile when Mildred saw that he noticed them. He pointed at several birds perched on a wire. She told him they were barn swallows. "They eat insects. See them darting around? They catch flying insects right out of the sky." He thought they were the same birds he'd seen at the Sweet Springs pool. Mildred went inside to clean his room and change his bed. Phil came outside and said he'd be leaving soon to go to church. When he asked Wayne if he wanted to attend, Wayne declined.

Wayne looked at the statue across the highway and was strangely reassured by its presence. He sat for a half-hour, watching the birds and clouds when he saw a large bird alternatively flapping and soaring overhead. He picked up the binoculars that were on the table next to him. The bird had a whitish underside with grey and brown splotches. It had bright yellow legs and talons. It had a long, rectangular tail and angular wings, both with black-tipped feathers. He was sure it was a bird of prey, but it looked more angular and athletic than the red-tailed hawk in his room.

As he watched it, a pigeon flew from behind the house. The hawk folded its wings and pointed itself downward and smacked into the pigeon, talons first. Bam! Feathers flew everywhere! Wayne gasped. The hawk and pigeon plunged to the ground not thirty feet away. The pigeon looked dead already. The hawk stood immobile over the pigeon with its wings spread, as if trying to cover the prey and keep it hidden. The hawk turned its head and looked at Wayne. Wayne could see its dark, round eyes, framed in yellow skin, and its black cheek-pads. It had a regal face with a prominent brow above the eyes. He had never seen such an awesome display of speed and power.

Wayne felt the rekindling of an appreciation for nature from his days in the Boy Scouts. He wondered what Phil or Truman might think of him if they saw him so enthralled by a bird. It occurred to him that he and his son, Eddie, had never shared a moment when an act in nature had impressed him.

Wayne and the bird stared at each other for many minutes, as if sizing up one another. The hawk finally emitted a hoarse scream, like the sound of a steam whistle. It turned its head to the west and took flight, laboring with the weight of the pigeon on his left talon.

A few hours later, Phil returned from church. He ambled onto the porch up the stairway, bypassing the wheelchair ramp. He took a rocking chair near Wayne. Wayne had forgotten to bring his pad of paper, but he was eager to share what he'd seen with Phil, so he spelled the word hawk in the dust on the windowsill, pointing to the yard.

Phil, misunderstanding Wayne's implication, said "Oh, yes. I promised to tell you about Ruby, the stuffed hawk in your room. Ruby is a red-tailed hawk. After I left for college, my father got into falconry, the sport of kings. Falconers keep and raise hawks and train them to hunt. Centuries ago, the hawks would provide food for the masters. But now falconers just do it for sport. Many kings in the 18th and 19th centuries were wealthy enough to hire people to keep and train the hawks for them."

Wayne scribbled in the dust again. Beside where he'd written, hawk he wrote, killed bird and pointed to the lawn.

"Oh, you saw a real hawk in action? They're pretty impressive, aren't they? There's a man in my Rotary Club, Reed Rathmell, who is still a falconer. I thought I'd take you to the meeting with me this week if you feel up to it. I'll introduce you.

"Anyway, there are many types of birds of prey around here. The hawks are generally of four families: vultures, hawks, eagles, and owls. There are two vultures around here, the black vulture and the turkey vulture, often called the buzzard. There are two eagles: the golden eagle and the bald eagle, the national bird. There are sightings of golden eagles a hundred miles to the north of here in West Virginia's biggest mountains and bald eagles are becoming increasingly more common along the rivers, as they are fish-eating birds. The osprey is smaller than true eagles, but is also a fish-eater. The hawks include accipiters, buteos, and falcons. Accipiters are small hawks with long, straight tails and short, rounded wings. Falcons are small hawks, like the Peregrine falcon, the pigeon hawk, and the sparrow hawk, often called the kestrel. They have angular wings and straight tails. Buteos are the soaring hawks. They have broad, rounded wings and broadly fanned tails. Ruby is, or I should say was, a red-tailed hawk, which is one of the buteos. Reed Rathmell keeps a red-tailed hawk at his home."

Wayne thought what he saw was a falcon. Bird Book? he wrote in the dust.

"Yes," said Phil. "I'll get it for you."

He walked inside and returned with a well-worn, small softcover book. Wayne flipped through the pages until he found the hawks. He pointed to a peregrine falcon. Phil said, "Is that what you saw? Peregrines are rare around here. If you saw one, it was probably on its fall migration. They're magnificent fliers, the fastest birds in the world. I'll never forget the first one I saw. I was hiking at Mesa Verde National Park in Colorado in the 1950s. I don't imagine you'll ever forget what you just saw, either."

Phil went inside to take a nap. Wayne continued thumbing through the bird book, noticing how many birds in the yard he was beginning to recognize: chickadee, titmouse, cardinal, blue jay, purple finch, gold finch, house wren, flicker, and mourning dove. His incapacity had made him more aware of his surroundings. He tracked the movement of the sun and for the first time in his life realized that on the day of the full moon, it rose exactly as the sun set, something he felt he should have realized much earlier in his life.

He had begun thumbing through Phil's collection of books and had finished the voluminous book on Stonewall Jackson. He had never been much of a reader of anything more challenging than magazines. But he started reading *Guns, Germs and Steel* and was fascinated by it. It gave some theories as to the circumstances that allowed European conquistadors and explorers to travel to and surmount the Americas and not the other way around. The world of learning strictly for the pleasure of learning was foreign to him as his frenetic pace had never allowed the luxury of study as a leisure time activity before.

+ + + +

September 21

Two days later, on Tuesday, Truman took Wayne to a physical therapy session. When Truman returned to the clinic to pick him up, Truman said, "When I drop you off, I'm picking up Phil for our weekly Rotary meeting. We always are encouraged to bring guests. Would you like to go with us?" Wayne nodded affirmatively.

As Truman wheeled Wayne up the wheelchair ramp at the Kalico Kitchen, a man gave a friendly hello to Truman, then turned to Wayne and said, "I'm Burton Jones, president of the club. Good to have you with us." Jones was a tall, thin man with a resonant voice. Wayne liked him.

Wayne received a kind word of personal welcome from most members, several of whom were elderly. Franklin McRoberts III, a former state senator, was there. So was Stuart Cummings, publisher of the *Monroe Watchman*, the weekly newspaper.

Wayne, being unable to eat, sat awkwardly while everyone else enjoyed a lunch of barbeque pork, cole slaw, and potato salad, all washed down with the ubiquitous sweet iced tea. Wayne sat between Phil and Stuart Cummings. Cummings asked Wayne, "Is this your first visit to West Virginia?"

Wayne nodded affirmatively, not wanting to elaborate on his trips to the race track at Summit Point in the eastern panhandle.

Between bites of lunch, Stuart asked, "Did you know West Virginia was formed at the outset of the War Between The States, solely from Virginia counties? In fact, it is the first and only state that was ever formed from another state without the parent state's consent."

Wayne nodded. He wrote on his pad, I like history.

Stuart said, "Very well, then. Let me tell you more about my beloved West Virginia. Our state has always been rich in natural resources. But little of that wealth has found its way into the hands of our residents. In 1940, the per capita income of West Virginians was better than that of Virginians. But not any more. West Virginia has generally been in decline, both in population and in its economy, for half a century. Today, we are among the poorest states in the country and near the bottom of scores of welfare indexes. We have the smallest percentage in the nation of foreign-born people and the lowest percentage of residents that speak a language other than English at home."

Wayne thought about how different that was from his bustling, multi-racial, multi-ethnic area of Northern Virginia. Wayne had always thought English was the only language Americans should speak. But Stuart's tone sounded as if Stuart thought more diversity would be a positive thing and welcome in West Virginia.

Stuart continued, "We are the only state that in the last census had a natural decrease in population since the prior census. More people died than were born.

"We are statistically among the nation's unhealthiest people. Huntington, the state's second largest city, has been called the Fattest City in America, because of its high percentage of overweight people. We printed in the *Watchman* an article from the wire services the other day that talked about sleeplessness as a function of where people lived. It has been documented that sleeplessness is greater in West Virginia than in any other state. This is correlated to our high incidence of obesity, smoking, diabetes, heart disease, and various other infirmities, many preventable. According to the article, as many as one in five West Virginians admitted to not having gotten a single good night's sleep in an entire month. I imagine that with your injuries, this is something you can identify with."

Wayne shivered with consternation, thinking about the intensity and frequency of his nightmares.

"There is a causative correlation between sleeplessness and obesity – one feeds on the other," Stuart continued. "I am certain that the depressed economy contributes to the problem as well. We joke about this but it isn't funny: West Virginia is in a permanent recession."

Truman was listening nearby. He said, "I got my degree in economics at the University of Virginia. I came home to Union to visit with my folks on Christmas break during my senior year and a banker who was a friend of my dad's offered me a job. If I'd stayed in Charlottesville, with the way it has grown, I would have likely made tons more money during my career. But I've never regretted coming home to Union."

Phil also joined in, "Wayne, you'll be surprised by the number of intelligent, worldly, and well-educated people here in Monroe County. The State's two pre-eminent universities are West Virginia University in Monongahela County and Marshall University in Cabell County. But I'll bet there as many PhDs per capita in Monroe County as either of these, and we have no university at all. Monroe has always been a magnet for intelligent people."

Stuart said, "Union is a bit like Mayberry, from the old *Andy Griffith* television show. We're like a Norman Rockwell painting. We're what America used to be."

Club President Burton Jones interrupted this impromptu civics lesson by instructing the members to stand and recite the Pledge to the Flag. He then asked Reed Rathmell, a retired minister, to give a blessing. During the meeting's program, the club discussed improvements to the kids' athletic field just south of town. They planned a yard sale as a fund-raiser to pay for new bleachers on the softball field. Wayne sensed a congeniality among the members that only such a long familiarity can breed, something he'd not felt personally since his fraternity days at UVA.

+ + + +

September 22

The next day, Truman arrived to take Wayne and Mildred to the Old Sweet again. On their way through town, Mildred asked Truman to stop at her house as she had neglected to bring her wallet. "Normally I don't carry it, but I'd like to stop for some cheese in Gap Mills again."

Wayne looked at her house when she went in. It was a tiny, wooden clapboard house with green shutters and a green tile roof. It had flower-boxes in each window and the grass in the yard was nicely trimmed. The flower beds were mulched. Nothing was out of place. He wondered how many neighbors were black and how many were white.

Arriving at the Old Sweet, Wayne luxuriated in the effervescent water for 45 minutes, feeling viscerally its healing qualities he'd first doubted. It dawned on him that the poison oak rash on his leg had virtually vanished the day after his last visit to the healing waters.

Afterwards, Truman drove him to a commercial garage on Main Street in White Sulphur Springs. "Your bike was taken here by a wrecker after your crash. Phil got a call from your insurance adjuster saying it was here. We thought you might like to have a look, see if any personal effects were left behind."

When they arrived, Truman exchanged pleasantries with the shop owner. Wayne wheeled himself into a dark backroom alone. Oleaginous goo covered the floor, coating the wheels of his wheelchair, leaving a stain on the sleeve of his jacket. The Harley leaned against the front fender of a wrecked Chevy Malibu, the roof of which was totally collapsed and bloodstains still appeared on shards of windshield glass. The Harley's front forks were bent and crusted with mud. The front wheel was flat. The right footpeg and rear brake lever were bent to hell. The exhaust pipe from the rear cylinder where it curved in front of the crankcase was ripped apart and there was a gash in the crankcase itself. The right mirror was broken as was the front brake lever. The Harley's faux gas tank was still indented from when Donna had dropped it.

Wayne's eyes darted from the oily floor to the dried blood on the windshield of the car to the broken Harley. The room was a pall of angst, destruction, and remorse. He replayed in his mind the crash, the impact and interminable wait for help. The same sickening feeling he experienced that horrible night washed over him again.

He turned to roll himself back to where Truman was waiting for him, but his arms wouldn't turn the wheels. He became resentful towards Donna for what she'd done to his possessions and his Harley. But he overwhelmed that notion with embarrassment and regret over what he'd done to precipitate her action. He rued his past behavior, the cheating, lying, and stealing.

He looked again at his Harley. The broken mirror's shards remained in place. Quite by coincidence, they reflected his image back to him. Donna was not in his mirror; he was. He need only blame himself for his misfortunes, not her.

+ + + +

Wayne took a long nap in the afternoon. After dinner, he took out his laptop computer for the first time since his arrival. He was surprised that his computer found a wireless network in range and thought to ask Phil about it. He downloaded 1443 e-mail messages. Most were junk-mail pitches for Canadian pharmaceuticals, Acai Berry diets, fake diplomas, and penis enhancement pills. Penis enhancement, he thought! Given his current condition and the events which precipitated it, he was stuck by the cruel futility of such a notion. He was hopeful his sexual equipment still worked but the pain in his hip convinced him to not think about it.

He got a message from Arnie Heckleman saying the insurance claim for the stolen Hummer was ready.

> Wayne, Should I mail it to your house or do you want to come by and pick it up personally? Please reply at your convenience and let me know. Rgds, Arnie

Wayne hit "Reply" and wrote,

> Arnie, I crashed my motorcycle and am stilll recovering from my injuries. I'm staying in West Virginia for now. Please send it here.

He gave Arnie Uncle Phil's Union address and hit "Send".

Wayne Googled the apartment complex where he'd signed a lease to get an email address. He wrote and explained his situation and begged to be relieved of his contractual obligation. Several minutes later, he received a reply. The manager agreed to void the lease, keeping only his first and last months' payments.

He logged onto the rant site, *www.redhawk.com*. Someone had sent a link to a video which Wayne decided to watch. It showed gang warfare amongst the African American men of Memphis, Tennessee. Several of the men interviewed in the video had shot several other men and had been shot themselves. It seemed like Memphis, Tennessee was a distant planet from Union, West Virginia. He had no emotional energy to vent as he had often done before, nor really anything to say. QUARRELLER stayed quiet on the web.

He checked on his investments and was delighted to learn that several were doing well, counter to the overall markets. He resisted doing any trading.

Phil walked in and said, "It may be none of my business, Wayne, but have you communicated with Donna since your accident?"

Wayne shook his head back and forth.

"I'm not your parent. But don't you think you should?"

Wayne nodded. Phil walked away. Phil wasn't Wayne's parent, but Wayne felt he'd been scolded nonetheless. Regardless, he entered Donna's email address and typed,

Hi Donna. I'm sure you know about my accident. Uncle Phil and his nurse are taking care of me. We have some things to talk about. Please let me know you and the kids are okay. Wayne

+ + + +

September 23

Wayne awoke the next morning to find the scene from his window shrouded in fog. He rolled into the bathroom and did his morning testimonials. He wheeled himself to the front door and let himself onto the porch. The tall spruce pine 30 feet from the house was a ghost in the mist. As he sat and watched, the fog began to lift, allowing sunbeams to illuminate portions of the yard. At one point, a bright beam shone on the monument across the roadway, giving it a surreal gleam.

Phil joined him outside and said "Good Morning! How are you?"

Wayne nodded affirmatively, and then raised his eyebrow as if to ask back.

Phil said, "I got myself out of bed again!" He ambled down the long driveway to the highway to retrieve the weekly copy of the *Monroe Watchman* newspaper. While he waited for Phil's ambulation that seemed to take an hour, Wayne realized he hadn't watched television or read a newspaper since his crash and was anxious to learn what was going on in the world. The entire paper was only 20 pages in a single section. The lead article was about the plans for a natural gas drilling company to negotiate mineral rights from some landowners in the northern part of the county between Wolf Creek and Alderson. The landowners, mindful of the long history throughout the state of poor mountaineers selling mineral rights for way less than their actual value, were actively sharing information and negotiating cooperatively.

Wayne wrote on his omnipresent pad, "nat/ world news?"

Phil said, "The *Watchman* has been around for over 100 years." He pointed at the masthead, that said, 'Published in Union, West Virginia, since 1872,' and 'The Noblest Motive is the Public Good.'

"When I was a youngster, it covered lots of national and world news. Newspapers were more prevalent in everyone's lives. Today there are lots of sources of news. There's TV and radio, and now that we have high-speed wireless broadband here in town, lots of people use the Internet.

"You'd be surprised how well-informed people here are. I think it may have resulted from the spa culture we had in the prior century. Each summer, lots of wealthy, influential people came to the area. Local people glommed onto their every word, eager for information and ideas from outside the area. Don't be surprised if the local farmer starts talking with you about Global Warming, the earthquake in Malaysia, or the drought in Australia. People here have always had a strong interest in and understanding of politics. They know what Federalism and Socialism are. They know the difference between a democracy and a republic and what is meant by States' Rights.

"As you know, I was once a professor. True to the stereotype, I have always loved to educate. I realize you are a captive audience, so I fear I'm becoming overbearing by lecturing to you all the time. Are you okay with that?"

Wayne nodded affirmatively. Surprising himself, he found his great uncle fascinating.

"Then let me tell you about Nathan Bedford Forrest, the man whose portrait you covered with a towel in the library. Oh, and the Confederate sentiments of Monroe County and of Abraham Lincoln."

Another sunbeam hit the monument and lit it

as if under a spotlight.

Phil said, "People in this area, and by that I mean Monroe County and Greenbrier County, our family ancestors included, have always closely affiliated themselves with the rest of Virginia. That Confederate monument indicates this area leaned strongly Confederate. But I am certain that sentiment was mixed even within the county. As in many Border States, the stresses of war were inestimable. The pro-Union people here would have been under tremendous pressure, facing the dangerous choice of either speaking their convictions and facing grave harm, or moving northward, or perhaps even feigning sympathy towards the Confederacy as simply a necessary expedient for survival."

Wayne was puzzled, thinking that sentiment was more consistent.

Phil said, "Before I spin this yarn, I should tell you that history has always been a fluid thing. What I'm going to say cannot be construed as the truth, not because I am a liar, but because in history real truths are fleeting. Is it the truth that Franklin Roosevelt knew the Japanese were planning an attack on Pearl Harbor and he deliberately failed to warn the military so as to provide the impetus for our nation to declare war in 1941? Is it the truth that Lee Harvey Oswald acted alone in killing Kennedy or that Jack Ruby acted alone in killing Oswald? Is it the truth that George W. Bush and the highest ranking officials of his administration were at any level complicit in the attacks on September 11, 2001 for the same reason, as millions of people seem to think? Some things cannot ever be known with absolute certainty. What I will tell you is my interpretation of historic events, which you are welcome to challenge or accept as you wish.

"To understand the United States at the onset

of the Civil War in 1861, we need to revisit our nation's founding. By the 1770s, the colonies were still loosely confederated, but enough so to form armies to defeat the British and gain independence. Still, the King of England, in granting that independence, signed a separate treaty with each colony as if each were an independent nation. Through the next decade, the colonies became states and entered into two unifying agreements, the first called the Articles of Confederation in 1781 and then the Constitution in 1789, which boldly asserts itself as the foundational document of a 'more perfect union.' Founder John Adams was 89 when he wrote to a friend in 1824, 'I expressly say that Congress is not a representative body but a diplomatic body, a collection of ambassadors from thirteen sovereign States. A consolidated government was never alluded to, or proposed, or recommended in any part of the work; nor indeed, in any moment of my life, did I ever approve of a consolidated government, or would I have given my vote for it.' The federal union the founders created was nothing like what you think of, especially you as a resident of the DC area seeing the enormous power Washington asserts over the people of this country and the world today.

"Thomas Jefferson, in my estimation, was one of the most impressive humans the world has ever known. There's a well-known anecdote that when John F. Kennedy invited a large group of Nobel Prize winners to join him for dinner at the White House, he said it was the greatest assemblage of intellect to have ever occurred there since Jefferson dined alone. In Jefferson's mind, the more democratic the government the better, and the more local the better. Jefferson favored a weak central government. The reins of power should be held by the people, locally.

"The people of the era understood that membership in this union was voluntary and if necessary, temporary. The states signed on to be part of a larger nation. But nobody questioned their absolute right to voluntarily withdraw at any time from a union into which they voluntarily joined. How logical is that? Students at West Point before the Civil War, including Robert E. Lee and Thomas J. Jackson, the man we'd later call 'Stonewall,' were taught that the secession of a state is the prerogative of the state. This war was between the 22 non-seceding United States of America and the 11 seceding Confederate States of America. Civil wars are wars amidst a single government, fought over power to rule it. The American War Between the States was not a true civil war.

"My point is that people are not always what they seem to be or how their legends portray them. Let's consider Abraham Lincoln and Nathan Bedford Forrest, two men whose legacies were forged by the Civil War.

"Most Americans think of Lincoln as a thoughtful, sagacious man, the Great Emancipator and the man who saved our nation. Early in his career, Lincoln understood the Jeffersonian model. In fact, Lincoln told Congress 20 years before the War Between the States that people anywhere have the right to shake off an existing government and form a new one that suits them better. He apparently changed his mind as he ascended to the presidency.

"I believe Lincoln's sole purpose in waging war against the Confederacy was the preservation of the Union. Slavery merely provided a moral purpose to rouse Northern sentiment to fight the war. If you think about it, the Confederacy never needed to win the war. They just needed to not lose. If they fought to a stalemate or a negotiated treaty, they would endure as a new nation. The North had to win in order to abolish the Confederacy and re-absorb the seceding states.

"I need to jump back a few years. Obviously, slavery is morally abhorrent and intolerable here or anywhere else. Nobody can argue otherwise. Nevertheless, while many people, both in the North and in the South agreed with this, many others in both regions were active participants in the slave trade and were beneficiaries. The cities of Newport and Bristol, in Rhode Island, were the major slave markets in the American colonies and made many traders filthy rich. In the mid-1700s, Rhode Island had the largest percentage of black slaves of its residents as any colony in the North.

"In the years prior to the War, the Federal Government increasingly looked to the plantations of the South to fund itself. The South had 30-percent of the nation's population but generated 70-percent of the federal income, through taxes derived from cotton and timber exports, primarily from the South. This tax disparity, along with the fact that slave labor was essential to the economic viability of the South, were the primary causes of the secession of the Southern states. But again, they were not causes of the War, at least to most Southerners. The Southern states had exercised their constitutionally guaranteed right to secede. Lincoln's unilateral decision to invade Virginia – in the area now West Virginia – caused the War. Lincoln goaded South Carolinians into attacking Fort Sumter in April, 1861, whereupon he called for Northern troops to assemble.

"Lincoln's first strategic objective was to protect the Baltimore and Ohio Railroad, the only railroad in that day to connect the eastern Seaboard states of the Union with the West. It ran across what was then northern Virginia. This, then, was an invasion by the United States into the Confederate States. Virginia had been enthusiastic in its support of the foundation of the Confederacy all along, but this is what really brought farm boys from Monroe County and the other counties west of the Blue Ridge to arms, even though few of them owned slaves or benefited in any way from slavery. They took up arms to kick out the goddamn Yankees! As I said a moment ago, Lincoln did this unilaterally; Congress was out of session and didn't reconvene until July. Lincoln did all this essentially on his own. Give the man credit; if he was anything he was decisive.

"Nevertheless, if Thomas Jefferson had been alive to watch Lincoln's machinations, he would have called them treasonous. Lincoln's actions effectively destroyed Jeffersonian Democracy.

"So what about slavery? Lincoln was the great Emancipator, right? He wrote in a well-known letter in 1862 to Horace Greeley, then Editor of the New York *Tribune*, 'My paramount object in this struggle is to save the Union, and is *not* either to save or to destroy slavery. If I could save the Union without freeing *any* slave I would do it, and if I could save it by freeing *all* the slaves I would do it; and if I could save it by freeing some and leaving others alone I would also do that. What I do about slavery, and the colored race, I do because I believe it helps to save the Union; and what I forbear, I forbear because I do *not* believe it would help to save the Union.' Most people of the era, Lincoln likely included, considered black people to be intellectually inferior to whites and not deserving of equality. Few Northerners wanted freed Southern slaves to migrate there. Lincoln's Emancipation Proclamation, issued in two executive orders, in September 1862 and January, 1863, declared freedom to all slaves *in the Confederacy*, what was then a separate nation! This was a public relations move, pure and simple. Imagine how the slaves in Rhode Island felt when Lincoln freed the slaves in Confederate Alabama and not them! Lincoln used the moral imperative of emancipation to conduct an illegal war, and the mythology that has emerged from the war persists to this day with that justification.

"Here's something fun for you to wrap your head around. As I said, Lincoln's Emancipation Proclamation freed only the slaves in the Confederacy. It was finalized on January 1, 1863. By June of 1863, West Virginia was admitted as a free state. So in the meantime, the slaves in West Virginia must have been in some sort of political limbo. My guess is that many became contraband property of war.

"The military-forced preservation of the Union was an unconstitutional act which destroyed the dreams of the founding fathers. In many ways, it weakened the Constitution to the point where many presidents since have ignored it at will. When George W. Bush was confronted by aides with the fact that many provisions of his Patriot Act were unconstitutional, he reputedly yelled, 'Stop throwing the Constitution in my face! It's nothing but a goddamn piece of paper.' Widespread acknowledgement of the illegal acts of Lincoln and the Union would vindicate the Southern cause and that simply cannot ever be done. Lincoln, the martyred hero, is a national icon and will always be so. We have a magnificent monument in Washington, DC and his stern visage on our five-dollar bills to crystallize his status. Do you know anyone who thinks Lincoln isn't a saint?"

Before Wayne could think to answer, Phil continued.

"Now then, I want to tell you about Nathan

Bedford Forrest, the man depicted in the portrait you've covered with the towel."

Remembering his recent nightmare, a shiver went up Wayne's spine. If Phil wondered why Wayne covered it, he didn't say so nor did he tease Wayne about it.

Phil continued, "Other than the fact that he was a tall, imposing man like Lincoln, and they both came from modest backgrounds, they have little in common, and other than that they were contemporaries and their legacies are ambiguous and controversial to this day.

"Have you ever heard of Nathan Bedford Forrest?"

"KKK" Wayne wrote. He couldn't remember where he'd learned about the association.

"Good for you! Yes, there is an involvement with the Ku Klux Klan."

"Forrest Gump," Wayne wrote, laughing to himself. His chest hurt under his healing ribs.

"Yes, you're right there, too! Forrest was born in central Tennessee in 1821. His biographers said he lacked education and refinement. He was a ruffian, and was basically illiterate. But he was a swashbuckling character, with a fierce temperament, brute courage, and iron will. He reputedly killed more than 30 men with his own saber and fists. He was 6'2" or 6'3" tall, huge by the standard of the day. He was rich as a businessman, investing in real estate, trading slaves, and running plantations. By the time the War broke, he was one of the richest men in the South with an estimated worth of nearly $2 million, a considerable sum in those days.

"He volunteered as a private in the Confederate Army. He quickly rose through the ranks. He was highly successful as a military commander. Robert E. Lee said after the War he regretted not taking better advantage of Forrest's skills.

"I'll be back in a second." Phil walked into the house and returned with a dusty book with a frayed, copper-colored cloth cover. He turned to a dog-eared page and continued. "In his farewell speech to his troops after surrender, Forrest said, 'Civil war, such as you have just passed through, naturally engenders feelings of animosity, hatred, and revenge. It is our duty to divest ourselves of all such feelings; and as far as it is in our power to do so, to cultivate friendly feelings towards those with whom we have so long contended, and heretofore so widely, but honestly, differed.' Does this sound like a madman to you? Not to me. Forrest was eloquent, direct, and conciliatory.

"The typical Southerner considered himself gallant and debonair, especially compared to the Northerner whom he considered bourgeois and mechanical, certainly unqualified to rule him. And yet carpetbaggers, opportunists, and politicians were flocking south in search of power and profit. From this discord many socially disenfranchised and marginalized Southern men organized exclusive white supremacy groups intended to resist Northern dominance and perpetuate their power and esteem. One became the Ku Klux Klan.

"One of the organizers told Forrest about the formation of the Klan and according to local legends, Forrest was sympathetic. Because of his imposing presence and proven leadership skills, he was soon elected Grand Wizard, the national leader. But Forrest always denied leadership. He told a Cincinnati newspaper in 1868 that he had no formal connection to the Klan. Nobody today can know what was in his mind at the time, but I don't think he supported the violent and racist direction the Klan was taking. I think he was looking for a counter to the reconstruction movement

that was overwhelming the South. He had participated in the slave trade prior to the war, so in that
sense he was a racist. The secretive and violent
nature of the nascent Klan obscures a true picture
today of Forrest's involvement. However, he gave a
speech to black Southerners in 1875 in which he
argued for a positive agenda of harmony and toler-
ance between black and white Americans. He was
known to have called for the admission of blacks
into political and professional classes. He was a
true warrior, and the nature of warriors is often
misunderstood. I know this from personal experience.

"Remember my story of World War II? I personally killed two German soldiers in combat. A week
after I'd escaped from the Germans, I was back
with my company. We found four Germans hiding
in a wrecked barn. They had their weapons but
no ammunition and no food. They were shivering
convulsively from hypothermia and defenseless.
Our company commander had seen the insane
brutality of the Nazis. When we found these four
guys, revenge was on everyone's mind. He ordered
another soldier and me to execute them. As we executed them, I envisioned their wives, soon to be
widows, and children, back home. And yet I knew
that they would have unflinchingly executed me,
as they almost did, had our roles and fates been
reversed. This was over 60 years ago now and the
memory still haunts me. I have never physically
hurt another person since then. I often imagine
what Forrest must have gone through emotionally.

"After Forrest's death in 1877, many monu-
ments were erected and schools named after
him. In recent years, because of the controversies
around his life, many have been dismantled or re-
named. The controversies over Forrest continue.

"The portrait of Forrest in the library is there because my grandfather, who was a career Army man, respected his military acumen. Grandpa was either oblivious to Forrest's racial legacy – unlikely – or suspect of it. Grandpa was not a racist. People don't cotton to racism around here. I like to think we got over that decades ago.

"I hope you see my point in this, that legacies are fickle, fluid things. Lincoln shares a holiday with Washington, has his princely face on the five-dollar bill, and has a fantastic monument overlooking the seat of our Federal Government where Martin Luther King, Jr., delivered his 'I have a dream' speech. Forrest was a shrewd military leader with a controversial racial legacy. Keep all this in mind as I continue telling you your family history."

By this time, Mildred had arrived. She said, "Wayne, let's get you back inside so we can get you fed."

Phil said, "Next time, I will continue my story about Andy, my great grandfather."

That evening, Wayne checked his email. Donna had written him back. She said,

> Wayne. We have many things that at some point will need to be discussed, primarily with regard to finances and child support. I am not of a mood to deal with this yet. My guess is that you aren't either. Please write back in a few weeks. Donna.

Wayne noted how absent was any anger or conciliation. He really couldn't tell anything about her emotional state and wondered with apprehension what she was thinking.

Part 3

The next morning after breakfast, Wayne again wheeled himself outside to the front porch. The air was noticeably cooler than the previous few days. He sat for only a few minutes before he retreated to the front hallway to borrow one of Phil's jackets which he removed from a hook above by using a wrapped umbrella as a tool. He rolled back outside. As he did, Truman arrived for a visit. Wayne nodded affirmatively when Truman asked about his recovery.

A few minutes later, Phil emerged carrying his ubiquitous cup of tea. Truman said, "Good morning, Dr. Phil! How are you doing?"

Phil said, "I got myself out of bed another day. Want me to continue telling you about great grand-dad Andy?"

Truman said yes and Wayne nodded. Wayne knew that Uncle Phil enjoyed telling him the family history. To his own astonishment, Wayne realized he was enjoying it, too. He was connecting with a family, something he never thought he needed to do. But here he was, sitting on the porch with his uncle, listening to family stories. He was eager to hear more, while still not quite knowing what to make of the newfound feeling.

"Let me think," said Phil. "Where was I?"

Phil took a sip of his tea and began again, "A month before Andy and Allie's daughter, Alicia's birth, seven southern states had declared their independence from the United States of America. Two days after Alicia was born, in the harbor of Charleston, South Carolina, a band of soldiers representing the new Confederate States of America attacked a fort called Sumter, held by troops of the United States. The War Between the States ensued. Four days later, Andy and Allie's beloved state of Virginia joined the other states in the new nation, the Confederate States of America.

"From what I've read in Andy's memoirs, I infer that Andy, Wes, and most of their friends were ambivalent about the maelstrom encircling them. They had no strong ties to either faction. They knew the war was largely about the contentious issue of slavery, yet they knew few families who had slaves. Only a handful of the farms in Monroe County were large and prosperous enough to afford slaves. Their strongest allegiance, if they had one, was to Virginia rather than to the United States. They felt that Virginia, as a sovereign state, had the right to make decisions about its own future. But they all hoped for peace amidst ominous clouds of anger and violence.

"In June, 1861, Andy and Teresa's older brother, Tom III, wrote to say he had made his way to Wheeling and had joined a Union regiment. He was neither heard from nor seen again.

"A few weeks later, Andy's and Wes' friend Nathaniel Bolt, who had joined the Confederate Army, returned from fighting in a Confederate victory near Bull Run Creek southwest of Washington, D.C. He tried in vain to convince Andy and Wes to take arms in defense of Virginia. They pleaded that this war was not of their making, and they had no stake in it.

"By early September, Bolt was back, this time with more conviction. As they met in Wes' and Teresa's cabin, he said, 'Confederate recruiters are everywhere these days, lookin' for all able-bodied men. They ain't takin' 'no' for an answer. Word has it that two brothers in Bath County refused to join.

Recruiters shot 'em and hung their bodies from a tree for refusin' to defend Virginia. Within a few months, you may be forced into service at gunpoint.'

"Andy and Wes talked this over at length with their wives. Nobody wanted to fight. But they loved Virginia and were certain that as a border state, the war would come to them regardless of their actions. Within two weeks, a recruiter from Lewisburg arrived and the men joined the Confederate Army.

"September 23, 1861 was a beautiful early fall day, with the oak trees just beginning to show the colors of autumn. Wes and Andy, accompanied by Teresa, Allie, and the children rode to the Salt to meet the other recruits. Just beyond the Indian Creek covered bridge, he saw a large column of turkey vultures kettling overhead and was horrified by the omen it brought.

"A newspaper saved with Allie's artifacts says that Mr. Warren, the proprietor of the Salt, welcomed a crowd of 45 people who gathered at the departure. His staff served free lemonade and sweet biscuits. He spoke glowingly about the patriotism and pride of the community in support of their beloved state of Virginia. 'You boys will kick those Yankees' butts! You'll all be home soon.' Mr. Warren had arranged a photographer from Union to be on hand to take photos of the soldiers as they departed.

"Once they were finally ready to depart, Andy and Wes were joined by five other boys from the Centerville area: Harish Grover, the stonemason, and friends Archibald Ganoe, Bartley McNeer, Bryant Cook, and Edwin Vawter. The men gave their wives, girlfriends, parents, and children hugs and began their ride from their beloved Monroe County to the train that would take them to war.

"Simple Howie, a man who spent much of every day sitting on the steps of the general store, followed along to bring their horses home. They traveled The Salt Sulphur Turnpike over Peters Mountain and Salt Pond Mountain, and down to the Sinking Creek Valley in Newport, then over twin mountain ridges of Gap Mountain and Brush Mountain, through Blacksburg and into Cambria, the village adjoining Christiansburg, through which the East Tennessee and Virginia Railroad ran. They were met by a Confederate quartermaster who assigned them to the 18th Virginia Calvary and booked them on a train to Lynchburg for combat training.

"The train stopped in Shawsville, Salem, Big Lick – which is now Roanoke – Blue Ridge, Bedford, and Forest, picking up more recruits. In his memoirs, Andy wrote about talking with the conductor about the steam boiler and the mechanisms that drove the wheels. He learned that the train was able to travel at almost 25 miles per hour, twice as fast as a horse could trot and eight times faster than a man could walk. The conductor opined that trains would have a dramatic impact on this war. What neither of them realized was that the North had significantly more locomotives, rolling stock, and track than did the South.

"Once they arrived in camp in Lynchburg, Wes, Andy and their friends were assigned to a light artillery brigade and began their training for operating a mountain howitzer. Each man worked hard to understand each specialized position and responsibility. At their first experience with live powder, the boys were astounded by the intensity of the percussion.

"With a few days of practice, the boys learned the teamwork to maneuver the cannon and reload quickly, even if one or more was hurt or killed. Andy's first letter was written a week later. Let me get it."

Phil withdrew into the house and returned with a leather satchel which appeared to be as old as the letters it contained. He began to read from one of them.

My dear wife Allie, The days away
from you are aready filled with longing.
Each man on the train from Cambria
seemed lost in sorrow. There were many
veteran Confederate soldiers on board
with the reassignment of a divsin from
Georgia to the front in Virginia. These
men were homesick but were eager to
met the enemy and win the war. Their
uniforms were regl and I found myself
looking forward to one of my own. We
stoped in sevral towns along the way
where more recruits joined us on our
way to training camp.
When we arrivd, we were issued our
uniform, blanket, haversak, canteen,
and oil cloth for rainy weather. I have
enough close. I have 3 flannel shirts, 2
linsy shirts, and 2 pairs of drawers. We
eat brekas of beef and baked bisquit.
Wes and me is learning to fire a
cannon. The days have been filled
with practice, parade driling, and war
tactics. Many of the boys from the
mountains are aready skilled with their
rifles but the boys from the flatlands
are gating good training. Praise God
from him all blesings flow.
Your loving husband, Andy

"On October 18, Andy and Wes were given furloughs for four weeks to return home to prepare their families for winter. They were able to telegraph their travel plans back to the Salt and Simple Howie brought their horses across the mountains to meet them in Cambria.

"Once home again, Andy and Wes worked feverishly to harvest the crops and gather firewood for heating. They killed one of their hogs for winter meat. They also harvested several bushels of apples from the orchard. Apple peelings were a social event as well as a nutritional necessity. Twenty people attended the peeling at the Littletree cabin, and the Littletree and McGranahan families went to several neighbors' houses to attend their peelings.

"Andy and Wes spent several days hunting, filling the smokehouse with meat for the winter. Allie and Teresa went on almost every trip with their husbands and the women insisted upon cleaning, reloading, and shooting the flintlock muskets. It was largely unspoken but each of them understood that while the war went on, the women might be called to do jobs that previously had been done by their men.

"Andy taught Allie how to load and shoot both the Brown Bess flintlock rifle and the English flintlock pistol that he intended to leave behind. He fashioned a small drawer under the dining table and placed the pistol in it. He placed a knife with a six-inch blade beside their bed mattress for her protection should she need it in the night.

"The weeks passed too quickly and soon the boys were back in Cambria awaiting another train. Andy brought along several needles, an awl, and some thread to do boot repair, something desperately needed by the Confederate soldiers."

Truman said, "Sorry to interrupt you, Phil. But I'm getting cold. I see Wayne has his coat, but I neglected to bring mine."

Phil said, "Now that you mention it, it is a bit chilly out here. Let's move inside." Wayne rolled while Truman and Phil walked into the library, where Phil continued his story from his favorite chair.

"After their furlough, orders took them south. On January 19, 1862, they saw their first combat at the Battle of Fishing Creek in Pulaski County, Kentucky. Andy was particularly graphic in his descriptions of this battle, perhaps because it was his first experience with real combat.

"Because of the rain and mud, artillery pieces were late getting to battle and Wes' cannon fired only six shots before the Federals retreated. After the battle, Andy saw areas where Confederate artillery had killed several Federal soldiers who had taken shooting positions behind a hedgerow. Multiple corpses lay strewn about, many horribly mangled. He saw one torso without legs. He saw another man whose face had literally been torn from his skull. It was astounding to him the damage a cannon like theirs could inflict. Andy was familiar with life and death, but he was unable to eat his evening dinner and he walked away from camp to the edge of a meadow where he bawled for an hour.

"The spring passed with only minor skirmishes in southern Kentucky. So the commander of the Monroe troops convinced superiors that his command would be better motivated by defense of their native Virginia. On May 15, 1862, Andy, Wes, and their 77 Monroe Countians were transferred into the command of the legendary Thomas J. 'Stonewall' Jackson in the Shenandoah Valley." Phil pointed at the portrait of Jackson on the wall of the library. "On their way, one of the train's regular stops was in Cambria, but the boys were forbidden to leave the train. All were desperately homesick.

"Andy's next letter home was dated May 16."
Phil unfolded another letter.

> My dear wife Allie, We arrivd at Mt.
> Solon in the Shenandoh Valley today
> and joined the Virginia 27th army in the
> First Brigade, which everyone calls the
> Stonewall Brigade, under the command
> of Stonewall Jackson. The day we ar-
> rivd, some members of our company,
> have their twelve-month conscripn
> expired, demanded discharge. When
> Colonl Grigsby asked old Stonewall
> what to do, Jackson said, if they mu-
> tiny, shoot them! I watched as a line
> of soldiers aprochd them with loaded
> muskets. They decided to remain in
> service to Virginia.
>
> General Jackson is nothing impres-
> sive to look at, stoic and unkempt, but
> the boys would follow him into hell if he
> commanded them.
>
> Everyones boots has holes in them. I
> am busy making repairs.
>
> The enemy is all around us and we
> are sure to see action soon. Hopefully
> our quick victory will end the war and I
> will see you soon. Your loving husband,
> Andy

"Within four days of their arrival, Andy, Wes,
and the entirety of Stonewall's Army had marched
some sixty miles and were within a day of Front
Royal at the northern end of the Shenandoah Valley. The rapidity of this march took the enemy as
much by surprise as it exhausted the marchers.
But on the unbearably hot day of May 23, Con-

federates routed a stunned Federal force which hastily abandoned the town. At the onset of battle, the Confederates were prevented from overrunning the town by two Federal artillery pieces, but the arrival of Wes's piece, along with several others, saw the Federals retreating rapidly towards Winchester. The retreating Federals were able to destroy a bridge which would have allowed Wes' cannon to continue pursuit, but Stonewall forged on without artillery and an estimated 3000 Federals were killed or captured with the loss of only 26 Confederates killed or wounded.

"Andy wrote again that night after having received a letter from Allie. Hers was filled with everyday tidbits regarding the children and the garden.

My dear wife Allie, Thank you so
much for your recent letter and I am
glad you and the children are fine. It
is so exiting to hear that baby Alicia is
starting to stand up on her own.
I have diarea something awful. All
my socks are tarn. I constanly repair
shoes for other soljers.
We encountered the enemy at Front
Royal and routed them. Ole Stonewall
has the Federals befuddled and scared.
Our General Stonewall is a genus. Wes
and I are exhausted but victory in the
Valley is in site. Your loving husband,
Andy

"While the Monroe boys were in the Shenandoah Valley, Union soldiers under the command of Brig. Gen. Jacob D. Cox were threatening the East Tennessee & Virginia Railroad. The Federals made a foray into Pearisburg in mid-May, but were repulsed to the north of Peters Mountain. As they prepared for another raid on the railroad, they received word that Confederate Brig. Gen. Humphrey Marshall and the Army of East Kentucky had arrived in the area from Abingdon. In three days of fighting near Princeton Courthouse, Mercer County, from May 15 through 17, Marshall's Confederates overwhelmed Cox's two Brigades. Combined casualties were 129.

"Cox's Brigades marched to the northeast to assist in the defense of trans-Allegheny Virginia. In information I have pieced together from Union Army records and from Andy's memoirs, I have learned that three of Cox's solders were brothers, Anthony Pasko, Joseph Pasko, and Silvio Pasko. Anthony was 30, stately and debonair. Joe was 26, heavy and uncouth. Silvio was 17 and boyishly handsome. All were from the rugged port town of New London, Connecticut and fought with the 28th Connecticut Brigade.

"Cox's Brigades march from Princeton led them through Oakvale into Glen Lyn, where they ferried across the New River. From a bluff on the east side, a lone sniper shot a single shot and struck Silvio Pasko in the neck, killing him instantly. By the time their ferry landed, the marksman had escaped. Anthony and Joseph were overwhelmed with malice and revenge, furious at the loss of their beloved younger brother.

"General Cox was a religious man with a degree in theology, but had a fierce temper. By afternoon he found himself infuriated by a woman in Peterstown. Franklyn Humphries was a lawyer and his house, on the corner of Pinhook Road and the Union Pike, was the finest in town. His wife, Elisabeth, had three prize show horses. Upon entering town, Cox had ordered his men to seize the best horses they could find.

"That afternoon, Franklyn was at work in the courthouse in Union. When Elisabeth confronted the Union soldiers stealing her horses, she found herself face-to-face with General Cox. Bystanders said she called him a 'son of a bitch' and spat at him. A moment later, he ordered her tied to one of the two grand maple trees in her yard, facing towards her house. Then he had the house torched. As Cox's army marched from town, intense heat from the fire singed her eyebrows and scorched her face, causing severe burns. By the time neighbors cut her free, her house was an inferno. Twenty minutes later, Franklyn Humphries emerged from court and saw smoke in the sky from the direction he'd traveled the previous day, some 24 miles away, and he wondered in trepidation what was burning.

"By the following day, Tuesday, May 20, 1862, Cox's Brigades had marched through Linside and bivouacked at the Salt. There were no Confederate soldiers in the area and the women and children left behind posed them no danger. At Raines Corner, Cox sent a detail of 13 men including the two remaining Pasko brothers to raid Centerville.

"Six infantrymen rode horses, two rode a quartermaster's wagon, and five marched. The soldiers first destroyed the saltpeter powder mill. They robbed money and jewelry from the workers. Then, at Mr. Stanley's gristmill, they commandeered eight large sacks of flour and cornmeal – all the grain their wagon would carry – and then set that mill afire as well. Mr. Raney watched as his workshop, with all his tools and work, succumbed to the flames. They robbed the millhands there as well. As the Yankees drove away, the millhands tried to throw buckets of water from the mill pond on the fire but the heat was too intense. Within an hour, the mill – virtually the sole grain-produc-

tion capacity of the community – was a smoldering
ruin, along with the bulk of the manufacturing
equipment.

"This detail of Yankees rejoined Cox's full company just before they arrived at the Salt, where
they commandeered from the Resort all the food
and supplies their wagons could carry. Cox ordered Warren to evict all his guests. Cox and his
officers made themselves at home in the largest
guest lodge and instructed Warren to force his
cooks to provide meals for his soldiers.

"Unaware of the heinousness engulfing their
community, Andy's and Wes' family were living
their lives as usual. Allie and Teresa had hitched
their wagon and driven it to the Salt to sell eggs to
the Resort's restaurant.

"After completing the sale, the sisters-in-law
and Allie's children entered the general store which
housed the apothecary. Allie sold the Jew some
ginseng she had collected. Anthony and Joe Pasko
entered the apothecary to buy some liniment for
Anthony's sore left shoulder. He had strained it
during the fight at Princeton.

"Allie turned away from the counter and bumped
into a tall, mustachioed man in a Federal uniform.
Startled, she looked into Anthony's eyes, not ten
inches away. Instantly registering in her mind this
was a Union soldier, she impassively said, 'Sir,'
and demurely turned away. She quickly found Teresa and baby Alicia, and they left the store. They
situated themselves on the wagon and drove away
to the south, Orion loping along behind.

"Anthony Pasko approached the counter and
asked the Jew for liniment. Then he said to the
Jew, 'Who was the dark-haired woman who just
left the store?'

"'Her name is Kate Adams,' the Jew replied.
'She lives in Willow Bend.'

"Pasko sensed the Jew was lying. He decided he'd kill the Jew before leaving town the next morning. 'Good day,' he grumbled, feigning politeness, and he left.

"On the porch, Simple Howie sat, whittling a pipe. Pasko said to him, 'Two women just left the store and rode away on a wagon. Who was the dark-haired woman?'

"'Allie McGranahan. She lives three miles south on the Peterstown Pike. Turn left just past the schoolhouse and she's up the hollow to the left.'

"'Thanks,' said Pasko, flipping him a U.S. penny.

"On their way home from the Salt, Teresa went to Allie's cabin to help her get Bobby and baby Alicia settled. Then she went to her own cabin, leaving Allie with the children.

"After supper, Anthony Pasko said to his brother Joe, 'Let's go pay a visit to the woman we saw in the store today.' They snuck out of the encampment along with Roscoe Steele and Sirgio Correggio. As they walked back southwestward on the Peterstown-Union Pike, the setting sun shone in their faces. They crossed the covered bridge over Indian Creek, passed the two-story log schoolhouse and turned left, off the main pike. They crossed Indian Creek again, this time by fording, and ascended the hollow of Humphrey's Run. At the junction, a sign pointed left to 'McGranahan' and right to 'Littletree'. The four of them went left, climbing steeply.

"Alison had fed young Bobby supper and he was playing with sticks. She was breast-feeding Alicia when she heard the geese honking outside. The next instant, she heard the dog leap from the porch, barking frantically. She pulled back the shade and in the dimming light saw four men approaching her cabin. One pulled a knife from his belt and threw it at the dog, striking her in the chest. The dog yelped and fell.

"Teresa Littletree lived three-quarters of a mile away. At that distance, she had never been able to hear Sasha bark. But as she sat on her porch knitting some socks, she heard the faintest sound of barking. Instinctively she knew something was wrong. She dropped her knitting and flew inside to get her Remington derringer.

"Allie bolted the door. Quickly and frantically, she put Alicia in her cradle and grabbed Bobby by the hand. She took him to the cedar chest, ripping out some linens to make room for him. She instructed him to lay inside without making a sound. She grabbed the Brown Bess flintlock musket from above the mantle and checked to see that the single-shot flintlock pistol was in its drawer under the table. Both were already loaded.

"In a moment, there were footsteps on the porch and pounding on the door.

"Allie yelled, 'Go away. Leave us be.'"

Phil took a deep breath and closed his eyes for a moment. He took another sip of tea and said, "The events I'm about to describe to you come with a caveat. This is how I envision the situation to have occurred, based upon journals and stories from the War and other personal accounts I have read. So again I ask you to pardon the artistic license.

"Anyway, Anthony rammed the door with his good shoulder, once, twice. On the third time, the bolt sprung from its molding, and he stood in the doorway, staring into the dark eyes of Alison McGranahan and then the barrel of the flintlock. She fired. About the time his eyes saw the spark and his brain registered what she'd done, a spherical bullet was on its way. It pierced his uniform and the small bible in his breast pocket. It smashed into his left third rib, shattering it, and then ruptured the artery just above his heart. He gasped twice and collapsed. Baby Alicia broke into a wail.

"'Goddamn it!' yelled Joe Pasko, as he jumped over his fallen brother and grabbed Alison by the blouse before she could move. He slammed her into the floor like a doll. Her left shoulder hit the black cooking pot, still hot from dinner, burning her and breaking her left scapula. He returned to his brother whose eyeballs had swiveled under his upper eyelids.

"Steele, who was right behind the brothers, came into the room. He crouched over Anthony and examined his wound. He said, 'He's a goner, Joe.'

"Pasko looked back at Allie, then at Anthony's body. 'Damn it, woman!' Staring vacantly at Allie, he pondered the situation for a moment. He had lost his two brothers within the span of two days, neither in actual combat. Allie reminded him of a girl he'd known with fondness as a child who had never shown the first interest in him. He wondered again why Anthony had brought them to her cabin in the first place. He looked again at his fallen older brother, and rage overcame him. He said to Steele and Correggio, 'Get him out on the porch. We'll deal with him in a minute.'

"As Steele and Correggio moved Joe's body outside, Baby Alicia continued to wail. 'Shut up!' He yelled at the crying baby. He hated babies. He walked over to the cradle. He pulled his knife, and slit the baby's throat. Her wail turned to a gurgle and then went silent. He shook his head once, turned to the men, and said, 'Shut the door and wait outside.' Then he turned to Allie.

"He walked to where she lay and in one motion, bent to the floor and with his left hand, picked her up by her gown. He grabbed the arrowhead that hung around her neck and yanked it backward, snapping the stout leather strap. He pitched it into the fire and looked back at her, gritting his teeth sardonically. He took his knife, now dripping with the infant's blood, and sliced her gown from the top between her breasts to her navel, slicing her skin at the same time. He dropped the knife on the table and with both hands, ripped the rest of her gown apart. He threw her on the bed.

"As she cowered and watched in dread and paralyzing fear, her shoulder crying in pain, she watched him take off his jacket and boots. He took off his belt with attached pistol holster. He removed his shirt and lowered his pants. He was as corpulent as the pig they'd slaughtered the previous autumn, and covered with dark, matted hair. He removed his drawstring underwear. He was the most vile, grotesque creature she'd ever seen. His stench overwhelmed the smell of gunpowder. He came towards her, and clenched her neck with his left hand, propping himself with his right elbow. He lowered himself onto her and penetrated. He began to thrust. Spittle, tinged with tobacco, spilled from his beard onto her forehead.

"She fought and squirmed, wriggling herself towards the wall. He heaved and groaned, heaved and groaned. He closed his eyes and tilted his head back. As he did, her right hand found the knife Andy had left for her. As he reached the throes of climax and lost himself, she struck, plunging the knife up to the hilt into his left lower back and yanked sharply forward to his ribcage, slicing his kidney and lower intestine. He arched back and screamed in pain. She struck again, this time at his neck, slicing his left carotid artery. Blood spurted over her face. In his rage, he slapped the knife from her hand with his left hand, and then reached with both hands to strangle her. For terrible moments, she was unable to breathe. She began to faint. Suddenly, his seething rage turned to panic: from fight to flight. He leapt away and fell heavily against the table. He dropped hard to the floor. He clutched the gaping wound in his throat and gurgled, 'Goddamn it!' for the last time.

"With the geese still cackling and nipping at them outside, Correggio and Steele had no awareness of the carnage inside. Correggio, increasingly restless, said to Steele, 'This ain't right. I'm heading back to camp,' and he turned and ran down the hollow.

"Steele waited for a few more moments, and then approached the door again. 'Pasko, what's going on in there?' He could hear nothing inside over the cacophony of the geese. 'Pasko!'

"Allie was stunned from being choked and wracked with pain in her loins and shoulder. She heard Steele's voice outside and pleaded with herself to regain her composure because her danger was not yet over.

"She got up from her bed, drenched in blood and Pasko's fecal material. She stumbled over Pasko's convulsing body and fumbled beneath the table for her pistol. She took it in both hands, imploring herself to stop shaking and hold it firmly. She pointed it at her front door. The third time Steele yelled for his fallen comrade, she fired at the door, hoping her aim was accurate at the target unseen behind. The bullet penetrated the hardwood door where it lost most of its momentum. Still, it hit Steele in his right eye, on the way shattering his eyeglasses. The bullet exploded his brain. He was dead before he hit the plank porch. She opened the door tentatively and found Steele crumpled there. She saw no one else.

"Allie dropped the pistol and looked inside at the cradle. Blood from her baby Alicia soaked through the linens and dripped to the floor.

"She picked up Pasko's belt and removed his

gun from the holster. Pasko was still convulsing on the floor, his left hand still clutching his neck wound. His eyes were wide. She took aim with his gun at the bridge of his nose, and then withdrew. She laid the gun on the table. She took a poker from beside the fireplace, walked to Pasko and swung it as hard as she could into his genitals. He gurgled a scream and curled into a fetal position. Then she picked up the pistol again, and from six inches away, fired a bullet which penetrated his face, then his skull, and then lodged itself in the wood planking below.

"She laid the gun on the table again, held her right hand over her eyes, and apologized to Jesus for her sadism.

"As Teresa ran to the junction of her hollow with the McGranahans, she saw a figure in the dim light running downhill, towards her. She hid behind a sugar maple trunk. Correggio ran past. She took one shot with her Derringer. She knew she hit him when she heard him yelp. He tumbled to the ground, but then got up again. She saw he was limping as he continued downhill. She ran as fast as she could to the McGranahan home.

"Teresa found a ghastly scene. Sasha was dead in the yard, lying in a pool of blood. The body of Anthony Pasko lay at the base of the porch stairs, still bleeding from a chest wound. The body of Roscoe Steele lay crumpled with its head against the door. She lifted his head by the hair and saw where the bullet had pierced his eyeball. She moved him out of the way and opened the door. She saw Allie sitting in her chair, the same chair in which an hour earlier she had breast-fed her baby. Allie was clutching Bobby in her arms, crying silently on his little shoulder. She was bleeding from the slit in her chest. Her gown in tatters was crimson stained. The naked hulk of Joe Pasko lay before her feet in a massive pool of blood. His face looked like mincemeat.

"Sirgio Correggio didn't stop running until he'd forded Indian Creek. He looked at his left calf. The bullet had grazed it and wasn't imbedded. But he was leaving a trail of blood. He took his kerchief and fashioned a bandage, but it quickly soaked through. He reassured himself he only had three miles to walk back to camp and he'd be safe. The moon was waning and wouldn't rise for several more hours, but the dim light allowed him to find his way along the Pike.

"Then Correggio heard a scream that stopped him cold. It sounded like the wail of a cat, then like the shriek of a woman in intense pain. Was it in front of him or behind? His head turned wildly and his eyes watched frantically for movement in the forest around him. He thought of the pretty woman in the house he'd left behind with Pasko. He thought of his own wife, about the same age, another black-haired woman, who had arrived from Italy four months before he left for war. He heard the scream again. As his eyes scanned the forest floor nearby for signs of movement, his skin prickled and his hands felt numb and cold. His heart pounded in his chest. He swallowed hard and his throat tightened. He ran for a few seconds but his leg ached in pain, and he slowed to a walk. He heard the scream a third time and he genuflected, begging his maker for mercy.

"At the cabin, Teresa ran to her sister-in-law and hugged her. They both cried. Teresa looked at the baby's cradle. She saw the blood dripping from it and said nothing. She noticed the blood streaming from Allie's chest and said, 'We've got to stop the bleeding.' She took a needle and thread from Allie's embroidery closet and put in six stitches. She heated some water and tenderly rinsed away the blood. She made a sling for Allie's arm and helped her put on a clean dress.

"Using all her might, Teresa dragged the body of Joe Pasko to the porch with the others. She put Sasha's body in the springhouse for later burial. She wrapped the corpse of the dead infant in a white linsey-woolsey cloth from the cedar chest where Bobby had hidden during the melee.

"She gathered up Allie and Bobby, and extinguished the oil lamp. Picking up the baby's body, Teresa, Allie and Bobby walked together to Teresa's cabin. Teresa put the infant's body on the kitchen table and sat with it overnight in a wake to keep the dead baby's spirit company while Allie and Bobby slept together in Teresa and Wes' bed.

"The next morning before dawn, Brig. Gen. Cox got word from Sergeant Bledsoe that four soldiers were missing. Cox ordered Bledsoe to send Privates Freeman and Erickson to look for them. Freeman guessed correctly that the missing men had gone south on the road from which they'd marched the previous day. Within a mile, they found the partially eaten corpse draped in the shredded uniform of a Federal soldier. The corpse wore a tiny metal plate hung by a leather strap over its neck with the word, 'Correggio' stamped on it.

"Freeman saw paw prints nearby that looked like they were made by a cat, but larger than any he'd ever seen before. Erickson ripped the tag and returned with it to camp for Sergeant Bledsoe. When Bledsoe presented the tag to Brig. Gen. Cox, Cox said, 'We must continue northward. We have no time to look for the others.' Bledsoe knew if the others were ever found, they'd be shot for desertion.

"In the morning, Teresa fixed breakfast for Allie, Bobby, and herself. She went back to the Mc-Granahan house and found the bodies of two of the three dead Federal soldiers. Apparently wolves had already drug the body of the older Pasko away.

"Teresa dragged one of the corpses, with already gas-distended midsections, to the woods. The bigger, hairy one was too heavy for her to drag, so she amputated his legs with Andy's wood saw and carried body parts in several trips. She cut off what remained of their uniforms and burned them, along with the tattered remains of Allie's gown. She hid the Federal weapons in the smokehouse. She dug a grave for Sasha in the apple orchard and said goodbye to her.

"Then she spent most of the rest of the day cleaning blood from the floor and furniture of the McGranahan cabin. The fireplace fire had gone out, but she noticed a white, ash-stained particle to the side, which she retrieved and wiped with a rag. It was the arrowhead from Allie's necklace. She placed it on the mantle.

"She returned to her own cabin late in the day with the soiled bedding. Two women from the Indian Creek Valley had come to her home unsummoned. Somehow each had identical lurid premonitions. The four women and one boy washed the bedding and prepared supper. Allie, Teresa, and Bobby slept together in Teresa's bed for weeks.

"A week after the attack, Allie wrote a letter to Andy." Phil shuffled through his stack of letters and found one marked, May 27 and read it to Wayne.

"My dear husband Andy, the children and I were attacked in our house by Yankees. Bobby and I are okay but baby Alicia was killed. We buried her Sunday in the graveyard besid the church. When you come home from the war, you will need to carve a headstone.

Your loving wife always, Allie
"P.S. Please come home soon. We
miss you so dearly.

"Allie stoically said nothing about the terror
she'd endured."

The three men were silent for several moments,
absorbing the horror they'd experienced vicarious-
ly. The clock chimed in the hallway and a cardinal
perched at the sunflower feeder outside the window, scattering the smaller chickadees, goldfinches
and slate-colored juncos.

"How much is true?" Wayne wrote.

"I don't know," Phil replied. "I remember a game
we played when I was a Scoutmaster when our
troop went camping. We would write the same sentence on two pieces of paper. We'd divide the troop
into two groups and have the scouts stand in lines.
We'd hand one sheet to each of the kids at one end
and ask him to whisper the sentence to the next
scout, and then pass the message on down the
line. Then we'd compare what the two last scouts
in line heard. It was always completely different
from what we'd first written on the paper.

"That's a long way of reiterating what I told
you earlier: all history is a fluid thing. I probably
haven't told this jeremiad in twenty years. I'm sure
I told it differently than the last time and perhaps
significantly differently than my granddad told me.
More than anything, I hope I conveyed the dread-
fulness of war.

"Whenever I tell it, I'm overwhelmed with emotion. Although the horror of war grips me again,
it invariably makes me profoundly grateful. I feel
a surge of gratitude whenever the lights turn on
at a flick of a switch, whenever there's food on
the table, and whenever hot water comes from my
showerhead. When you ask me how I'm doing and

I say I got out of bed one more morning, I'm sure it sounds facetious. But I don't take that blessing, or any of the other blessings of life, for granted. The courage, fortitude, and indomitable will that Allie and Andy possessed, in fact or in legend, is always inspirational to me. I'm also filled with gratefulness that I have a family legacy and heritage. Continuity with the past on a personal level is another blessing of my life."

What Phil didn't say but Wayne understood was that Phil was pleased to be imparting this continuity to him.

"Allie faced inexplicable evil in her own home and overcame it. Andy, as you will learn soon, faced his own demons at war, as did I in Alsace-Lorraine. I suspect you are facing some demons yourself. Each era has its own challenges and each individual has his or her own demons. What makes us who we are is how we allow them to shape us."

The three men sat quietly for several more moments. Wayne fixated on Phil's use of the word, "allow." Our demons don't shape us; we *allow* ourselves to be shaped. Phil stood up. Without saying a word but by expression only, he indicated that he was emotionally drained from telling the story and went upstairs to take a nap. After Truman took his leave, Wayne stared out the window pensively at the monument, across the way, in the pasture. The notion of a family legacy or history had never occurred to him and he'd never appreciated the value. He wondered if someday he'd be telling this same story to Willa and Eddie and be similarly gratified by the opportunity.

+ + + +

September 28

The following Tuesday, Truman picked up Wayne and drove him to the Lewisburg Medical Center where he had been treated after his accident. A nurse drew some blood for analysis. Dr. Meier, the orthopedic surgeon took some x-rays. He showed Wayne the film, where the resolution was good enough to see the threads on the screws in his femur and ankle. He told Wayne his wounds were healing well.

Dr. Ram stopped by to say hello. "How are you and Phil getting along?"

Wayne wrote, "Good! Nice man!"

Keith Pearsall, the maxillofacial surgeon, walked in. He spoke to Wayne about his jaw and his food. "If all goes well, a week from now I'll remove your wires and you can begin eating real food again. But you suffered a pretty serious laceration from your mouth to your jaw. The wound will heal but I doubt you'll regenerate the severed nerves. Your face will likely permanently wear a bit of a scowl as the corner of your mouth will show the scar that will make that side of your face turn downward. Every time you look in a mirror, you'll be reminded of your accident."

Wayne thought about what he might say when he could talk again and what his first words in weeks would be. He thought about Dr. Ram and how he'd felt nothing but contempt for her when she stuck him with a sharpened tube. He had come to realize that this little, dark woman with the silly accent had saved his life. Perhaps she was a much more skillful and intelligent doctor than he'd previously allowed himself to believe. As she turned to walk away, Wayne thought to mumble the word, "Thanks," but couldn't get himself to do it.

Truman and Wayne drove back to Union to pick

up Phil for their Rotary Club meeting. A speaker came from the Bedford Energy Company. He was introduced by member Franklin McRoberts III. McRoberts had served for several terms as state senator and was the area's most enthusiastic economic development advocate. He had invited this speaker to explain about a proposed new economic development initiative from Bedford Energy to place a series of commercial wind turbines on Peters Mountain.

"This will bring new jobs and new growth to the area," McRoberts said. "Wind energy is clean and eternal. As you all know, our country will soon face an energy crisis if we continue to rely on coal, oil, and natural gas to meet our energy needs."

The speaker told the group that commercial wind turbines are graceful. "They are gleaming white and they are huge. When you look at them from here in town, you will see this line of propellers on the mountain, gently spinning out free, renewable energy.

"Not only will these turbines reduce our dependency on imported energy, but they will also reduce carbon pollution, mitigating the impacts of global warming. My company will not only pay the county an annual tax, which can be used for services like schools and fire and rescue departments, but will pay the landowner as well. I can't imagine how anyone could be opposed to them."

On the way home, Phil said to Truman and Wayne, "This Thursday is the fourth in the month, the lecture Chautauqua day. I'll be giving a lecture on the geology of the area. It dovetails nicely with the proposal we've heard about the wind turbines. You'll be attending won't you, Truman?"

+ + + +

September 30

Of the six people who attended the Chautauqua, Truman was the only one Wayne knew, although one other man had been at the Rotary meeting. Everyone introduced themselves. Wayne wrote on a card, "Wayne, Phil's nephew, from NoVA." Everyone smiled when he showed it to them. Phil welcomed everyone and began speaking.

"Today I'm going to talk about geology. As always, I'll have a special focus on our local geography, here in West Virginia. Geologists are in general agreement these days of a theory called plate tectonics." Phil, typically informal and glib, became instantly more pedantic and professorial. "For as long as cartographers have had good maps of the earth, even schoolkids have recognized that the east coast of South America looks like it dovetails nicely with the west coast of Africa. And yet until the 1960s it wasn't widely believed they once were contiguous.

"The continents sit upon the earth's mantle like pancakes on a greased griddle. There are also many smaller sheets that move independently from the neighboring continents. Interestingly, the ocean floor is also on plates, counter-intuitively heavier than the continental plates. All these plates slide around on the earth's mantle, which is molten and thus fluid. The sliding is almost unfathomably slow, but continuous.

"Understand that they move independently of any fixed points. It's their movement relative to one another that is of interest to us.

"For example, the Asian Subcontinent, which is mostly India, Pakistan, and Bangladesh, is on a plate that is moving northward relative to the rest of Asia. This slow-motion crash is building the highest mountains on earth, the Himalaya

Mountains. Similarly, the boot of Italy is inching northward into the European plate, creating the Alps.

"Sometimes plates slide against one another on lines called faults. This is the case with many of the California Faults, including the most famous, the San Andreas. When plates scrape against one another, there must be periodic relief at the fault line. This is when earthquakes happen. The more time has elapsed between the earthquakes, the more severe they are because the greater the distance the land has to shift.

"The poles of the earth are where, if you'll pardon my analogy, the needle goes through the ball around which the earth spins. The continents can move anywhere relative to the needle. Right now, there is land at the South Pole – Antarctica – and the world's smallest ocean at the North Pole. It has not always been this way.

"In our distant past, our continent of North America has appeared drastically different. For one thing, what is now the continent of Africa was once coterminous. The collision of North America with Africa caused the upwelling of mountains here in the Appalachians, which at one point may have exceeded 25,000 feet. Few are over 4000 now. It's hard to imagine time frames that would show us the movement of Africa to 6000 miles away and the erosion of the mountains to mere remnants of their former selves.

"Meanwhile, keep in mind that the various land masses moved relative to the poles and the equator. This is important because it affects the flora – that's the plants – and the fauna, the animals that live on them at the time. But the poles, which are now the coldest places on the planet, haven't always been cold. There have been ice-free periods even at the poles.

"Patterns of plant fossils show when and where different climate zones occurred. Here in West Virginia we now have a cool, temperate deciduous zone. Further north and in higher elevations even here in West Virginia we have zones that are more dominated by pines, spruces, and ferns, which have been adapted to cooler climates.

"This is really interesting, I think. As our world has continued to warm after the last Ice Age, these cold-weather plants have move both northward and to higher elevations. The plants on West Virginia's highest peak, Spruce Knob, are in effect now on a high-elevation island, surrounded not by water but by warmer temperatures. As the climate continues to warm, they will be pushed upwards to oblivion.

"Scientists are in general agreement that fossil fuels: peat, coal, oil, and natural gas, were formed by heat and compression over time from plant material. Much of West Virginia contains these fuel resources. What happened over many cycles is that a warmer period would ensue, causing great swamps and forests to flourish. Their material would drop and decay under new layers. Erosion from the peaks covered these carbon-based materials and under successive layers of both, over millennia, would produce the fuels we now exploit. Sometimes these areas were under the sea, due to rising seas from global warming and sometimes they were above sea level.

"Fossil fuels are rare things, formed under special and specific conditions, where organic productivity would have generated hydrocarbons. Our society is now extracting and consuming fossil fuels at a rate around a million times faster than the earth regenerates them. In my October presentation, I'll talk about depletion of these resources.

"Anyway, the linear mountains to the south

and east of here, all the way to the Blue Ridge, are from what we call the Allegheny Fold Belt. The creation of these mountains by the folding of colliding sheets terminated about 260 million years ago. These mountains are made primarily of limestone and they do not contain hydrocarbons. To the west and north are the coal-bearing mountains of West Virginia, Western Virginia, and Eastern Kentucky. As I said, they were formed by deposits of sediments that flowed from the limestone mountains to their south and east.

"Originally the limestone mountains were of immense proportions. Meanwhile the sandstone areas, the coal-bearing areas, were flat and at sea level. Through the millions of years, the limestone mountains eroded to today's modest proportions, although retaining their general linearity. Meanwhile, the same erosion produced the still more modest, but more intricately shaped sandstone areas. It takes a real stretch of the imagination to believe that the coal-bearing areas of Appalachia were once flat and at sea level, but the fact that we occasionally find fossils of oceanic plants and animals in the strata reinforces the accepted explanation.

"Here's a summary. The African plate crashed into the North American plate, causing the upwelling of long, high ridges. Flows of rock, both from glaciers and landslides, sent deposits to cover flatter lands rich in organic material. That material, over time and with heat and pressure, became fossil fuel, primarily coal and natural gas around here. The areas that have coal now were once at sea level. At times there was ocean on both the east and west side of today's Appalachians."

A woman Wayne didn't recognize interrupted. "Did you say there wasn't always ice at the poles?"

"Yes," said Phil. "For three-quarters of the earth's history, there was no ice at the poles. Our current situation is not typical. As I mentioned, continents slide around relative to the poles and equator. Ice ages correspond to times when there is land at the poles because continents cool faster than seas. Right now, there is land at the South Pole: Antarctica. There is a small ocean, the Arctic Ocean, at the North Pole surrounded by North America, Greenland, and Russia, which behaves as a landmass. During the recent spell of Global Warming, the poles have warmed faster than the mid-latitudes. During most of geological time, there have been greater expanses of ocean at the poles, making the planet warmer overall. When the planet is warmer, greater areas of the continental plates are inundated, further warming the earth because water warms faster than land.

"We are still on the downside of warming from the last ice age, around 10,000 years ago. Humans have accelerated that action by the release of carbon into the atmosphere via industrial processes and fuel consumption. The problem we have as a civilization is that now hundreds of millions of people live in low-lying areas which will become inundated by rising seas and all of us depend upon food production from a stable climate. Many of the major cities of the world are on coastlines with elevations close to sea level."

Truman said, "Phil, you said the mountains were once 25,000 feet high. That would make them almost as high as Everest."

"Yes. It's hard to imagine, isn't it?

"That concludes my presentation. Thank you for your attendance and attention."

A woman named Mrs. Adams brought some brownies for everyone. Phil went into the kitchen and returned with a teapot and eight cups and saucers. Conversation ensued, primarily about the recent delightful weather. Wayne sat and listened, impressed that these people linked social events with learning. So much for his Jed Clampett images of rural West Virginians!

+ + + +

October 1

The next morning, Phil ambled outside with his cup of tea and found Wayne already on the porch. Although this was a warm, calm early fall morning, the maple trees across the lawn were beginning to brighten with fall colors. White, wispy clouds drifted lazily over Swoopes Knobs to the west. Wayne showed Phil the note he'd written the day before, "Andy?"

Phil said, "Oh yes, I promised to continue our story. Where did I leave off?" Phil said absentmindedly.

Wayne wrote, "Allie attacked."

"Yes, thanks. Unbeknownst to Allie, Andy's week had been similarly hellish. The night after the Front Royal rout featured unrelenting rainfall. Andy, Wes, and their company had spent the night without tents, spooned together on the ground, using all the oil cloths they had for covers. The next day and then the next, Jackson's Army chased the retreating Federals under the command of General Nathanial Banks, first through Cedarville, then Middletown, and then Bartonville on the way to Winchester. Since the typical order of advance was the cavalry, then infantry, and then artillery, Andy's artillery division was near the rear and faced sparse skirmishes as the Army moved rapidly forward. The men were exhausted and famished, but Stonewall's push was relentless. Andy's diarrhea had continued, and he stopped to relieve his bowels frequently. He lost eight pounds in a week from his already trim body and his ribs were clearly visible on the rare occasions he bathed in running streams. He had blisters on both feet that ached with every step. Seemingly everyone was sick or wounded and everyone was famished.

"On Sunday, May 25, 1862, Jackson's army caught up to the Federal General Banks' Army in Winchester. Banks was so confident that Jackson would rest his troops before assaulting the city, he retired to his headquarters to rest. His warm bath was interrupted only when he heard musket fire to the south and the roar of his retreating Army along Braddock and Cameron streets, with Stonewall's men in hot pursuit. By May 26, Banks and the bedraggled remains of his army fled across the Potomac from Williamsport, Virginia into Maryland.

"For the next few days, Stonewall's men rested and enjoyed the warm support of the people of Winchester whose town had been under Federal control for two months. Andy's diarrhea abated, and he regained a few pounds.

"Lowly soldiers like Andy were unaware of the overall implications of Jackson's strategic achievements, but they were many. The Army had, in a dozen days, routed a force of more than 12,000 Federals, seized valuable supplies in Front Royal, Strasburg, Winchester, and Martinsburg, taken 2000 prisoners, and threatened the North with invasion to the point of disrupting Lincoln's plans for the invasion of Richmond. By May 30, Jackson's Army had marched 170 miles, an average of more than 14 miles a day. Some days they traveled more than 30 miles. Confederate casualties were a meager 613 officers and men.

"Federal strength in the Shenandoah Valley and environs was 62,000 men. Jackson commanded a mere 16,000. Jackson's brilliance and temerity were unquestioned, but mistakes on his part, even small ones, would not be suffered without considerable losses. With better recognizance, Federal generals' assumptions about Jackson's strength became more realistic. Jackson saw the reconstitution of Federal threats in each direction. Mindful of General Lee's overall strategy, Jackson abandoned the assault northward towards the Potomac and moved instead southward.

"Under unrelenting rains, Jackson's army retreated up-valley unimpeded from Strasburg along the Valley Road through its string of villages: Toms Brook, Mauertown, Woodstock, Edinburg, and by June 4 to Mt. Jackson. A mile south of Mt. Jackson, Confederates set fire to the bridge over the North Fork of the Shenandoah. The raging river impeded the pursuing Federal army for a day before the Federals constructed a new bridge. On June 5, Jackson's infantry and artillery, including Andy, Wes, and their battery, made camp at Cross Keys, a village south of Harrisonburg, in one of the widest and most open areas of the upper Shenandoah Valley.

"On the afternoon of June 7, Andy, Wes, and their gun crew set their cannon on a high embankment above and south of Mill Creek between the villages of Cross Keys and Port Republic. They had been told to expect an attack. Andy and his mates were delighted at finding such an ideal strategic location.

"Throughout the following day, an eerie quiet settled over the region as both commanders anticipated movement from the other. The bulk of Jackson's army stood seven miles away at Port Republic. The men camped under a waxing moon that arose after midnight. Around 2 a.m., Andy stumbled to the camp latrine, a fifty-foot long pit, a foot across and a foot deep, filled with human feces. His diarrhea had returned. The stench was overwhelming. Andy used leaves to clean himself.

"The morning of Sunday, June 8, 1862, dawned still and silent, other than the distant crowing of a rooster. Andy gazed at the grand Massanutten Peak to the north and wondered what the view would look like from there. The great range of the Blue Ridge Mountains loomed over his right shoulder. A barred owl sat perched on a huge chestnut tree behind him, an ominous sign to Andy.

"From his vantage point a hundred or so feet above the Mill Creek Valley, he could see a long line of advancing Union troops. Several Union artillery batteries took positions at the base of Longs Hill. Andy's battery, with four guns and 30 men, was given the order to prepare their guns for firing. The captain of the brigade gave the first order to fire. Andy and the other men opened their mouths to protect their eardrums from the intense percussion and the first cannonballs flew.

"Andy watched the first round of projectiles strike near the main Union column. He watched several men cut down by the explosion. He quickly joined his comrades to prepare the gun for subsequent shots. He moved repeatedly from the limber chest to the howitzer lugging prepared rounds.

"On his eleventh trip, with the battle barely begun, a Union cannon shell plowed into their emplacement. Shrapnel hit their howitzer. Harish Grover, the stonemason who had built the chimneys for the McGranahan and Littletree houses, was decapitated. Archibald Ganoe lost his leg above his right knee and yowled in pain until he bled to death. Bartley McNeer's body was obliterated. Bryant Cook's face was blown off and he never regained consciousness. Chester Phlegar was blown over by the concussion and slammed so hard against a rock that it fractured his skull. Edwin Vawter lay alive but unconscious. Wes, Andy's best friend and brother-in-law, lay clutching his gut where his abdomen had been ripped open and his intestines were spilling out.

"Andy had been running away from the howitzer towards the limber chest for more ammunition when the shell struck. He was knocked down by the concussion. As he tried to leap to his feet, he realized his right ankle had been broken. He crumpled to the ground again. His left hand ached. The ribs on the left side of his chest hurt like hell and his left cheek had a long laceration. Blood ran into his eyes from a gash at the left edge of his mouth as he crawled back to the gun emplacement. The barrel of their howitzer had fallen from its fractured carriage and lay askew on the ground. He made his way to Wes, who was delirious. Andy stroked his brother-in-law's hair. Wes sobbed and choked. Andy thought of dragging Wes away from the battlefield, but even if he could have done such a thing with his broken ankle, he saw it would be to no avail. As a bullet smashed into a log not a foot from where they sat, Wes wailed mightily and said, 'Tell Teresa I...' and began to choke. Then he moved no more.

"Andy went over to Edwin Vawter and could feel his breath on his hand. He shook his face and gently slapped him. As Vawter regained consciousness, he slowly opened his eyes. Andy somehow gathered enough strength to pull both of them to stand and together they retreated from the emplacement. Each, at times, supported the other, as they hobbled 40 yards towards the horses. They sipped water from Vawter's canteen. Smoke and the stench of sweaty, terrified, and dying men scratched his nostrils.

"Andy got to his feet and found a stout stick

to brace himself so he could walk on his injured leg. He turned to Vawter and said, 'I'm goin' back,' and began walking towards the remaining howitzers. Vawter yelled an expletive but began to follow him.

"Mere seconds passed until the next shell arrived, knocking both men into the air and killing Vawter instantly. Andy fell to the ground and lost consciousness, bleeding from his forehead.

"In his conscious moments, Andy hoped for a quick rescue. But none came. Night fell, leaving Andy amidst the stench and sorrow of the corpses of his dead compatriots. By morning his forehead wounds had coagulated, but he was lying in a pool of his own blood, urine, and excrement.

"The next day, just five miles away to the east at Port Republic, Stonewall Jackson's army first defeated an advanced portion of Union General James Shield's force and then turned to repulse another force commanded by Brigadier General Erasmus Tyler. The Valley Campaign was a great victory for Virginia and the Confederacy.

"By 4 o'clock that afternoon, villagers from nearby Goods Mill walked the battlefield and found unspeakable horror, a vast field of rotting flesh of both man and horse. These people lit fires to burn the horseflesh. They dug shallow graves for the dead of both Union and Confederate armies.

"Mr. and Mrs. Walker Crain, a couple in their sixties, surveyed the bloodbath surrounding the cannon emplacement of Andy's howitzer. Walking past the dead Confederates, they saw Andy, with blood over his face but still with color in his skin. Crain held his hand above Andy's upper lip and felt his breath, weak but detectable. They instructed their great grandsons, mere schoolboys, to carry Andy to their parlor where they placed him on a flat board covered with an old carpet. Crain had heard the schoolhouse on the Port Republic/Cross Keys road had been converted to a hospital. He sent one of his grandsons to fetch Dr. Downey. His grandson returned an hour later, saying Downey was overwhelmed by the dozens of patients already in his care. The Crains would need to care for Andy themselves.

"Crain learned Andy's identity by reading the letters from Allie that Andy carried. And, he got an address. The next morning, he wrote to Allie."

Phil pulled another letter from the satchel and began to read.

Dear Mrs. McGranahan. Your husband Andrew has been severely wounded on the battlefield near our home. The vilage doctor is unavailable to us and we are atempting to keep him alive. I will write to you again if he survives and can be properly dignosed. Rgds, W.Crain, Goods Mill, Virginia

"Several days later, Crain's letter arrived at the Salt along with a telegram about the deaths of Grover, Ganoe, McNeer, Phlegar, Vawter, and of course, Wes Littletree. The Jew – Mordeci Mishkin – and his wife Rivka drove their wagon southward from the Salt on the Peterstown–Union Pike. They turned left at the old schoolhouse and forded Indian Creek, now low with water. They went right at the signs that said Littletree' and 'McGranahan' and found Teresa feeding her chickens. Rivka spoke to Teresa, 'We have a telegram from the battlefield. Your brother, Andy, has survived but Wes is dead.' Teresa wailed. The Jew and Rivka comforted her as best they could.

"The three of them walked back to the junction, then uphill to see Allie and give her the news and the letter.

"Allie and Bobby had only returned to their cabin a few days earlier. The flintlock musket had been reloaded and placed again over the mantle. The pistol had been returned to its drawer and the knife had been cleaned and was back by the bed. Persistent bloodstains still coated much of the floor and Allie had decided that she would cover them with a rug as soon as she could. The bullet hole in the front door was yet to be plugged. Another bullet was still lodged in the planking of her floor.

"The Jew, his wife, and Teresa found Allie tending a pot of beans on the stove and young Bobby playing nearby. Allie's left arm was still in a sling, but her arrowhead necklace was back around her neck, atop a healing vertical scab.

They watched as Allie read Mr. Crain's note. She closed her eyes and took a deep breath. 'Lord be with my Andy,' she said. That Sunday in church, the minister blessed the souls of all the lost boys of Monroe. 'Let not your heart be troubled; you believe in God, believe also in Me. In My Father's house are many mansions; if it were not so, I would have told you. I go to prepare a place for you. John 14:1-2.'

"Forty days later, the current edition of the *Charleston Gazette* arrived at the Salt with word that the Congress of the United States of America, working with Northern Virginia Panhandle politicians had established a new state called West Virginia, which included Monroe County. Everyone at the Salt poured over the lines of copy in disbelief and anger. Without ever leaving their new homes, they had been ripped away into a new state, away from their beloved Virginia.

"Allie had received a letter saying that Andy was well enough to travel and would be departing Cross Keys soon to return home. Days later, Mr. Warren had gotten word by telegraph from Cambria that Andy had arrived by train. He sent Simple Howie to retrieve Andy while sending word to Allie when Andy was expected to arrive.

"When he arrived at the Salt, Andy was unable to put any weight on his right leg, so three men helped him from his horse. He unstrapped a crutch from his saddle and hobbled to Allie and Bobby. They embraced as tears flowed. Oblivious to him, a crowd had gathered while he and Allie hugged. When he looked to them they erupted in applause."

Wayne was struck by the similarities in Andy's wounds and his own and wondered suspiciously whether Phil had modified his story to make them seem that way.

Phil concluded, "I've got some work to do in the greenhouse just now. I'll tell you more of this story soon." He walked inside.

Sunbeams streamed through the window onto Wayne's shoulders, warming him. Swallows darted to and fro. He wondered about his own homecoming. When would his injuries heal so he could return to Northern Virginia? Who would be there to greet him? Cynthia was surely gone from his life forever. Was he in love with her or merely in lust? Would Donna ever be a part of his life again? He missed her more than he'd previously realized. How could he face her again and what would he say? Would she and he ever lie together again in loving embrace?

What would the children think of him? Would he be a part of their lives, two years, four years, or ten years later? If he told them Andy's story, would they realize the parallels? Questions ricocheted through his mind like bees at a hive.

+ + + +

October 5

A week after his last hospital visit, Truman took Wayne back to Lewisburg Hospital to have his wounds checked. Keith Pearsall, the maxillofacial surgeon, removed the wires from Wayne's mouth. He told Wayne that he was unable to fully repair Wayne's lower lip on the left side. Wayne would be left with a flat, drooping of the lip. Pearsall suggested facial exercises that Wayne could do immediately and told him that he would still need to be careful with the food he ate, avoiding hard, chewy foods.

Wayne was examined by Dr. Meier, the orthopedic surgeon, who told him his hip and ankle were healing but he would still use his wheelchair from time to time for months to come. Each day, he needed to spend more time on his feet using crutches.

Leaving the hospital, Truman said to Wayne, "I have a special treat for you today. Phil tells me that you have an interest in hawks. One of our fellow Rotarians, Reed Rathmell, is a falconer. I called him last week and arranged for you to view the work he does with his birds. He suggested we go hunting together after the Rotary Club meeting today."

"Yes," Wayne said, testing his newly liberated jaw. "Uncle Phil once spoke of him. That'd be fun."

After the meeting, Truman and Wayne followed Reed Rathmell westward over a small gap in the Swoopes Knobs. They parked in an open field just beyond a sign that said, "Knobs Unincorporated." Reed had a covered pickup truck. Inside was a cage covered with a sheet. The three men shook hands and exchanged pleasantries, Reed congratulating Wayne for his recovery and his ability to speak again.

Reed put on a heavy welder's glove and reached inside and took out a magnificent red tailed hawk. Rathmell said to Wayne and Truman, "I'd like you to meet Thor. We'll sit for awhile. Thor and I typically begin our day's hunt sitting together, scoping things out. She and I look around, marveling at the world before us in our own way. She sees so many things I cannot see."

"She?" Wayne asked.

"Yes," Reed said, chuckling. "I caught her three years ago. I thought she was full grown and was a male. But she continued to grow, eventually growing larger than a male should be, so I decided she was a female. It's hard to tell for sure a bird's gender. You can't just lift the skirt to have a look at the equipment." He chuckled at his innuendo.

Wayne noticed that Thor was similar in coloration, although darker, than Ruby. He wondered if the difference was due to the fading of Ruby's feathers over the years or simple differences between two specimens in the same species.

Rathmell showed Truman three lightweight lawn chairs in the truck and asked him to carry them into the field. The three men and one raptor sat in bright sun looking over a tall, waving brown grass. Trees were every shade of yellow, orange, ochre, and crimson. The sky was brilliantly cloudless and calm. The air had a crispness and cleanliness that Wayne had never experienced before, totally unlike what he knew from Northern Virginia. It felt good in his lungs as he breathed.

Reed spoke. "Falconry is the sport of Kings. Arabic legend states that the first falconer was a King of Persia. Another legend has that Ulysses brought a falcon to Greece after the siege of Troy. The most accepted story is that Europeans learned falconry from Attila the Hun in the 5th Century. By 900 A.D., falconry was widespread amongst the nobility of Europe and the British Isles. Popes participated in falconry and generals took falcons to battle with them.

"Frederick II – Holy Roman Emperor who reigned from 1210 to 1250, wrote a six-volume book, *De Arte Venandi cum Avibus*, the Art of Falconry. His obsession with falcons was the first scientific work in the field of ornithology. He described the bird's anatomy, the mechanical aspects of flight, and nesting, mating, and migration habits. Frederick's book is still studied today for advice on the sport and intimate looks at medieval traditions.

"Falconry reached its zenith in the 1600s with Louis XIII, the last great European falconer king. Thereafter, the invention of buckshot made for a more efficient way to provide food for the table. Falconry was gradually relegated to hobbyists.

"The species of the bird was related to the rank and status of the owner, with the larger birds like golden eagles belonging to emperors. Impersonation of a higher rank by the ownership of an improper bird was punishable by amputation of a hand."

Thor saw a crow overhead and emitted a scream. To Wayne, it sounded primordial. He was transfixed just looking at the magnificent bird.

"Falconers use hoods to calm the birds, typically for transport. Once we get them to where we'll be hunting, we remove the hood so they can scope things out. Thor really freaks out the crows.

"Anyway, falconry today is for sport rather than for food. Falconers train their birds in much the same way it was done centuries ago. I particularly like that aspect of it. Here in an open field in West Virginia, we are experiencing the same thrill a king or knight in Sweden, Scotland, or Bavaria might have experienced 400 years ago."

Thor emitted another scream.

Rathmell said, "I think she's ready to go hunting." He removed the straps from her talons and threw his arm forward. Thor went airborne.

"As you can see, she is totally free to fly away at any time. I weighed her this morning and she was 3.8 pounds, which is her flying weight. I need to make sure she is slightly underweight, which tells me she is hungry. If I let her loose when she isn't hungry, she'll find a nice, high tree and just sit there while I wait for her. I let her loose before telling you this, 'cause I don't want her to hear me, but for as regal as she looks, she isn't the brightest bulb in the proverbial chandelier. Hawks can sit for hours in what I jokingly call hawk hyper-space. She's not much fun to be around if she isn't animated, and she isn't animated unless she's hungry. She is motivated not by love, habit or friendship with me. She has no fondness for me in the way we typically think of a pet, and she isn't cuddly."

Wayne spoke slowly and gingerly. "I saw a hawk at Phil's house the other day. I think it was a peregrine falcon. It swooped from the sky and killed a pigeon. Took my breath away! The hawk looked stunned afterwards."

"Yes," Rathmell said. "Hunting is apparently tremendously taxing on a hawk. Hawks in the wild must be successful during the hunt or within a few days will lose the strength they need to continue hunting and will die. Falconers usually keep dead rats, mice, squirrels, and the like to feed their birds."

By this time, Thor was perched in the branch of a large tree on the edge of the field. Rathmell pointed across the field where a rabbit ran from one briar patch towards another. Thor took flight. Ten feet above the sprinting rabbit, Thor leveled somewhat, tightened her wings, and pounced. Thor reminded Wayne of the old war movies he'd seen, looking like one of the German Stuka bombers. Both predator and prey went sprawling across the ground. Thor righted herself above the rabbit which emitted a loud, painful wail that sent shivers up Wayne's spine. In twenty seconds, it was dead. Wayne realized he hadn't breathed for many moments. His eyes were wide and his heart pounded inside his healing ribcage. "Holy heart failure, Batman!" he murmured.

Rathmell ambled towards Thor. As he approached, he distracted Thor by tossing a chicken leg from his pouch a few feet away. He held up the rabbit to show Wayne and Truman and yelled, "Dinner!" He took the rabbit and stuffed it into the large pocket of his jacket. He fed Thor with some squirrel parts he'd brought along.

On their way back to town, Truman asked Wayne what he thought of the experience. Wayne said, "It is fascinating. Thor is beautiful. I'm intrigued by the relationship Reed has with her."

As they drove home, Wayne pondered the link Thor provided to an ancient time. Everything in his Northern Virginia experience was historically new. The oldest structures in the District of Columbia were barely 200 years old and the choking sprawl of Arlington and Fairfax counties was still newer, a product of the auto age. Falconry was elemental: a man, a bird, and prey. Modern suburban life was chaotic, frenzied, hectic, and artificial. The adrenaline he'd just experienced was primordial and real. The haste and stress that had marked his life seemed no longer relevant or appropriate.

+ + + +

October 6

The next morning, Mildred burst into his room in her usual ebullient way. "How are we this morning?" She exclaimed.

"It's not 'we,' it's 'me.' My mouth moves," said Wayne gingerly. "I can talk again."

She said, "Well ain't that just something? Congratulations! I have to say, I was looking forward to the end of carrying the conversational load by myself all these weeks."

He said, "I can eat soft food as well. Fix me some oatmeal."

She returned a few minutes later with his food. As she set it down in front of him, he said, "You forgot the butter."

He began to eat his breakfast. He said to her, "I never saw yesterday's paper. Bring it to me."

She left the room and returned a moment later with the paper. He took it from her and began reading it. She went into the kitchen to tidy up the stove. When she returned, he said dismissively, "I'm finished with breakfast. Take my plate."

She took his plate and turned towards the kitchen. She stopped cold, then returned and slapped his jaw on the unbroken side.

He yelled at her, "Goddammit, woman!"

She grabbed a desk chair and positioned it directly opposite his. She pursed her lips and she looked at him squarely in the eye. She said, "I've had enough of your condescension! It is hard for me to believe that anyone can be as rude as you. Since the day you landed here, flat on your back and broken, you have been under the care of complete strangers who literally saved your life. We have carted you from place to place, fed and clothed you, and nursed your health. To my knowledge, none of us have asked anything in return other than civility and common decency. Every day I have handed you a dose of medicines. I could have easily killed you. Believe me, after reading some of the things you have posted on the Internet, I've been sorely tempted."

"What are you talking about?"

"Do you think we're all idiots here? There are a few things you need to learn about living in a small community. We look after each other. We are civil towards one another and we expect that civility in return. We know each other well. Nobody is anonymous."

"Now wait just a minute," he protested.

"Hush! We like to get to know newcomers when they arrive. The Internet has provided some exceptional new tools for us to do that. You have made no attempt to disguise what a vile and disgusting human being you are. What's all this stuff about 'jungle bunnies' and 'Jigaboos' and sending blacks back to Africa?

"What was all that trash about immigrants destroying our country? Who the hell gave this land to your people, white boy? For thousands of years before your people arrived, Native American people lived in relative peace and harmony with their environment. They had great leaders and honorable traditions. As shameful as the actions of white Americans were towards black Americans, they were much worse towards Native Americans. Why do European-Americans have any greater claim to this nation than African-Americans, Asian-Americans, Latin Americans, or Native Americans?"

He started to get up, but she pushed him back on the bed.

"I'm not done. The reason so many people in this community have worked so hard to keep you fed and alive is that we are by nature hospitable people. It is certainly not because anyone has any affection for you whatsoever."

Feeling like he did when he was caught cheating on a test at UVA, he hoped the moment would pass quickly, but it seemed unlikely.

"As a black woman, I may be a bit oversensitive to abuse, as my people have suffered through three centuries of subservience in this country. Black people have dug the coal and built the cars and sowed the crops and fought the wars that made this country great. Yet until our last presidential election, we never felt that we were full citizens within our own country. Still, we treat strangers with every possible kindness because it is our cultural experience. Black people, at least the ones I know, have every reason to be angry. But instead, we give a kind word to everyone we meet and we praise the Lord for His kindness and generosity. We are blessed people.

"You are my patient and I am your nurse. I have no control over what odious or loathsome thoughts ricochet between your ears. I can, however, demand a measure of civility and respect. From this moment on, you will act as if you understand that, or you can find someone else to take care of you. Now then, did you have something you wanted to say?"

Wayne was stupefied. He tried to fashion a plausible response, but nothing came to him.

She rose and walked towards the kitchen. As she reached the door, she stopped, then turned and walked back to him. She said, "My behavior just now was inappropriate and slapping you was inexcusable. I apologize."

Then she said, "The occasional apology is good for the soul. You might try it sometime."

He rolled himself to the porch.

After straightening his bed, Mildred came outside to say goodbye. Wayne said, "Mildred, I

apologize for the way I've treated you and appreciate what you've done for me. I have been rude and
condescending, which is unforgivable. You will see
new, improved behavior from me from now on."
    She smiled and nodded.

+ + + +

That evening, Wayne wrote to Donna again.

> Hi Donna. My injuries are healing. I'm
> moving around better and I'm able to
> talk and eat again. I hope you're okay.

He thought about what else to say. He wanted
to tell her he missed her, but couldn't get himself
to do it. He continued:

> I have been thinking a lot about our
> relationship.

He thought about his spat with Mildred. He
wondered what would have happened if he'd
crashed his motorcycle closer to home. Donna
would have been forced to take care of him. How
would she have treated him so soon after learning
he'd been unfaithful to her? Would she have been
the faithful wife and nursed him back to health?
He rather thought she may have poisoned him. He
was thankful that he never had to find out.

> My experience here has helped me to
> understand how hurtful I have been to
> you and I apologize.

He wondered how would Donna react to that.
Should he apologize for specific transgressions?
Should he promise any changes in behavior, and if

so, which? Should he swear to a lifetime of fidelity if she would take him back?

> I'm still not well enough to travel and be back in NoVA and I don't know how to resolve our relationship. I miss the kids and I thank you for taking care of them in my absence. Wayne

Part 4

At the following week's Rotary meeting, a new face was in the crowd. Wayne was introduced to Ansel Cummings, the son of Stuart Cummings from the *Watchman*. Wayne and Ansel sat together. After introducing himself, Ansel said, "I live over in Mercer County. I work in coal mining. Most of the time, I run the roof bolter in a drift mine."

Wayne said, "I didn't realize anyone mined coal any more."

"Are you kidding? More coal has come out of West Virginia each year in recent years than ever before. These days mining is highly mechanized. Some of the larger mines are like factories underground. There is also a lot of mountaintop removal mining going on."

"I've heard about that. Isn't it controversial?"

"Yes. Coal is buried underground in thin seams, like icing in a layer cake. In underground mining, we remove the icing while working under the cake, allowing it to collapse as we make our way back out. In mountaintop removal mining, or strip mining, we take all the cake, blast it loose, and then dump it into the hollows and valleys below. Then we can take the coal away. There is typically a ratio of 20 to even 100 to one between the rock and the coal.

"I have been mining 'met coal.' Met means metallurgical, the coal used to make steel. It's the most valuable coal we have, but its market is volatile. With the recession and the troubles the auto industry is having, there's no demand for met coal right now. Our mine closed a few months ago and

I was laid off. I've been staying with my lady in our family cabin near Waiteville."

Wayne thought Ansel had the physique of a football player, perhaps a running back. He had a "been there, done that" grizzled look to him. He had dark eyes, a couple of missing teeth, and a soldier's crew-cut that didn't quite mask a large scar across his skull. He had a tattoo on his left forearm that said "Marines" and "Semper Fi" and another on his right forearm that said "Desert Storm."

"Is the family cabin a weekend retreat?"

"Dad and mom bought it for that reason. But lately for me, it's become more of an apocalypse hide-out. I think this country is facing catastrophic times. I needed a place that I could fend for myself and not be swept away in the coming mayhem."

Wayne admitted he'd had similar thoughts about the future of the nation. As they chatted, they realized a common interest in firearms. Ansel said, "Our family has always had lots of guns."

Wayne said, "I like to shoot, too. I haven't had a gun in my hand since my accident, but until then I always carried a gun."

Ansel said, "If you'd like to come over to the cabin, I'll show you the collection. I load my own ammunition, too.

"I come to town most weeks to shop for groceries with the lady. Today, she's in Pineville visiting with her folks, so I thought I'd join dad at Rotary. I have an appointment with my shrink at the Veterans Administration hospital in Salem next week. But the following week, I'll stop by after the meeting and pick you up. You can visit for a few hours, and then I'll give you a lift back to Union."

"Right on, brother!"

+ + + +

During dinner that evening, Phil said to Wayne, "I've been meaning to ask you about your trip here in the first place. Now that you're talking again, do you mind telling me what precipitated your visit? You said when we spoke by phone you were interested in some of the furniture."

Wayne's mouth was already open with a fork of mashed potatoes on its way. "Yes. I think you know Donna kicked me out of the house. It was the day before I called you. Mom had called a few weeks earlier and said you had some to give away. So all of a sudden, I needed some furnature for the apartment I rented."

"Do you mind if I ask what caused Donna react the way she did?"

"I'd rather not go into the gory details. I admit that her action was not undeserved. The rest I'd prefer to leave unsaid."

"What plans do you have? Do you expect to go back to her?"

"Right now, I'm not sure what to expect. I'm not at all sure she'd have me back. This is a tough thing for me to admit, but I think if I were in her position, I wouldn't be all that eager. I really miss my kids. I suppose I miss her, too."

"Regardless of why you came, it is good to have you here." Several moments passed before the old man spoke again. "If you miss her, you owe it to her and to yourself to tell her so."

+ + + +

That evening Wayne got a note from Donna.

> Hi Wayne. I'm glad to know you are feeling better.
> I have been thinking a lot about our

> relationship, too, and am as uncertain as you seem to be about its future. I think the wounds are still too raw for either of us to deal with it. But if you can send me $750 a month to help pay the kids' expenses, I'll put off calling my lawyer for a few more months. Donna

He hit "reply" and typed,

> Hi Donna. You're acting better towards me than I deserve and I appreciate it. If there is any way I could see the kids, would you be willing? Wayne

He was about to hit the "send" button, but decided to add,

> Yes, the $750 per month you've asked for is reasonable. I will mail a check tomorrow.

+ + + +

October 14

Two days later, on Thursday, a young woman with blonde hair came by the house with a guitar case. Wayne remembered Phil mentioning that today was a Chautauqua Thursday and that it was a day for music rather than for a lecture. He hobbled on crutches into the living room as Phil led her in.

Phil said, "Wayne, I'd like you to meet Gibby Robinson."

"Hello," he said. "It is a pleasure to meet you."

She said, "Yes, it is my pleasure, too. Professor McGranahan told me about your accident. It looks like you are recovering well."

Phil said, "Gibby lives up the road in Pickaway, towards Lewisburg. We've known each other since she was a baby."

Wayne said, "What do you do now?"

She said, "I am studying biology at the community college in Lewisburg. I hope to become a pharmacologist someday. Dr. McGranahan has always inspired my learning. He is a legend in the biology world."

"I see you play guitar, too."

"My great aunt taught me how to play when I was eight years old. I have written a few of my own songs but I always enjoy singing songs from the great folk musicians."

Phil said to Wayne, "This area is the epicenter of traditional Appalachian music."

Wayne said to Gibby, "I look forward to your concert. It's nice of you to come and sing."

By this time, a group of five people had appeared on the porch and were exchanging greetings with Phil. As they came in to take their seats, Wayne said hello to each, happy to be able to speak again.

Gibby began her concert. Her voice was high and clear. As she performed, Wayne was struck by how alluring she was. Wearing no makeup, she had a youthful glow and exuberance that enchanted him. Around her neck, she wore a string necklace with a cross medallion which sat above her bosom. It reminded him of the way Cynthia wore her cross. It was the first time he'd been aroused since his accident.

Her concert contained a number of songs about the struggles of mountain people. She ended with the classic Irish melody, Danny Boy.

Oh Danny boy, the pipes, the pipes are calling
From glen to glen, and down the mountain side
The summer's gone, and all the flowers are

dying
'Tis you, 'tis you must go and I must bide.
But come ye back when summer's in the
*   meadow*
Or when the valley's hushed and white with
*   snow*
'Tis I'll be here in sunshine or in shadow
Oh Danny boy, oh Danny boy, I love you so.

Several members of the audience were visibly emotional. After the concert, his uncle brought some cookies from the kitchen. As Gibby was ready to leave, Phil handed her an envelope and said, "Thanks again for coming. Here's something to help with your college expenses."

That evening during dinner, Wayne said to Phil, "Gibby sure has a great voice. It was a pleasure to hear her sing."

Phil said, "When a man gets to be my age, there are few things left to live for. One of them is to have this house filled with song. I like just about every type of music there is. As I mentioned, this area has a wonderful heritage in traditional music. Somehow, I always envision the woods of the walls and hardwood floors resonating to the tones of an instrument the same way the woods in a guitar or violin does. In my mind, the music seeps into the walls and stays there for several days. I feel the richness and structure of the music as held by the fibers and textures in the wood. It makes me so happy!

"I fear that our younger people are losing the musical skills that have always permeated this area. It's fine with me that our high schools teach the trombone and the clarinet but I think they should be teaching the banjo and the autoharp as well. I enjoy thinking that music is in the blood of every Monroe Countian, even the non-musical like myself. It's part of who we are.

"Gibby is a particularly lovely young woman. It always brightens this house to have her here. When she was younger, she would spend many summer afternoons working with me in the garden. She absorbed information about living things like a sponge. She was like the granddaughter I never had. That she has a voice that makes Baltimore orioles envious makes her that much more endearing."

Wayne was taken aback by the old man's admission, placing a sexual connotation on it. Do people in their nineties still have sexual urges? He'd never really thought about it. He was sure Phil implied no sexual attraction and was embarrassed that his mind had gone there. His mind played the song, *My Generation*, by The Who, with the line, "I hope I die before I get old." He had never given much thought to his own longevity expectation. Would he want to die before he became ninety-four? He had seen so much personal pain lately he wondered whether he could endure decades more of his life if they played out similarly.

Changing the subject, Wayne said, "When you spoke about Thomas Jefferson a few weeks ago, you piqued my interest. I did some reading about him from a couple of books in your library and on the Internet. Having attended his university, UVA, I always thought of Jefferson as an architect. But I'm sure you know he was also an inventor."

"That's right," Phil said, "but much more than that! Statesman. Botanist. Geographer. Archaeologist. Jefferson really could do it all. I think of him more as an innovator than an inventor, taking ideas other people had created and improving on them. Before he was president, Jefferson served the nation as George Washington's first Secretary of State. When Jefferson was in Europe, he observed the Dutch moldboard, which is the front of a plow, the part that lifts and turns the soil. The designs he saw were inefficient so he set his mind to improve it."

"I read about that. What astounded me is that Jefferson never patented his idea, magnanimously believing it should be readily available for the good of the people, not for his own monetary benefit. Can you imagine that level of selflessness today?"

"I was going to ask you the same question," said Phil.

"The sad part of his generosity is that at his death, he was penniless and his heirs had to sell Monticello to pay his debts."

"Did you read his thoughts on the influence of religion in politics?"

"Yes! I was surprised to learn he thought the religious leaders of the day, especially the Calvinists and Catholics, were as culpable as the kings in suppressing freedom by making their followers adopt obscure doctrines instead of thinking for themselves. Surprisingly, the Baptists of the day agreed with him about the absolute need to separate the government from the churches. If he was around today, I don't think he'd be able to reconcile the sway organized religion has on the political process. I'm not sure how he would have felt about the decisive social issues of today, but I certainly think he'd be appalled at the overbearing influence religious groups like the Southern Baptists have on the Republican Party."

"You're right about that. For a true Jeffersonian Democracy to be successful, the governed people really need to be informed and active. Our representatives in Congress are a sorry lot, spineless, self-centered, and in the pocket of the major international corporations. But in tolerating their mischief and malfeasance, the people are equally to be blamed."

+ + + +

October 16

Saturday, Wayne got a call from his old friend Martin Kneeland. "Wayne, old boy! I heard from Donna that you've had a bit of a problem in West Virginia."

They chatted for awhile. Martin was calling from the clubhouse where he and Wayne played golf together. Wayne told about the crash the best he could remember it, including the intense pain and the fact that he thought he was close to death.

"How are my kids?" Wayne asked.

"I've only seen them a couple of times since you left. You know how kids are. They change so fast. They seemed all right, if a bit edgy."

"I really miss them."

"Say, Cheryl's sister and her family live in Salem, Virginia. That's not too far from where you are, is it?"

"It's only an hour from here."

"We come down several times each year to visit with them. Maybe Donna would consent to having us bring your kids along next time we come so you can see them."

"Yes, I'd like that. I'll write Donna and ask her if it's okay." Wayne explained that he had no vehicle of his own and still couldn't drive, but would ask around for a ride. Martin said he'd be in touch when they planned their next trip.

Later that afternoon, Wayne wrote an email to Donna and explained Martin's offer and asked her permission. She wrote back to grant it.

+ + + +

October 19

The following week at the Rotary meeting, Wayne sought out Reed Rathmell. Wayne said, "Thanks for inviting Truman and me to your falconry hunt. It was one of the most exciting things I've ever seen. I've always loved speed, but I won't be going anywhere fast for awhile. This sort of scratches the speed itch I've been having."

"No problem," said Rathmell. "I enjoy showing it off. Falconers spend lots of time with their birds. All of us love having new, enthusiastic people along."

"You are retired, aren't you? What kind of work did you do?"

"I was a Brethren minister. I had a church in Tazewell County, Virginia for several years. My wife died a couple of years before I retired. After that, I decided to move back to Monroe County, where I grew up." Rathmell turned to a younger woman beside him. She wore a blue jean dress and lots of colorful beads. "I'd like you to meet my daughter, Juliet."

"Hello," said Wayne.

"It is nice meeting you," said Juliet. "I understand you've had a bit of an accident."

As Wayne recounted his accident, focusing on the rescue and recovery, he looked her over. She had pearly-white, crooked teeth, red hair and blue eyes, with thick, wire-rimmed glasses. She looked to be in her mid-thirties. He asked her about herself and learned she had a degree in biochemistry from Concord College, now Concord University, in nearby Mercer County. She'd joined the Peace Corps after graduation and worked in Honduras, then Peru, then Argentina, and finally in Bhutan. She said she spoke six languages.

"These days, I'm close to finishing my PhD in Psychology at Virginia Tech down in Blacksburg. I also teach one class in social work at the community college in Lewisburg. So two days a week, I drive north to Lewisburg and two days I drive south to Blacksburg. It's a brutal schedule and it seems like I'm on the road all the time. I live at dad's place in the old slave quarters behind the main house. Dad fixed it up as a guest house. I try to spend as much time as I can with him now that mom's gone."

The meeting got underway. Afterward, Wayne said to Juliet, "I've enjoyed meeting you. Will you be attending again next week?"

Juliet said, "I am busy right now with school, so I only attend occasionally."

"Can we get together sometime, if it fits into your schedule?"

"Yes, I would like that. I'll let you know."

+ + + +

October 22

With each passing day, Wayne felt his recovery was progressing. He could move around without the wheelchair using the crutches. Phil had a lift on the stairway, and though Phil never seemed to need it, he suggested Wayne use it so he could move to an upstairs bedroom. Wayne was pleased to do so, feeling he'd have more privacy and Phil would appreciate having use of his library again.

Wayne realized that in the face of his skepticism, the waters of the Old Sweet Springs had actually accelerated his healing. Soaking in the waters certainly felt better than the painful physical therapy sessions and he felt certain the waters had a curative effect.

Around 9 a.m., Wayne saw Mildred's car approach. She emerged from the passenger seat with two bags of groceries and walked to the house. He walked with his crutches to the front door and opened it for her.

"Thank you kindly," she said.

"Our little conversation the other day helped me see that I should be doing more of this, particularly now that I'm on the mend."

"I'm glad what I said made a positive impression on you."

"It did, indeed."

She smiled. "My husband, Sherwood, dropped me off. He has a quick errand to run, but then he'll be back to pick us up. He's going to the Old Sweet with us.

At the Old Sweet, Mildred, Sherwood and Wayne all partook of the healing waters. On the way home, Wayne asked, "Where are you from originally?"

Sherwood said, "I am from Union. Mildred is from Gap Mills, where the Mennonite cheese store is. We met at a dance while we were in high school. How about yourself?"

"I grew up in Northern Virginia, not far from where I live now... or where I lived before my accident. Other than when I attended UVA, I've been there most of my life."

"Do you like it there?"

"Not particularly, but it's what I'm used to. The traffic is awful and everything is really expensive, especially housing. The summers are brutally hot and humid. There are lots of stressed-out people who seem like they're on an endless treadmill. I guess I'm one of them. There's also a lot of racial tension." He was angry with himself about bringing it up. The silence that followed was heavy. Trying to break the mood, he said, "There doesn't seem to be much of that around here."

Sherwood pointed out his window at seven deer grazing in a pasture. He said, "Racial issues have driven national and world issues forever and nobody can ever overstate the impact. That said, I never think about race. We socialize quite a bit. We are accustomed to being in a tiny minority. Often at parties we are the only blacks. We accept everyone and just about everybody accepts us. We know we are black. Everyone else knows we are black. We don't try to be white. We try to be who we are.

"We choose to be active and involved. Blacks haven't always had choices in society. The only blacks that would have been seen at the Old Sweet Springs one hundred years ago, even fifty years ago, would have been hired help. Blacks changed the beds, washed the linens, cooked the meals, and performed every menial job for the visiting whites. Even in our childhood, we would never have been able to participate in the Old Sweet Springs experience as customers. When I say that, it is not a negative statement about Old Sweet. The same situation would have existed at The Salt, The Greenbrier, The Homestead, or any of the other luxury resorts.

"Today we have choices. Most of the barriers we faced growing up are gone. West Virginia integrated its schools in the mid-1950s, earlier and with less tension than Virginia. Part of the reason was the cost savings, more so perhaps than enlightenment. I was one of the first black kids at Union High School. I encountered lots of new experiences. I had never heard about choosing classes. But most of my friends were white so these were the same kids at school.

"We learned from our parents, and we taught our kids when we became parents, that if we wanted to excel we needed to be more than almost as good. We weren't taught or encouraged to be better

people, because every person is equal in the eyes
of God. But we were encouraged to be better at the
task at hand. We needed to be better to be seen as
being even."

Mildred said, "Mine was the only black family in
Gap Mills. Like Sherwood, I grew up accustomed to
being with white people. We grew up surrounded
by mutual respect. I remember when I was six my
dad calling together all the families with school-age
children. He told the kids that although we were
neighborhood friends, we'd be going to different
schools because the state hadn't yet integrated.
We were disappointed. It was very sad for us."

Wayne didn't say so, but he thought about all
the urban blacks whom he'd met who felt completely differently, that many economic doors were
closed to them.

Sherwood said, "One night when I was a teenager, I was bumming around with a group of friends.
All were white except me. We decided to stop by
the new diner in town. It was owned by a man
who moved here from Connecticut. The other boys
walked inside, but when I did, the owner stopped
me and said, 'We don't allow Niggers in here.'
The other boys looked at him, then at each other,
and without saying anything, we all walked right
back outside. I never spoke about what happened,
but within a couple of weeks, word had spread
throughout Union High School. Pretty soon, there
were fewer and fewer cars in the diner's parking
lot. Next thing we knew, there was a 'For Sale' sign
and the owner was never seen again. It made my
heart feel good to have the support of my town.

"My brother was in the Army in the 1970s. Afterwards he worked in an underground coal mine.
He told me once that the Army always talks about
being a band of brothers, but the camaraderie was
nothing like he found in mining. Whenever people

have a shared purpose and face a shared danger, race is no longer an issue."

They drove through Gap Mills. Mildred Webb pointed at a cluster of houses to the left of the highway and said, "That's my home area over there. I moved to Union when I married Sherwood. I was a stranger to everyone except Sherwood's family members. But negative interactions are exceedingly rare."

Wayne said, "Most of the black people I know in the DC area are angry. Why aren't you angry?"

Mildred said, "My parents explained to us when we were young what we had to face. We knew discrimination was wrong and we trusted that someday, America would figure it out. I am proud that West Virginia figured it out earlier than most of the South. Many of the states of the Deep South looked to West Virginia as a model for successful integration. Particularly when coal mining was hiring lots of workers, many blacks came from the South because opportunities were better and situations were more equitable. The blacks here demanded equality."

Sherwood chimed in with a similar tone. "In many ways, I have felt that racial strife was one more stressor brought to West Virginia by outsiders. People here have always gotten along. We feel our heritage is shared as is our destiny. From the earliest days of European and African immigration to Appalachia, the exploitation of our land, water, timber, and mineral resources by outsiders has been the greatest source of stress. Our stresses haven't come from other Appalachians, either black or white. When I see videos or read stories about gang activity and violence in the inner cities of America, or read the terrible statistics about the number of black men behind bars, I'm as appalled and dismayed as you are."

Wayne thought about his own experience with black people. His childhood friends thought blacks were inferior and unworthy of equal treatment to whites. They were violent and destructive, deserving of antipathy and resentment. Before he could say anything, Sherwood continued. "We are religious people. For the most part, even though our churches are generally still segregated, the blacks and whites of Appalachia practice their religion within the same denominations and worship the same God, through his son Jesus Christ. God tells us that anger and hatred are worthless and destructive emotions."

Mildred spoke next, "Now I have a question for you, Wayne. Why are you so angry?"

Wayne was speechless. He thought unsuccessfully for an answer. A mile passed before he said, "I am angry because my father was killed in a useless, unwinnable war before I ever met him. I'm angry because my brother was killed in freak highway accident. I am angry because anger has comforted me. Anger is a cop-out, an easier emotion for me than the others.

"What's more, I am proud of my anger. Angry people have always been comfortable to me because I felt they were more realistic about their views. It's difficult to explain and to admit. I am a hard, suspicious man, with a devious mind. I expect everyone to be selfish and to take advantage of everyone else. I have always been ready to hurt people before they hurt me."

It was moments before he spoke again. "I have been thinking about it a lot since my accident and I am less comfortable all the time with my conclusions. I have begun to question who I am. I am ready to be someone else, someone less angry. I'm trying to figure out how."

Sherwood laughed, "Mildred told me about the

little discussion she had with when you got your jaw unwired. Listening to you now, I'd say you've already taken the first step."

+ + + +

October 26

The following week, Ansel was waiting in the parking lot of the Kalico Kitchen when the Rotary meeting ended. He sat in a Toyota pickup truck with a bumper sticker that said "We *dig* coal" and another that said, "Welcome to the South. Now leave your daughter and go home." There was an empty gun rack behind the driver's seat. The tailgate was rusted and badly bent to the point where Wayne wondered if it would still open.

Ansel got out. He greeted Wayne and exchanged pleasantries with Reed and Phil. He said something to Stuart, his dad, but Wayne couldn't hear it and it sounded terse and argumentative. Ansel came and greeted Wayne, and then helped him into the passenger seat. Ansel put Wayne's crutches in the back with the groceries. Ansel drove south towards Willow Bend and Zenith, hard against the slope of Peters Mountain. The road was little more than a paved path.

Ansel said, "You'll be surprised by Waiteville, how remote it is. It's on the other side of Peters Mountain. For some reason I've never understood, that little rectangle of land ended up in Monroe County and in West Virginia, rather than Craig County in Virginia."

They began the ascent of Peters Mountain on what Ansel called a "layover road," which had a thin paved section in the middle with two gravel shoulders. Ansel said when two cars meet, both need to lay-over their outside wheels on the gravel.

The ascent alternated from forests to open fields with incredible views. Wayne couldn't remember seeing such grandeur.

On the south side of Peters Mountain, in the center of the valley, was Waiteville, a tiny, unincorporated village with no commercial establishments. A white building that had the telltale architectural style of a railroad depot had been converted to a private home.

To Wayne, the Waiteville Valley looked like a photo from Montana he'd seen on a calendar. The leaves on the trees had changed to a gorgeous mix of crimson, ochre, yellow, and orange in the October afternoon. Ansel turned left, to the northeast, and ascended on a dirt road in a cove so tight and wooded Wayne felt claustrophobic and antsy.

After what seemed like an hour, they emerged at a rustic cabin on a small, wooded bluff. No other habitation was in sight in any direction. Wayne said, "I didn't know places like this still existed in the Eastern United States."

Ansel chuckled and said, "I'm sure there are more bears within five miles than people."

Upon arrival, Wayne grabbed his crutches and began walking towards the cabin. Ansel carried four plastic grocery sacks inside. Entering, Wayne's first thought was how messy it was. Two walls had large, velvet art posters of Western scenes. There were multiple weapons around, some in glass cases, some simply propped in corners. Several pistols were on the living room and dining room tables alongside stuffed toys and children's books. Wayne recognized ammunition-loading tools at a workshop desk. Ansel murmured, "Make yourself at home. Not much to look at, but nobody bothers me up here." He put away the perishables, and opened a plastic bag full of marijuana which he spilled onto the Formica surface of the kitchen table. Both men sat at by the table as Ansel rolled a joint and lit it. He took a drag, and then pointed it at Wayne. "Hit?"

"Better not," Wayne said. "I haven't been stoned since my UVA days." Alcohol had become his drug of choice.

"Suit yourself."

Ansel took another hit. The aroma hit Wayne's nostrils. "Maybe I will take a hit," he said. Ansel handed the joint to Wayne. Wayne took a drag, suctioning it deep inside his lungs. The smoke felt good. Starting to exhale, he choked and then coughed. He coughed again and again, the muscles of his chest spasming, shooting pain through his healing ribs. "Jeez!" he shrieked. Ansel chuckled. Wayne said, "Thanks anyway, friend, but I'll pass on this from now on." Still, the one hit was enough to make his head spin.

Ansel took several more hits.

"I've been up here almost full-time since the layoff last winter," Ansel said. "With what's going on in Washington these days, the end of this great nation is near. Too many God-fearin' law abidin' citizens are being sucked dry by the parasite class, the maggot welfare feeders. We will need to fight to regain our liberties to live quietly on our own. The people of Appalachia have always been able to fend for themselves. We don't need no government in Washington running our lives. At a Rotary meeting months ago, dad introduced me to our congressman. I said to him, 'When you go back to Washington, do me a favor and do nothing. I don't need you to feed me, provide my health care, take care of me when I'm old, or protect me from myself or anyone else. The best thing you can do for me is nothing.'"

"They seem to be involved with everything these days," Wayne agreed. "Finance, food, cars, energy, healthcare. What happened to free enterprise?"

"I swear to God, when they come to me to pay the medical insurance for the shirkers who won't work, they'll need to come with their guns 'cause I ain't surrendering."

Wayne reached to the floor and grabbed a stuffed bear and sat it on the kitchen table. Ansel said, "That belongs to my lady's daughter. My lady's name is Annie and her daughter is Sarah, who is four. Annie's ex-husband, Sarah's dad, died in a mining accident a couple of years ago. From what Annie told me, he was abusive to the both of them. So his death was no loss.

"Annie is 24. She treats me pretty good. We got engaged a couple of months ago and we're going to get married in the springtime. Do you have a family?"

"Yes. My wife and I split just before I came to Union, a couple of months ago. Let's just say I did some things she didn't approve of. I have two kids, a girl and a boy. I really miss them. A friend said he'd be willing to bring them to the Roanoke area to see me next Saturday if I can get there to meet them."

"I'll take you," Ansel said. "I shop at a couple of building supply stores over there."

Wayne felt grateful to this guy who was willing to go out of his way to do him a favor. They made arrangements to go together.

"Let's go outside. I want to show you something," said Ansel. The men walked across his small lawn to a wooden lean-to with a tin roof. On the way he continued his diatribe, "As I was saying, the collapse of our empire is any day now. With all the nastiness involved, it will be mighty unpleasant. The industrial food machine will fail and marauders will roam the streets of our cities. This mountain has thousands of deer. When city-slickers see rabbits or squirrels, they think they're furry and cute. I see dinner. Squirrels are stringy and gamy, but they'll keep a man alive. I'm not going to go hungry. Six months? Nine months? Nobody can predict the future, but the death spasms of our nation are certainly no more than a year away. It'll start with the assassination of our lying, treasonous president. The shit will start hitting the fan pretty hard from there."

Wayne agreed, saying, "You got that right. My home area will be ripped apart. There are so many latent animosities; it's hard to know what side people will take."

Inside the lean-to were a table and bench, with two large wooden boxes. Ansel opened one of the boxes and pulled out an assault rifle with an integral tripod. He placed the weapon on a table. "This is a Barrett M82A1 sniper rifle. See the target over there?" Ansel pointed at a distant, wooded ridgeline.

"No," Wayne said, squinting.

"There's a trash can lid hanging from a tree limb." He handed Wayne a pair of camouflaged binoculars. Wayne finally saw it, although it was too small to see without power lenses.

"Keep an eye on it," Ansel said. He loaded a cartridge which looked to be ½" in diameter and almost 4-inches long into the chamber. He peered through the sight telescope, took a deep breath, and fired. The sound jolted Wayne and the concussion echoed through the hollow. Wayne saw the trash can lid bounce.

"Holy Bill of Rights, Batman!" Wayne murmured. Ansel asked Wayne if wanted to do some shooting. The memory of choking on the marijuana and the pain in Wayne's chest convinced him to decline.

Ansel fired off several more rounds, all the

while taking hits from his joint. A set of hearing protection muffs hung on a wooden dowel from a nearby wall, but Ansel never moved to put them on or offer them to Wayne. Wayne was impressed that while Ansel continued to smoke and appeared to be increasingly stoned, his shooting skills never wavered. Wayne, with his ears ringing, his chest aching, and his head swimming, became increasingly uneasy in this man's company. Wayne said, "You're a damn good shot."

Ansel said, "I fought a war this way." He took another shot and the target bounced under the impact. "I was a sniper in the Army. I fought in Iraq in Desert Storm. The service ranks have always been filled disproportionately by West Virginians. I think a lot of us join for a couple of reasons. One is that we ain't got many job opportunities. The other is that we are a patriotic, belligerent, conviction-driven people, willing to fight and die for what we believe in.

"I'm a Christian soldier. This nation is being flooded with spics, cow-kissers, camel-fuckers, and Hebes. If the immigrants begin to threaten Christianity, there will be war."

Wayne thought how similar Ansel's tone had sounded to his own rants, but Ansel's level of vitriol and militancy, combined with the inebriation and guns, scared him. Wayne had long fed the anger machine that had come to dominate civil discourse in America, but here he was seeing a different view and maybe, he realized, he wasn't comfortable with what he was seeing.

Ansel fired off a dozen more rounds. Large bullet casings were strewn on the ground nearby.

Wayne redirected the conversation to coal mining, hoping Ansel would become less agitated. "I'm sure coal mining was a horrible occupation."

"You know, I love coal mining. I did some construction work and some hauling after I got out of the war, but I've never done anything I like as much as coal mining. People in the military talk about being in a band of brothers, but it's nothing like the camaraderie you share with a group of guys 1,000 feet below the earth. It's tough to explain to someone who's never been in a mine how working under a three foot roof in the dark can be fun, but I'd go back underground in a heartbeat if there were jobs. It pisses me off that after the Wall Street masters of the universe wrecked the economy and ruined my livelihood, our government bails them out with my tax money. I'm mad enough to kill people."

Wayne asked Ansel to drive him home, feigning weariness. Ansel drove slower on the way back, but was easily distracted by the deer and birds he saw. Wayne thought Ansel's driving was more affected by his inebriation than was his shooting. Ansel went off the road several times before dropping Wayne off.

+ + + +

October 28

Two days later was Chautauqua Thursday. Truman and six other people came to hear Phil speak. Wayne sat in one of the high-back upholstered chairs in the back of the living room.

Phil began, "My topic today is energy and its impact on our society, particularly as it relates to our area in Southern West Virginia.

"All of us are aware that the price of a gallon of gasoline is much more expensive than it was just a few years ago. I'm going to talk about what we can expect in the future, both near-term and more distant.

"Energy is defined as the ability to do work, and it is the life-blood of all living things, including humans. The earth never supported more than one billion people before 1800. When I was born in 1915, there were fewer than 2 billion. Now there are 6-3/4 billion and the number is still rising. The reason the earth has become capable of supporting that amazing growth is this: we discovered an endowment of non-renewable fossil fuels, primarily oil, coal, and natural gas, always literally buried right below our feet, and turned that resource into food and along with it unprecedented mobility and unimaginable wealth. Today 85% of all our energy comes from fossil fuels. Energy is as basic a factor to human life as air, earth, and water.

"When I was I child, the only people I knew from Union who had ever gone overseas went during World War I. Now, many Americans have gone. How many of you have traveled overseas?"

Four of seven people raised their hands.

"The amount of travel everyday Americans do is indicative of our access to seemingly endless, affordable energy. Energy consumption and economic activity have always closely correlated. In particular, over 99% of all transportation is fueled by petroleum. Petroleum is essential to food production and distribution; it is a primary ingredient in plastics, pharmaceuticals, petrochemicals, and clothing. All our institutions are dependent upon oil, the lynchpin resource that keeps the economy humming and allows it to grow.

"Fossil fuels are depleting, non-renewable, and limited. Once we've consumed about half our endowment, our production trend stops rising and peaks, and then declines inexorably forever. This is as inevitable as the morning sunrise; it's neither negotiable nor arguable. When I started college, we were consuming 4 billion barrels of oil a year and finding 30 billion. Today we are consuming 30 billion and finding 4 billion.

"The U.S. domestic peak occurred in 1970. It's called Hubbert's Peak after King Hubbert, the scientist who proposed it. That means that there was never a year before, nor has there been a year since, when this country produced more oil. How many of you knew this?"

Truman alone raised his hand.

"The peak left us vulnerable to artificial shortages like we saw with the Arab embargo, which left millions of motorists waiting in queues at the pump and blasted our economy. Those shortages were artificial and temporary. The next will be real, permanent and will worsen every year.

"Meanwhile, domestic consumption is increasing. We have made up the difference with imports. Today we import over two-thirds of our consumption. The geopolitical and national defense ramifications of our dependency are frightfully serious.

"The worldwide peak is predicted to happen at any time and may in fact have already happened. My latest analysis shows that the world in fact peaked in 2008.

"Our economic system reacts poorly, often tragically, to shortages. A 5% shortage won't mean a 5% increase in price. Expect a 300% increase in price instead. Predicting the future is always a risky proposition, but my guess is motorists will be paying perhaps $8.00 per gallon with a weekly allotment within a few years. The effects will ripple throughout the economy.

"The few countries on earth that are still producing more each year are clustered around the Persian Gulf and many are ruled and populated by people who hate us. Even friendly producers will begin to use more of their own domestic resource and will slash what they export to us as they pass their own peaks. The notion the rest of the world will nourish our gluttonous appetite indefinitely is a pipe dream, if you'll pardon the pun." Phil laughed at himself.

"I am convinced that no known or dreamed-about energy source singly or in combination with others will come to the rescue – especially where transportation is concerned – and allow the rapacious consumption we now enjoy. Oil is but the first of the fossil fuels to face peak, but coal and natural gas are also on target to peak within the next few decades. Coal, our main source of electricity, is becoming scarce in many countries and more expensive here and we're permanently destroying thousands of square miles of our Appalachian mountains to get more of it, especially here in West Virginia. People have long thought of coal as being essentially limitless. But recent studies show that in about 15 years the world may hit a peak in its production. Natural gas – the secondary source of electricity generation – simultaneously will be at or past its peak, poses a threat to our supply of electricity. We will not be able to switch our cars to run on natural gas, coal, or even electricity. With transportation in particular being almost entirely fueled by oil, I can't see how to reach any other conclusion than that we will be forced to adjust to much less moving around.

"There are many other energy sources: solar, wind, and geothermal. These will contribute, but in the foreseeable future, there are no proven technologies for using these sources for transportation."

Wayne thought about all the fuel he'd used in thousands of miles of driving around the DC area and the fuel his race-car consumed at Summit Point. He tried to imagine how much gasoline was consumed every day just in the greater Washington, DC area.

Phil continued, "Projections for future activity, from automobile miles driven, to economic development, to overall population, are typically made by superimposing the past on the future to the point where growth has been an institutionalized aspect of our economic system. But with cheap, easy energy diminishing, that will not continue. So while the 20th Century was one of unparalleled expansion, look for the 21st to be one of significant contraction. Our current economic downturn will not be part of a cycle as have been previous downturns but instead the beginning of a permanent decline.

"If mobility is constrained and life becomes fundamentally more local, what will be the impact in rural communities like Union? The people, neighborhoods, towns, cities, and states that take impending threats seriously and prepare will fare better than those that don't. I am an old man. Almost the entirety of the oil age has occurred during my lifetime. Until now, extraction has been all uphill. The amazing growth of populations and materialism has given the people of my generation the opportunity to live amazingly rich and interesting, although not necessarily any happier, lives. For a child born today who might live to my age, the world will have become very different, because the next 90 years will be on the downslope. I hope the stresses brought about by downscaling aren't tragic.

"I'll take questions if anyone has them."

One woman said, "My family has been in farming for generations. How will this affect us?"

Phil said, "It is difficult to know fully. On the negative side, there will be more work done by the muscles of people and horses. On the positive side, there will be less food at the grocery store brought from distant places providing an opportunity for more of it to be produced locally. Perhaps we're on the cusp of the next golden era of farming. Everybody has got to eat."

Another woman said, "My son and daughter-in-law commute to jobs in Narrows and Covington. They burn lots of gasoline. What will happen to them?"

"I don't mean to be the harbinger of doom, but the more dependent people are, the more problems they'll have. The people and organizations that work on a small scale, locally, I believe will fare better."

After the meeting, everyone left except Truman and Wayne. Wayne said, "You're a brilliant man, Phil, but I just don't buy your entire discussion. That was nothing more than fear-mongering, and frankly I'm surprised you'd engage in it. We have brilliant scientists and engineers in this country. They'll solve this."

"Energy and technology are not the same, Wayne," Phil said. "A 747 jet has incredible technology, but without energy, it won't leave the runway."

"We'll move from oil to the next energy source."

"Really? What do you suppose that will be?"

"I don't know. Maybe hydrogen. Maybe nuclear."

"There are no hydrogen mines. Hydrogen does not exist in a free state. It must be produced using some other form of energy. Hydrogen is an energy carrier, not an energy source. Nuclear was once hoped to be too cheap to meter. We haven't had a new nuclear plant built in this country for decades, primarily due to safety, proliferation, waste, and cost issues. It would require hundreds of new plants to replace the shortfall. Even now, nuclear power requires a significant subsidy from petroleum in order to operate."

"We'll come up with something. We always have!"

Truman said, bolstering Phil's argument, "It wasn't that long ago when the price of a barrel of oil almost reached $150. If a miracle fuel was going to emerge, it would have emerged at least in concept then."

Phil said, "I don't think it is wise for our society to bet its future on some unspecified breakthrough. Our entire lives have been during the age of increasing availability of fossil fuels. It's easy for us to think there will always be more. Other than during the oil embargos of the 1970s, energy availability has been as dependable as gravity. It is difficult for us to even imagine having less energy each year rather than more."

"If we've already peaked, why aren't we waiting in line for gasoline now?" Wayne asked.

"Because the economic crisis has made demand drop even faster than supply. Should the economy begin to rebound, the scarcity will become apparent."

Feeling frustrated, Wayne blurted, "How could your generation have done this to us?"

From the look on Phil's face, Wayne realized he had put him on the defensive and angered him. He had never seen Phil angry before. Truman stepped in. "Don't blame this on Phil's generation. His generation endured the deprivation of the Great Depression. They learned to live and be happy with very little. Your generation worships stuff. Yours is the most consumptive the world has ever known. When you point that finger at him, three more are pointing back at yourself."

Wayne said, "I still think our scientists will

solve this crisis."

Phil said, "Perhaps, but optimism alone won't solve it. Regardless, I won't be around to see it." He walked towards the kitchen.

Truman asked Wayne, "What type of work did you do before your accident?"

"I sold cars."

"I'm sure the topic of this little lecture means a lot to you, then."

"Yes, especially since cars and motorcycles have been an avocation even longer than my occupation. But once I'm healed enough to return to work, I may try something else." He never let on that he'd been fired from his job.

+ + + +

October 29

The next morning, a Friday, Phil walked to the mailbox by the highway and returned with two identical envelopes for Wayne. They were from his insurance company. One contained a check for the stolen Hummer. The other contained a check for the crashed Harley. These would provide some spending money for awhile. A new vehicle would have to wait. His ankle and hip still weren't healed enough to allow him to drive anyway.

Wayne endorsed and mailed both insurance checks to his bank and mailed a check to Donna. He walked the driveway using his crutches to place them in the mailbox.

+ + + +

October 31

On Sunday, Phil returned from church and

found Wayne reading one of his books on the history of West Virginia. Wayne greeted his uncle and said, "I finished reading one of your books on Stonewall Jackson. I learned he was born in what is now West Virginia, but I just read he never set foot in West Virginia as a new state."

"That's right," said Phil. "Let's talk about old Stonewall and see if my image of him fits yours. Stonewall Jackson was a brilliant tactician but perhaps because of his blind devotion to the Confederacy, many people think he was just another racist. Nothing could be further from the truth.

"Thomas J. Jackson was born to two Virginians in Clarksburg, which, as you learned yourself, was then in Virginia but now is in West Virginia. There were already two other children. His first brush with tragedy was when he was two. His sister, Elizabeth, died while Thomas was by her bedside. His father died three weeks later. His mother gave birth to another daughter the following day. So there were now three children and a widow mother. She remarried four years later, but her new husband rejected the children. When Thomas' mother died a year later, the children were orphaned. The family was split apart and Thomas and his sister Laura Ann were sent to live with an uncle near Weston, West Virginia. Weston is about 150 miles north of here.

"Thomas' personality was shaped by his terrible childhood. His uncle was a lout who had no affection for him. Nobody loved Thomas except his sister.

"Another boy from the area was accepted at the U.S. Military Academy at West Point, but was too frightened to stay. Thomas got the appointment almost by default. Because of the inadequate schooling he received prior, he entered at the bottom of his class. Through the determination that would mark his life, he quickly rose to the top.

"Jackson fought in the Mexican-American war from 1846 to 1848 and came home a hero for bravery under fire. It was during that war when he met Robert E. Lee. Afterwards, he accepted a position of Professor of Natural and Experimental Philosophy and Instructor of Artillery at Virginia Military Institute in Lexington. He stressed the military values of mobility, discipline, and commitment. He understood the value of assessing his enemy's strength while concealing his own.

"Jackson fell in love in 1853 when he was 27 with Ellie Junkin. She died fourteen months later while delivering a stillborn son. In 1857, Jackson married again to Mary Anna Morrison. Her first daughter died less than a month later. A second daughter was born in 1862, shortly before Stonewall himself died.

"When war broke out, there was little doubt which way Jackson would go. He was a conviction-driven man. He felt the Constitution of the United States was a divine document, literally from the hand of God. Lincoln's first strategic act in the war was ordering the invasion of federal troops into Northwest Virginia to protect the B&O Railroad. To Jackson, that was usurping the word of God."

Wayne said, "It seemed to me that the Confederate cause was almost Biblical to him. His determination and faith were always rock-solid and unquestioned. He never gave the first thought to losing. He believed prayer had power. God was behind everything. When he lost his arm in battle at Chancellorsville, he felt it was a blessing from God. What a madman!"

Phil agreed to a point. "While he was thought of by his students at VMI as a bit of a lunatic, the Negroes of Lexington revered him. He was instrumental in organizing Sunday school classes for blacks at the Presbyterian Church. In his teaching at the school, the pastor said he was stern and firm but kind and empathic.

"By 1861, he and his sister had become estranged. By 1863, he was dead. The only family members left alive were his second wife and third child. Like so many people of that era, sadness and tragedy marked his life.

"Jackson had a basketful of idiosyncrasies. He obsessed over one arm being longer than the other. He was said to be able to sleep any time and on occasions was found asleep with food in his mouth. He was tender with his wives and he adored children. Legend has it he gnawed lemons whenever he could and loved fruits. He was an ordinary looking man, a disheveled dresser and a poor horseman. He was taciturn and circumspect, and secretive, even to his own lieutenants. Interestingly, his horse, Little Sorrel, a small chestnut gelding, outlived him to the age of 36 and is now stuffed in a museum at VMI over in Lexington, Virginia.

"As a tactician, there was none better."

Wayne said, "What I found so ironic was that his enormous skill as a battlefield commander gave the Confederacy victories that prolonged the war, causing additional casualties on both sides."

"Andy, my great grandfather, frequently included observations about Jackson in his memoirs. There is no doubt of the reverence and admiration Andy felt for Stonewall, the warrior. This portrait of Stonewall has been hanging in the library for over 120 years."

Wayne said, "What do you think you'd have thought of Stonewall if you'd known him personally?"

"No, first you tell me what you'd have thought of him."

"My favorite story of him was when his students at VMI chided him for not running when under fire during the Mexican War. He said, I was ordered to stand my ground so I stood my ground. If I'd been ordered to run, I would have run.

"Like I said a moment ago, I would have thought he was a nut-cake. He was an automaton. I'm accustomed to thinking contemptuously about someone so mindlessly, unconscionably conviction-driven. I'm driven by self-interest and personal survival. If bullets were flying around me, I would have run. I'm not the kind of guy most soldiers want fighting beside them."

"I'll admit," said Phil, "a nation of hard-headed people like Stonewall wrought our most horrific conflict. But a nation of self-interested people stands no chance for a lasting future, either."

"I see what you mean," Wayne admitted. "Our country needs to have some cohesion and shared purpose."

"Now you just listen to yourself!"

+ + + +

November 2

At the Rotary meeting the next week, the first Tuesday in November, Burton Jones, the club president, explained, "A few weeks ago, we heard from a representative of Bedford Energy talking about their proposed wind turbines. Today we have a guest speaker, Professor Sisowath Nol, from the Engineering Department at West Virginia University, who will also speak to us about wind energy. I felt it was important to balance the pro-industry talk we heard earlier with a more scholarly viewpoint. Because this is a topic of such local importance, we have invited the entire community."

There were 38 people in attendance, rather than the average of ten. Professor Nol began his lecture.

"Good afternoon. I am here today to help the people of Monroe County understand the status of wind energy in the United States and around the world to help you make an informed decision about the planned wind farm atop Peters Mountain."

Professor Nol dimmed the lights and focused a PowerPoint slide on the movie screen showing a row of gleaming, white turbines atop a mountain that Wayne guessed was in California.

"As many of you know, the United States faces an energy crisis of epic proportions. Much of the energy we use every day in this country is imported, often from far away and from countries where the people and governments who run them don't really like us. Additionally, because so much of our energy comes from the burning of fossil fuels, we have significant pollution problems. Burning of these fuels is a significant contributor to the production of greenhouse gases which lead to global warming. Because wind energy does not generate any emissions or create any greenhouse gases, it has become increasingly attractive as an alternative energy.

"However, producing electricity from the wind is still considered an industrial operation and it has many impacts, both those associated with other industrial operations and those that are particular to it. Particular to wind energy are such concerns as noise and site effects to humans and effects on the natural life, especially with regard to bird and bat fatalities.

"In my discussion today I will try to relate back to wind energy in our mid-Atlantic region because I know that is the area of your greatest concern.

"Wind energy is nothing new. Sailing ships used wind energy to carry Christopher Columbus and other explorers to the Americas 500 years ago and ancient warriors used wind energy on ships plying the Mediterranean Sea well before that. Wind energy has been turning the blades of windmills in Holland similarly for hundreds of years. However, significant generation of electricity from the wind, at least in the United States, has only about 25 years of history. Even at that, wind today generates less than 1% of our total electricity production. By contrast, coal generates over 50%, even though it is our dirtiest fuel."

Nol showed a pie-chart of electricity production in America. Coal was half the pie while "Solar, wind, and other renewable energy" was a mere sliver.

"I touched briefly on the issue of the importation of fuels from other countries. That issue is beyond my scope today. However, our energy independence and security are inestimably important issues. This subject is better left to the politicians and policymakers.

"Most contemporary utility-based wind turbines in the United States are mammoth. The support pylons are free-standing tubular towers, often 200 to 300 feet tall. Most have three-bladed rotors that can be 200 to 300 feet in diameter. Picture these as huge, massive propellers. Typically an installation will not just have one turbine but many. In the mid-Appalachians it is uncommon for an installation, commonly referred to as a wind farm, to have fewer than 10 turbines. Some of the larger wind farms in the western states have thousands.

"The effects are both beneficial and adverse. The adverse impacts include viewsheds, landscapes, wildlife, habitat, and water resources. The positive effects are the reduction of air pollution and greenhouse gas generation.

"In some areas, for instance around Roanoke which has a commercial airport, aviation concerns come into play. For the most part, though, protecting birds and bats are the main legal constraints to wind farm development.

"The environmental advantage of wind energy is in its ability to displace other more potentially damaging energy sources. In other words, for every megawatt generated by the wind, one fewer megawatt need be generated by fossil fuel plants. There are two important caveats, however. Because most people are not well versed in technical terms such as megawatts, projects such as wind farms are often categorized by the equivalent number of residential homes that can be served. For example, if a single wind turbine generates 2 megawatts and a megawatt will power an average of 1000 homes, if a particular wind farm has 20 turbines, we might conclude that this wind farm will power 40,000 homes. The first caveat is that because wind is intermittent, wind turbines seldom operate at full capacity. Therefore, if the farm is generating only 25% capacity, then at that time it is powering only 10,000 homes. The second caveat is that sometimes the wind does not blow at all. Therefore, all of the electricity requirements must be made up from other sources. Because we are not content to use electricity only when the wind blows, wind turbines do not allow for the diminishment of any overall electrical capacity.

"Consider that if turbines were placed ¼ mile apart on the entire spine of the Virginias, the ridgeline of mountains on the border between Virginia and West Virginia, they would produce less power than a single new coal-fired power plant. But the power company would still need to build the plant, because if there was no wind, consumers would still need the power. None of our choices are easy.

"Different types of power generation have different operating conditions. For all intents and purposes all the electricity that is generated by power plants of any type is fed into an interconnected national grid. The electricity flows to where it is needed. Nuclear power plants, for instance, are run at a full steady-state capacity for months at a time. Natural gas-fired power plants, and to a lesser degree coal-fired power plants can be cycled on and off more readily. Wind farms generate power not in a steady-state and not necessarily when desired but solely when the wind blows.

"All power plants require some level of industrial infrastructure. While nuclear and fossil-fuel fired power plants require typically large installations including a cooling mechanism to complete the thermodynamic cycle of returning steam back to water, wind farms also require industrial facilities in addition to the turbines themselves, including but not limited to access roads, electricity management facilities such as substations, and associated power lines. Because the best wind is often removed from the cities, there is a greater need for transmission lines and equipment and there are greater transmission losses. Plus, a considerable amount of excavation must be done and concrete must be poured to provide an adequate foundation for such huge structures.

"The East Coast of the United States, for better or worse, does not have a significant amount of high-quality, exploitable wind resources. The best wind, particularly on-shore, is at the tops of the long ridgelines of the Appalachian Mountains. But off-shore wind is typically much better, being stronger, steadier, and more predictable.

"Unfortunately, ridgelines are the preferred flight path of many migratory species, including raptors. Large birds of prey have not evolved with the potentially lethal threat of a spinning turbine blade flying across the sky. While from a distance, it appears as though the blades are turning relatively slowly and gracefully. But given the enormous length of each blade the tips of the blades are moving through the air at considerable velocities, upwards of 220 miles per hour, faster than a bird's retina can process. At a site a hundred miles north of here, also in West Virginia, during a six-week period during the spring migration a few years ago, a wind farm killed approximately 2000 songbirds. Turbines become avian Cuisinarts.

"Bats are already suffering serious losses due to mysterious viruses. The presence of wind turbines is a significant additional stressor. Bats provide a tremendous service at limiting the population of insect pests. Turbines placed on our long ridgelines appear to be more dangerous to bats than those at lower elevations sites.

"The nocturnal passerines – passerines are what we consider mainly our perching songbirds – are the most common fatalities at wind farms, perhaps due to their relative abundance. However, because raptors are so majestic, we humans feel their loss more profoundly. Additionally, because raptors live longer than small birds and have fewer offspring, the loss of each one is more detrimental overall.

"With regard to impacts on humans, the number one stated impact is the aesthetics. Watching a row of huge propellers spinning on the top of a distant ridge line is either beautiful or abominable based upon the eye of the beholder. The mechanical action of the internal gearing structure and the action of air passing over the airfoil of each propeller blade can generate whirring noise. However, this noise is typically beyond recognition if the listener is farther than one-half mile away. So you can't really consider them to be noisy, although they may seem that way because they are often placed in quiet, unspoiled environments.

"Not to be discounted is the social impact of the potential rifts within a community between the proponents and opponents! I attended a public hearing once where a small group of people were almost at fisticuffs in their disagreement over a proposed wind farm.

"To me, this pretty much encapsulates the 'head' discussion. It is the 'heart' discussion that now must take place. There is a coal-fired power plant only about 25 miles from here on the New River in the town of Glen Lyn. There is a billboard outside. On it is the face of a miner with a wearing a helmet and a lamp. Across the top of the billboard are written the words, 'Coal, it keeps the lights on.' It goes without saying that all of us are consumers of electricity and that electricity must come from somewhere. I am of the mind that the cheapest, most environmentally benign kilowatt is the one that isn't generated at all because of conservation. But as you can see," he said, pointing upwards at the ceiling, "the lights are on in this room right now. My computer is running as well. These watts were generated somewhere.

"Because this project is proposed by a private company rather than a state or federal govern-ment, your community may have some input as to whether the appropriate certifications are granted or not. I wish you all the luck in the world making the right decision."

Club president Jones thanked the speaker and asked if there were questions. Mildred Webb was at the meeting. She said, "I've heard that backyard cats kill more birds than wind turbines. Is that true?"

Professor Nol said, "I'm certainly no expert on cat predation on birds, but I understand the impact is significant. I read somewhere that there are 90,000,000 pet cats in America and a similar number of strays. Each cat may kill dozens to hundreds of birds, snakes, and small mammals each year. What's so tragic is that predation by cats, at least those with homes, is totally preventable simply by keeping the cats indoors. The birds killed most often by cats are common backyard birds, whereas the birds killed by turbine blades are migratory forest birds."

Reed Rathmell the falconer said, "If the turbines are allowed to be built but prove to be killing the migrating hawks, what would happen then?"

Professor Nol said, "The turbines could be taken out of service, for instance, during the spring and fall migrations." He looked left and right, as if wanting to say something secret. "But I think it is unlikely that a multi-million dollar wind turbine might be purposefully shut off if the wind is blowing and there is power to be generated. There's too much invested to have them just sit there."

Burton Jones had a question. "What are the other financial impacts?"

"That's beyond my purview. I'm sure the turbines would generate income, because the electricity they generate would be valuable. If the county were to find a way to tax them, it could generate income for its roads, schools, and other services. I'm sure there's not a community anywhere in the state that wouldn't benefit from additional income. The investors who build them, like anyone who opens a business, has the typical loan, cost, and benefit issues. My guess is that most wind farm investors are merely looking to cover their costs in the near-term. The long-term prospects are brighter as fuel costs for coal and natural gas inevitably rise, whereas the wind is always free. But again, I'm not in the public policy arena and I can't comment on specific cost and income ramifications."

Jones presented the speaker with a gift, a specialty, locally produced brick of cheese, to thank him for his presentation. The meeting adjourned.

+ + + +

November 4

"Good morning, Wayne! How are we?" Mildred exclaimed as she arrived for her morning duties.

"We're doing fine. When I sneeze I don't feel like my ribcage is going to explode. I am actually trying to envision a totally pain-free day."

"I am so happy for you!"

"I've been reading about the history of West Virginia. And Uncle Phil has been telling me about the men of these portraits. It's been a real education."

"What have you learned?"

"Well for one thing, there have been some pretty colorful characters in American history."

"When you say, 'colorful characters,' is that a pun?"

"Oh, sorry. I didn't mean it that way. But now that you bring it up, I'm learning again and again how important racism has been as an issue in America."

She said, "Absolutely! After you, Sherwood, and I spoke about this in the car a few weeks ago, there were a couple of things I wanted to add. Prior to the Civil War, there were 4 million people enslaved, making the United States the largest slave nation in the history of the world. The Civil War itself was the most calamitous and disruptive event in our nation's history and has meant everything to the way America is today."

Wayne said, "I remember saying that black people seem so much more contented here than in the DC area where I'm from."

She said, "I don't think it's just black people. That may apply to everyone. In my estimation, rural life is by its nature less stressful than urban life. It's more connected to the rhythms of nature and the seasons than to traffic jams and crime reports. We've never had a terrorism attack. We've never had a riot or a random sniper in Monroe County. We're not as wealthy and nobody wants to be impoverished, but having more stuff has never made anybody happy."

He said, "I can't imagine that the minority population here in Monroe County is more than a few percent. And yet you seem perfectly happy living here. Have you ever wanted to live in a city like Winston-Salem or Petersburg where the population is overwhelmingly black?"

"No. There are about 800 black people here in Monroe, a county with about 13,500 people. My sister lives in Richmond. Don't get me wrong, Richmond is a charming city and over half the people are black. Richmond has many beautiful homes and a rich history. But for me, the history is underpinned by racial disharmony. Richmond has a beautiful divided boulevard called Monument Avenue. Every few blocks, there is a magnificent statue, most of which are Civil War heroes. I have never had a positive feeling about it. Sure, the Confederate monument that we see outside our window here in Union has many of the same overtones. But for me, he seems much more kindly and introspective than all the defiant, self-righteous generals in Richmond. When I was a child, I never knew he was the likeness of Professor Phil's great-grandfather, but somehow he always seemed genial.

"Black people living in predominately black

neighborhoods are no more contented than black people who live in predominately white neighborhoods. I don't know how this will come across but it is how I feel and so I will say it. I have never felt as comfortable in predominantly black cities as I feel here in Monroe County.

"I have no idea what your vision of central Appalachia was when you arrived or even what it is now. But Appalachian people, counter to stereotypes, are warm, welcoming, and open people. Sure, there are likely racists among us. But I choose not to see them. I am certain there are racists throughout the world. But fortunately for me and my family, there are enough fair-minded people in this community to have made it a wonderful place to live. I never hesitate to open my front door to anyone who rings the doorbell.

"Expectation is a huge part of life. Many people expect our modern society to give them something that earlier societies did not have. For too many people, particularly in urban and suburban environments, there is a constant struggle to achieve more, to obtain more, and to consume more. I cannot speak for everyone of my race, but for me, my expectations are much more modest. I want to live all of the days of my life in peace, harmony, and amiability with my neighbors. My goals are to be a good wife, a good mother and grandmother, and to see that the people under my care – including you – have the opportunity to be healthy and happy. For me, there is no better place in the world to do that than Union, West Virginia.

"How about you? What are you going to do now?"

"I was afraid you might ask. I hate to be evasive, but I will need to get back with you on that. All of my energy has gone into staying positive about my recovery. My expectations crashed with me and my motorcycle a few weeks ago. I'm still working to put everything back together again.

"I have suffered two physical indignities here in Union. The first was when I crashed. The second was when you slapped me. The former hurt a helluva lot more, but both changed the way I see things."

"How so?"

"I was mad as hell at you when you slapped me. But in retrospect, I deserved it. You did me a favor. You helped me see how the person most hurt by my anger was me. It was really a game-changer."

"Healin' is my business!"

As Mildred departed, Wayne realized that for the first time, he truly respected her as a person. She was assertive but not arrogant, intelligent but not overbearing. Beyond respect, he even liked her.

+ + + +

That evening he got on the rant website, *www. redhawk.com*. He read a long post where a Neo-Nazi man in Virginia listed the names, street addresses, phone numbers, and even the children's names of several civil rights advocates and attorneys who offended him. He suggested that if these people were killed, it would please him. Wayne imagined how terrified he would be if this happened to anyone he knew. He went to the login screen of the site and deleted his name and moniker. QUARRELER would never rant again, at least publicly.

+ + + +

November 6

The following Sunday, Truman gave Wayne

a lift to Paint Bank, in Virginia just over Peters Mountain from Sweet Springs. Truman and his wife often went to the Swinging Bridge Restaurant for Sunday breakfast. Every commercial building in Paint Bank had been purchased by a rich couple from Massachusetts a few years earlier and had been fully restored. There were several rejuvenated businesses where none had existed since the 1960s. Ansel drove down the Potts Creek Road and met Wayne there for the trip to Salem where Wayne had arranged with Martin Kneeland to visit with Willa and Eddie.

Ansel drove his pickup on SR-311 over Potts Mountain, a scenic and curvy road that made Wayne long for being on a motorcycle again. Making small-talk, Ansel said, "Tell me about your kids."

"My daughter, Willa, is seven and my boy, Eddie, is five. It occurred to me when I was brushing my teeth this morning that with my jaw being broken, I haven't shaved since the accident, almost three months. I can't imagine what they'll think.

"How about you? You said your lady had a daughter. Do you have kids of your own?"

"As far as I know, I've never sired a child. My lady's little girl is adorable. I've never even been around kids, at least in a parenting role. I hope once I marry her mom, this girl and I can have some kind of relationship. I've never really known how to relate to kids. This is a new experience for me. For the first time in my life, I think I'm ready to be a father. I can see already what a positive impact my lady and this little girl have made on me. For a few years after the War, I didn't have much to live for. Now I do."

The trip took the two men through the town of New Castle, which like Union was the seat of a county without a single traffic light. They crossed

Catawba Mountain and the Appalachian Trail before reaching the greater Roanoke Valley. They took the highway to the intersection where SR-311 reached busy Interstate 81. Ansel dropped Wayne off at the Shoneys to wait for his kids. Wayne called Martin on the cell phone to see where he was. He was just passing I-581 and would only be another ten minutes.

Martin opened the door to the restaurant. Cheryl and their boys came in followed by Willa and Eddie. Willa saw Wayne immediately and ran to him, giving him a hug. Eddie grabbed Cheryl's leg and wouldn't let go. Martin walked to Wayne and shook his hand. "How's it going, old boy?" Cheryl looked at him disdainfully.

Wayne looked at his friends, speechless. He hugged Willa tighter and kissed her. Little Eddie stared at his dad but seemed befuddled. "I've had quite a time since I saw you last," Wayne said.

They talked for a few minutes about Wayne's recovery. Martin said, "I'm going to drive across the street and get some gas. I'll let you and the kids have a couple of moments to yourselves." Martin, Cheryl, and their boys left the restaurant.

"When are you coming home, Daddy?" Willa asked.

"I don't know, sweetheart. I'm still not feeling very well and it's not good for me to travel." He knew this was only half-true. "I still have some healing I need to do before I can come home," which was certainly more true.

He bought the kids hamburgers and fries. He asked about school. Both kids were playing soccer regularly and Eddie loved kindergarten. Wayne was tempted to ask the kids about Donna, but decided against it.

When Martin and Cheryl returned, he asked them about Donna instead. Cheryl snapped at him. "So you care? You're a piece of work, you are, Wayne. She's having a pretty rough time. That's all I'd like to say about her. I have lots of things I've been thinking about saying to you, but I'm restraining myself. Do you have anything to say to her?"

"No. Not yet."

+ + + +

November 11

The next week was a Chautauqua week. When Wayne asked Uncle Phil about it, Phil said an Appalachian storyteller named Clyde from Bozoo, in the western edge of Monroe County, would be performing. Wayne was immediately curious.

Clyde McCall was a tall, wiry man who wore a flannel shirt and a coonskin hat. He reminded Wayne of the man who played Daniel Boone in a movie from his youth. Clyde was animated, moving his hands expressively as he spoke in a scratchy, high-pitched voice. "Storytelling is a traditional Appalachian performance art. West Virginia has several festivals of storytelling and arguably the finest storytellers in the nation.

"This little story I call, 'Teaching my baby to drive.' Awhile back, I was sitting next to my teen daughter, she in the driver's seat and me in the passenger's seat for our third driving lesson on a country road where we didn't expect any other traffic. I had a flashback. My mind drifted to the day after her birth, 15 years earlier. I was lying on my back and she was napping, her tiny stocking-capped head resting against my ribcage, each of us feeling the other's warmth and heartbeats. I remembered thinking about the wondrousness of birth, the immaculate beauty of a newborn, and the absorption capabilities of the modern diaper.

"Screech! I was jolted from my reverie by a dumped clutch as our family Plymouth lurched forward. 'Sorry dad,' she said, wondering aloud how her parents could be so thoughtless as to inflict upon her a manual transmission while all her friends were learning on automatics.

"It goes without saying my daughter, even at that age, was a competent young lady—intelligent, attentive, and dexterous. In my fumbling paternal way, I tried over the years to teach her a thing or two, but typically she already knew everything I knew and more. It was nice to have a fleeting upper hand, experiencing a skill I could do robotically and she couldn't do at all.

"Earlier that week, I sat through an excruciating evening presentation for young drivers and their parents at the old Union High School where a parade of pedantic teachers, administrators, and law enforcement people downloaded a weighty cargo of horrifying statistics about teens behind the wheel. For instance, your child, or shall I say *my* child, is roughly 126,000 times more likely to have an accident before her next birthday than the members of the Hell's Angels motorcycle club. Sixteen year olds have the attention span of cocker spaniels – with all due respect to cocker spaniels – and don't develop into functional human beings, attention wise, until at least their mid-twenties. Furthermore, these teens are physically incapable of just doing one thing at a time, like driving, and will preternaturally gravitate towards adjusting the radio, putting on make-up, or downing a 16-oz Mountain Dew, or some combination, every twelve microseconds."

Several audience members chuckled with sympathetic laughs.

"The presentation featured several gratuitous

angst-breeding documentaries, some more relevant having been filmed right here in the homes
and valleys of West Virginia, where real parents
of real deceased children choked through torrents
of tears talking about the senseless losses of little
Suzy and Tommy to avoidable traffic crashes. The
irony here is that my daughter didn't accompany
me to this meeting, as she had something infinitely
more important to do, like going to cheerleading
practice or somesuch. The presentation was completely wasted on me, as I was already more vexed
about her safety in cars than anything.

"Screech! 'Sorry, dad,' she repeats.

"Lastly, we got our sermon from the local Na-
tionwide Insurance agent. He didn't venture any
actual numbers regarding the projected increase
in premiums associated with adding a teen driver,
lest mass resuscitation efforts be necessary. But I
envisioned that if our current insurance cost $500
annually to cover my wife and me, it would rise
to approximately the gross national product of,
say, Romania. That was, of course, assuming we
could actually find an insurance company mindless enough to cover such an obvious risk as our
daughter.

"The bottom line is that the chance of your
child having a tragic crash the first time he or she
shifts into reverse is 344%. If you are a parent,
you would have to have a bucket of walnut shells
inside your cranial cavity where the grey matter
belongs to allow your baby to drive an actual car
on an actual road before that baby reaches the age
of, say, 43.

"That was eighteen years ago and she's never
had an accident!"

Everyone applauded.

"Here's another," Clyde continued. "I call this
one, 'A trip to the dentist.'

"Millennia ago, when I was a child and dinosaurs roamed Monroe County, my mother took me for regular visits to a dentist in Peterstown. I'm won't mention Dr. Crankpin's name publicly, for obvious reasons. But he was infamous throughout the Virginias.

"In those days, dental floss hadn't been invented and tooth care was still a black art practiced primarily by sorcerers and enchantresses in dark, steamy, subterranean caverns. One television commercial for Colgate, a toothpaste made from a mixture of Styrofoam and teachers' chalk, featured little Bobby who, at each trip to the dentist would hear the dentist cheerily proclaim, 'You have just one cavity!' My math led me to conclude that one cavity, twice per year, from age three to eleven, would produce sixteen cavities, one for every other tooth. And this was something to brag about?!

"Speaking of which, do you know what they call thirty-two West Virginians in a dentist's office? A full set of teeth!"

Two people guffawed sardonically. Phil hissed.

"Do you like this one better? Did you know the toothbrush was invented in West Virginia? Otherwise, it would have been called a teethbrush."

Again, muffled laughter.

"Self-deprecating jokes involving dental hygiene never seem to get old in West Virginia.

"Anyway, back to my story. Those were the days before municipal water utility companies added fluoride, bromide, chloride, plutonium, and other teeth enhancers to the tap water. We drank regular stuff from the well. So cavities were common.

"Dr. Crankpin's receptionist, Chastity, was thin and buxom, and wore skirts that made the word 'miniskirt' seem like an understatement, which now that I think of it must be a pun. Whenever Dr. Crankpin walked past her, his right eyebrow, which had hair so long it meshed with his eye-lashes, would shake and quiver. Since she'd been hired, Chastity had lured in men who hadn't seen a dentist since the Hoover administration, just there to watch her walk down the hallway. I was eight years old when I first heard the four-letter obscenity for sexual intercourse. I had no idea what it meant, but I was sure it had something to do with Chastity.

"The dental hygienist, a woman named Ploppette, had a disease that turned her skin as purple as an eggplant. Her whole body wasn't this way, but only a grotesque, puffy patch that covered most of the left side and chin of her face. This deformity was so beyond grotesque that if she could have traded it even-steven for leprosy, she should have jumped at the chance.

"There were two examination rooms, one painted green and the other, blue. Both featured mechanical, robot-like devices, which applied rotational forces to various dental tools. These devices had long, wand-like beams from which strings and pulleys sprang, emitting whirring, mechanical sounds. The Green Room was for people like me and my brother, at least so far. The Green Room's robot, although fearsome, was in a simpler, more benign league than the Blue Room's. The Blue Room's robot would shame the most malignant creatures of the modern *Transformer* movies in its sinister quality. Beside both robots were swirling, toilet-like bowls that acted as spittoons for dental fluids. Patients' chairs were equipped with straps like today's seat belts.

"The Blue Room was a fearsome place, reserved for those seriously deficient in dental hygiene, where jaw extractions, tongue amputations, and similarly grotesque procedures were performed with bulky, ferrous, medieval tools. Woe upon the unfortunate who found himself or herself strapped into the chair of the Blue Room!

"Old man Crankpin had disturbing brown eyes, cloudy with cataracts, hidden behind thick, dirty trifocals. He grimaced when he worked, showing a mouthful of gold-capped teeth, always making me wonder why I'd trust my incisors to a man who had no ability to maintain his own. His gown always had coffee stains on it, illustrating his inability to transfer a steaming cup from the table to his mouth. My brother and I were largely held defenseless in his clutches during the teeth cleaning process.

"On this day, peering seemingly through the back of my skull, he proclaimed 'You have a cavity, boy.' He walked away to ask Ploppette to prepare some Novocain. Sensing my last chance at survival, I crawled out of the chair and headed for the closet, where I'd planned to hide. Inside, hanging on a clothes hanger, I found a life-size skeleton, which I placed in the chair I'd vacated. Crankpin returned and with a needle that was no smaller than the sword Wart had pulled from the stone to transform himself into King Arthur, proceeded to inject the skeleton. While the painkiller took effect, Crankpin trimmed a couple of fingernails with his teeth, spitting the fragments into the swirling bowl. When he tried to small-talk with the patient in his chair about the recent weather, I'm sure he was surprised at how quiet it was.

"Crankpin then proceeded to drill the offending tooth, filled it with a metal paste, and proclaimed me as good as new. When he left to put the needle away, I switched places again with the skeleton, whereupon Ploppette gave me a candy cane for my good behavior."

Everyone clapped. "Tell us another," said Phil.

"Well, several years ago, I decided the Lord

had called me to preach the gospel. Not much has changed in some ways for those called to the ministry. When a man commits himself to the Lord's work, he must get a license, and then the church is responsible for what he does. I had earned my license, but the church hadn't yet assigned me my own congregation. So I told some of the other preachers in Union that if they ever needed me, I'd help them. I was determined to do a good job and to show other preachers my fervor.

"One day, one of the other preachers called and said, 'Clyde, two members of my congregation have died and both burials are on Saturday. I can't go to both. Will you do one burial for me?' So I said I would. He took the funeral for the banker in town, and I got the poor hillbilly in the country.

"The directions he gave me were doggone cryptic. 'Go to Glace and take a right towards Pedro. Go past the big oak tree and take a left beyond the creek." He pronounced "creek" as "crik." "Once you leave the paved road – Incidentally, you know you live in West Virginia when the directions to your house include the phrase, 'Once you leave the paved road' – cross the creek and go up the long hill. Anyway, to make a long story short, by the time I'd jump-started the Buick and gotten on my way, I was already late. I figured I was hopelessly lost when I finally arrived to see some workmen shoveling dirt into the hole on the ground. I jumped right out of the car and commenced preaching up a storm, sprinkled with one 'Glory Hallelujah' and 'Holy Jesus' after another. Forty minutes later, when I finally wound down, one worker wiped his brow and said to the other worker, 'That was the damnedest eulogy I've ever heard. If this preacher would do this for a septic system, imagine what he'd do for a deceased man!'

"It's a pitiful story and I'm sure there's a message in it. But I've never figured it out."

Wayne caught himself laughing out loud with the other guests, for a moment embarrassed that he'd sunk to the low level of humor of mountain people. But he was then carefree about it. He thought about the bartender at his local bar back home and realized this guy was in the same business, but better at it, and without the liquor.

+ + + +

November 12

The next morning, Truman came to the McGranahan house. He found Wayne and Phil on the front porch, staring at a chilly rain. Truman said, "I've got some bad news." To Phil he said, "You know Stuart Cummings over at the newspaper has a son named Ansel. He's been living off and on at the family cabin with his fiancée and her daughter over the other side of Waiteville."

Wayne said, "I just was with him last Saturday. What happened?"

Phil asked, "He was in the first Gulf War, wasn't he?"

"Yes," said Truman to Phil. "He's been mining coal over in McDowell County since his discharge from the Army. Anyway, night before last at his cabin he shot and killed his fiancée. He was high on something and he apparently mistook her for an intruder. She had a key and let herself in, along with her 4-year old daughter.

"Police have him in custody in town. As you can imagine, the little girl is devastated. The state's attorney will probably charge Ansel with involuntary manslaughter at best, murder at worst. Three lives are ruined: Ansel, the dead woman, and her daughter."

Wayne was dumbstruck, thinking about this tragedy. He remembered all the weapons at the cabin and wondered how many of them were illegal to be owned by civilians. He envisioned FBI officials combing the place, sorting through all the ammo, weapons, and drugs.

Phil said, "What a shame! I spoke to Stuart many times at Rotary meetings about Ansel. Ansel came back from the War in such bad shape, mentally. It seemed like his fiancée was helping him regain his humanity and emotional balance. Stuart told me that there had been several occasions since the war when Ansel's militancy and anger had scared Stuart. The casualties of war never seem to end once the battles are over." He looked wistful. "I have been lucky. With the love and support of my wife and friends, I was able to deal with what I saw in the snow of France. Others haven't been as fortunate."

Wayne thought to himself how old his great uncle looked.

+ + + +

When Mildred came by that afternoon, she was deeply disturbed by the news of Stuart Cummings' son. "Live by the sword, die by the sword," she said to nobody in particular, shaking her head over and over.

Truman came by again during the afternoon and told them what he heard from the news reporter doing a story on the killing for the *Monroe Watchman.*

"Ansel shot his fiancée, Annie. Ansel was stoned. He fell asleep. He didn't expect her back at the cabin until the following afternoon. Instead, she arrived around 10:30 p.m. with her daughter in tow. He must have thought she was an intruder.

God only knows what was going on in his head. Ansel awoke, heard commotion in the hallway, and shot the figure he encountered. According to the Sheriff, Ansel shot her once through the chest. Her daughter was right behind her. The woman slumped to the floor. Ansel realized his mistake and ran to her. Her wound was fatal. The girl alternatively cried and slept all night. They have no telephone out there.

"The next morning, Ansel wrapped Annie's body in a blanket and put it in the bed of his pickup. He and the little girl drove to Union. He took the girl by the hand and walked into the sheriff's office and told the sheriff what happened. The sheriff called the magistrate and an investigator. The investigator advised Ansel of his Miranda rights. Ansel readily admitted what he'd done and waived counsel.

"They walked outside and looked over the body. Ansel gave the gun to the sheriff, along with the spent casing. Ansel was questioned by the sheriff and the detective, and then put into a cell in the courthouse basement. The investigator drove to the cabin for forensics examination. The investigators determined the shooting occurred just as Ansel had described it. Ansel apparently had lots of illegal weapons and drugs at the cabin. He made no attempt to hide or dispose of any of it.

"Meanwhile, the girl sat for two hours, crying in the sheriff's office. The sheriff's receptionist tracked down the girl's grandmother, but she refused to drive over from Pineville to take care of the child. The girl was taken to Child Protective Services. They called Stuart who went there to obtain at least temporary custody of the girl.

"The sheriff certainly wasn't happy about the fact that Ansel waited all night to turn himself in. But there was freezing rain last night and thick fog on the mountain. Besides, he was stoned and likely not thinking clearly.

"The State's Attorney is in Charleston on another case. They're not even sure what he'll be charged with."

Wayne said, "When I visited with him up there, he scared the hell out of me. He had lots of drugs around and lots of guns. He had been in Desert Storm. I don't know much about warfare, but my guess is that he had some form of PTSD. When he took me to Salem recently he said he was on his way to see his shrink at the VA Hospital.

"What an awful situation," said Phil. "It's hard to know what to think. Sometimes the casualties of war don't surface until years later."

For the first time in years, Wayne thought about his father, dying in Viet Nam. He thought about Ansel and his tragedy, and the horror of the motherless young girl, now an orphan due to Ansel's mistakes. He thought of Phil and his recovery from the emotional scars of World War II. And he thought of Andy and Allie, his forbearers, who suffered so mightily in the Civil War.

Would the human race ever learn to solve its problems without massive destruction and killing? Would the voices of anger and vitriol ever give way to the voices of peace? For the first time in his life, Wayne connected the vitriol he'd used for so long in his rants on the Internet to the eternal march towards war.

+ + + +

November 13

The next day, Saturday, a brisk mid-November morning, Wayne walked to town to get his prescriptions filled at the pharmacy. He saw Juliet Rathmell across the street at the post office and called out to her. "Let me drop this letter and I'll come over," she yelled.

A moment later, she approached and held out her hand. "How have you been?"

He held her hand firmly and said, "Just fine. I'm feeling better every day."

"If you walked all the way from Phil's house, I'm impressed."

"I did! Say, do you have time for lunch?"

"Sure."

They walked two storefronts to the north towards the Kalico Kitchen, laughing at a bumper sticker they saw on a Hyundai sedan that said, "Beekeepers don't die, they just buzz off." They took a table near the picture window. She ordered a chef's salad and he ordered pork BBQ.

Juliet said, "Tell me more about yourself."

Wayne said, "You know about all about my accident. I live in Northern Virginia, near DC. I'm in sales. How about you?"

"There's got to be more to it than that. Are you married?"

"I'm separated. I have two kids. Once I get back on my feet, I'll need to get together with my wife and talk about custody and things like that."

"So your breakup was fairly recent?"

"Yes. In fact, it was just a couple of days before my accident."

"Wow! Sounds like you had a bad streak going."

"Worse than you could know. How about you?"

"I've never married. I was in a relationship with an engineer from Colorado. We were in the Peace Corps in Guatemala bringing clean water to the remote villages. We were together for about six years.

But that was years ago. I am not dating anyone now.

"I am working on my PhD at Tech and teaching at the community college in Lewisburg. When I'm not working or studying, I make stained glass panels. I also do massage to generate some income, but I don't have time for a regular clientele. I do falconry with dad. I have always been fascinated by his birds. I only wish I had the time and money to have my own."

"I'm fascinated by falconry, too!" he said. "Your dad may have mentioned that I watched him hunt with Thor a few weeks ago. I've always been into speed and power. Watching Thor scratched an itch for me that hasn't been scratched any other way for awhile.

"Don't get me wrong, Uncle Phil has been great. He's the smartest man I've ever met. And he's being a good host to me, especially given my physical problems. But I do have my moments of boredom here."

She said, "Not to preach to you, Wayne, but did you know that boredom is a modern construct? Nobody in the 19th Century had any idea what the word meant."

"You sound like a psychologist."

"Seriously, I'm sure there were times when people were listless or didn't have something meaningful to do. But boredom implies an expectation of entertainment or something of interest, not simply the lack of it. You're bored because you expect to be provided with entertainment."

"Fair enough," he admitted. "Folks like me are bombarded with stimuli. The weeks here have given me an inkling of what might be required to entertain myself. I'm not very good at it! I must admit the city life is intensely stressful. People seem more content out here. I bet people live longer, too."

"They certainly should and some do, but too many don't. Far too many people here die prematurely from preventable diseases that result from smoking, obesity, and lack of physical fitness. Public health officials have their hands full."

They talked more about the hawks and falconry. Juliet said, "When you feel up to walking a mile, let me know. There is a raptor observatory atop Peters Mountain. During this time of year, there is a fall migration of hawks flying down the long Appalachian ridgelines. Sometimes I've seen dozens of birds in an afternoon."

"Yes, I'd like to do that."

"I'd be willing to do massage for you. I think it would help with the healing of your wounds. No hidden agenda here; strictly business."

They finished lunch and she offered to give him a lift home. As she dropped him off, she said, "There are a number of rumors circulating around town about you. Unless I'm one day forced otherwise, I'm going to turn away from them. I like to make my own character judgments."

"Really? What have you heard?"

"Apparently some folks decided you posted some nasty things on the Internet."

"I beg the right to protection from self-incrimination. May I merely say that I've done many things that I'm increasingly not proud of? I doubt I'll ever live an exemplary life, but I'm working towards doing a better job as a human being," he said.

She smiled, knowingly and said, "Knowing you have a problem is the first step towards change."

"There you go being a psychologist again!"

She laughed at his teasing. She said, "I enjoyed seeing you again."

"Me, too. May we get together again?"

"Oh, I'm going to a wedding a week from Sunday. A neighbor from my childhood is getting married. Want to come with me?"

"Sure."

"Bring your wheelchair. The church has only wooden benches."

+ + + +

November 15

On Monday, Wayne hitched a ride into town with Truman, with the intention of trying to see Ansel. He went to the courthouse, a squarish, two-story brick building in the center of Union. He went inside and found the sheriff's office to the left of the main hallway. He spoke with a receptionist who said, "Our jail in the annex is under renovation. There are two prisoners housed in the basement. Go down the stairs and you'll see the jailer. He'll be able to help you."

Wayne hobbled painfully down the stairs using his crutches, and found the uniformed man. He explained that he was a friend of Ansel's and had come for a visit. "I'll get him for you. We don't consider him a flight risk, but we still need to keep him in chains."

Ansel came out of the cell and sat at a heavy, wooden table, with his feet and hands shackled. Wayne sat opposite him. Video cameras were everywhere.

"I'm so sorry about what happened to you and your fiancée," Wayne said.

Ansel sat silently for several moments, barely acknowledging Wayne. "This fucking place gives me the creeps. For years, I've heard it was haunted and now I know. There's a clock outside my cell that has a mind of its own. Yesterday dad came to see me. It was 11 a.m. A few minutes after dad left, it said 9 a.m. When my lawyer came at 2 that afternoon, it had corrected itself."

"Why did you shoot her, Ansel?"

"Fuck, I don't know. I was stoned. I didn't expect nobody to be around my place. I served three tours in Iraq. Combat is scary as hell. I thought every day would be my last. I'm jittery, man. I fell asleep. I awoke to the sound of my front door opening. It was as dark as the inside of a cow. I sensed a figure coming down the hall and I shot it. I would never have shot her on purpose. I loved that girl like nobody I've ever loved anybody before. She was helping me turn the corner..."

Wayne said, "What happens now in the legal process."

Ignoring his question, Ansel continued, "I'll be napping on my bed and my toothbrush will fall from the sink. They keep lights on in the hall overnight and I'll see shadows of birds and dragons. I can hear women's voices, but the other prisoners are men. One voice sounded like Annie's. This morning, I asked the jailer if he would look at the videotape from the camera. He said nothing moved all night long."

Ansel's face dropped and his eyes stared at his handcuffs. Wayne looked at him sympathetically, unsure what to say or do. "I'd better go now," Wayne said. "Let me know if I can help you in any way." He called the jailer who escorted Ansel back to his cell. On his way outside, Wayne thought how futile the suggestion was.

+ + + +

November 16

That Tuesday, Wayne was delighted to see Juliet in attendance at the weekly Rotary Club meeting and he sat beside her. She said, "The program today is being given by a geologist from West Virginia University. She's here to speak about gas well drilling. Dad's land appears to have potentially mineable gas under it. I wanted to hear what she has to say."

The speaker, Professor Sally Maris, began, "As many of you know, there is a formation deep underground here that is known to contain natural gas. The formation is called the Marsella Shale. There are plans to drill for this using high-tech directional drilling methods.

"Our nation runs on fossil fuels, and natural gas is one of the cleanest fuels we have. Sadly, for decades natural gas was considered nothing more than a waste product from coal and oil extraction. Billions of cubic feet of it – and it's measured in cubic feet because it is gaseous – were flared into the atmosphere. This not only wasted a valuable resource, it also contributed to greenhouse gasses in the atmosphere.

"The Marsella Shale deposit is around 6000 feet below us, which is over a mile. That seems like an incredible depth and a lot of pipe. But some of the new discoveries of oil in the Gulf of Mexico and elsewhere are almost 30,000 feet down.

"Fossil fuel energy is free to us, in the sense that we don't pay the earth for it. Our only cost is to extract and deliver it. So I never talk about gas 'production,' only 'extraction.' Extraction of natural gas here in Monroe County will be exceedingly expensive, but the cost may be dwarfed by the income from it. If wells are drilled successfully, somebody will make a fortune.

"So what about the community? I read in the County Comprehensive Plan that according to the people who live here, water is your most valued resource. I'm convinced there is no better water in the world than in Monroe County. The mining company will take enormous quantities of water and force it into the Marsella Shale at terrific pressures to liberate the gas and allow it to be captured. The water will be purposefully polluted with proprietary chemicals and particulates to assist with the process of liberating the gas. The proprietary nature of the mixture is justified by the company because they face competitive pressures. The general public and even those of us who study this stuff have no more than an inkling of what will be put in the water.

"Because this technique is new, we are unable to get a clear picture of what happens to this water. Will it seep to the surface, tainting wells? Most of our near-surface soils are karst, which means permeable limestone. Limestone soils produce the best crops and best grasses for grazing animals. Clean limestone is vital to the productivity of our farms.

"Once mining is done, my impression is that the water will need to be extracted from the mines and treated to return to the freshwater streams. Because the chemicals in the water are not disclosed in the first place and because its condition when extracted isn't fully known, we have no idea how successful purification efforts will be. The volume of the water will overwhelm our local rivers, the Greenbrier and the New. There is no infrastructure for the treatment plants, for the drilling apparatuses, for the influx of personnel or the housing, schooling, and transportation needs of the personnel.

"Similar processes are being employed in other states around the country. There are real and anecdotal stories of sickness and pollution in well water, and the like.

"The exploitation of the fossil fuel resource in

the Marsella Shale could bring significant income to your area. It could also lead to the ruination of your most treasured resource, your water."

In the question and answer session, Franklin McRoberts III asked Dr. Maris, "Who will be responsible for environmental issues and potential pollution problems from spills or accidents?"

Maris said, "The drilling company. But the regulatory agencies need to be diligent. In 1972, over in Logan County, the earthen dam at a slurry pond owned by the Pittston Coal Company failed. The resultant flood killed 125 and injured 1121 people. Lawsuits were filed in the hundreds of millions of dollars, but Pittston ultimately paid around 2% of the private losses. We all know what happened when the Exxon Valdez went aground in Alaska."

Phil McGranahan, said, "You mentioned that someone will make lots of money if this drilling is successful. Where do you think that money will go?"

The speaker said, "That question is not mine to answer, but surely the county can be a beneficiary if it properly taxes the extraction. The landowner will be compensated as well. But both had better be careful with negotiations. Energy companies have historically gotten the better of the deal." The meeting adjourned.

Wayne looked at Juliet. Her face was flushed. She walked out hurriedly. Wayne chased after her as quickly as he could move. "Wait, Juliet!"

"You may not want to talk with me right now. This makes me furious!"

"Why? Natural gas is clean burning energy. Mining it here lessens our dependency upon foreign countries. Our nation needs it for growth and development."

"Why do we worship at the altar of growth?" she snapped back. "We live on a finite planet; we can't grow forever. Why are we always talking about growth?"

"Everybody wants more prosperity and wealth. It's human nature."

"Perhaps," she agreed, "but not at the expense of clean air, clean water, and human health. Suppose our groundwater is contaminated with carcinogens. Would you trade your good health and a Yugo for throat cancer and a Lamborghini?"

"I've always wanted a Lamborghini," Wayne quipped, hoping to break the tension.

"Dammit, Wayne, can't you see that we're treating the earth as a cash machine, converting our resources into the illusion of prosperity while bankrupting our progeny? The cancers and pollutants and ruined rivers and landscapes are making rich people rich while impoverishing our people and especially our children. Everyone needs food to eat, clothes to wear, and shelter from the elements, but beyond that, I've never seen a correlation between wealth and happiness.

"West Virginia has given this nation immeasurable mineral wealth and today it is one of the poorest states in the nation. From the oil wells of the Middle East to the diamond mines of South Africa to the uranium mines of the American Southwest, everywhere extractive industries go, the people suffer."

"But communities that don't grow stagnate."

"Really? Monroe County's population 100 years ago was around 13,000. Fifty years ago it was around 13,000. Today I think it is around 14,000. We're growing only marginally, but I certainly don't consider us to be stagnating.

"Progress is measured lots of different ways, Wayne. You tell me what the rest of America has that we don't have that we need. TELL ME! We don't need Wal-Mart to come here and decimate our downtown and destroy our locally-owned businesses. We don't need McDonalds and Burger King to come here and poison our children with calorie-laden, nutritionally bankrupt food. We don't need your Gap, Nike, and Prada and all the other consumer crap that America worships. We don't need your traffic, your stress and racial tension. We need clean, flowing water, and breathable air. We need community schools, community post offices, and locally owned businesses. America's obsession with consumerism is killing the country. There is nothing, and I mean *NOTHING*, about natural gas extraction that will make this community a better place."

"I guess I've never looked at things that way."

"Maybe it is time you did."

Part 5

The next day, Truman arrived wearing a tortured expression. "Ansel Cummings hung himself. He is dead," he said to Wayne and Phil matter-of-factly.

"Oh, no!" Wayne said.

Truman continued, "It's the strangest thing. When the jailer started his shift this morning, Ansel's cell was empty, even though the cell door was still closed and locked. He radioed the Sheriff immediately. While he waited for the sheriff to arrive, he looked at the surveillance tape from the camera in the hall. Individual cells don't have cameras in them, as that is a violation of privacy rights. All night long, nothing moved. Somehow, Ansel had escaped without opening his cell door or being seen by the camera. The sheriff drove to Ansel's place, past Waiteville. If Ansel had an accomplice, he could have easily gotten there, but the neighbors didn't see a car come or go all night.

"The deputy drove up the long dirt driveway, and there were no fresh tire tracks or shoe tracks. When he arrived at the cabin, the door was wide open. He went inside and found Ansel's prison clothes folded on the kitchen table. Beside them was a note that said, 'Out back.' He went up the hill fifty yards behind the house. Ansel had dressed himself in his Marine Blue Dress uniform and hung himself from an old oak tree. There was a fallen bench that he'd kicked out from under himself. The sheriff's people are questioning the family and any friends.

"There's almost no way Ansel could have

walked those 25 miles through the night, but that seems to be what happened. A fit person can walk perhaps three miles per hour. Nobody saw him escape, walk the roads towards Waiteville, or ascend his driveway. Those roads don't get much traffic, particularly at night, but if he walked home, somebody would have seen him. It's surreal.

"Rumor is that the prosecuting attorney was leaning towards leniency, charging him with manslaughter instead of murder, although there would have been some narcotic drug charges as well. Ansel would probably have gotten off with a short prison term. Besides that, Ansel's bond hearing was to be in two days, and he may have been released on bond. My guess is that in his mind, the punishment was inconsequential, relative to the devastation he felt in killing his fiancée."

Phil said, "What will happen to the little girl?"

Truman said, "Two days after the shooting, Child Protective Services allowed Stuart Cummings and his wife to take temporary custody. They like the girl and maybe things can work out. She seems to have nowhere else to go."

Phil pursed his lips and shrugged. "It's a shame."

Wayne looked at Phil while trying to read his own reaction. Wayne was deeply saddened by the loss of his new friend, regardless of the fear he felt when in his presence. Wayne was disappointed in himself in not informing someone of the depression and delusion he sensed in Ansel during his visit at the jail. But he was unsure anything could have or would have been done by the authorities. They would not have released him, and they would not have had the wherewithal to watch him any more closely than they did.

He also realized that he hadn't shouldered his pistol since the day he arrived. For the first time since his teens, he concluded he felt no safer with it than without.

+ + + +

November 21

It was a Sunday morning in late November when Juliet came by once again in her old Subaru to take Wayne with her to the wedding of her friend. There was a sugary frost on the grass which had melted in places where the sun struck it, sending a gentle mist into the air. The trees had lost their leaves. Wayne watched as she emerged from the car and paused for a moment to look at the Confederate statue across the way. She was wearing a heavy woolen jacket with a multicolored scarf. He met her on the porch where she rolled Wayne's wheelchair down the ramp as he gingerly walked behind. He said, "I noticed you looking at the Confederate Monument. What do you think about when you see it?"

"Gosh, that thing has been here since way before me. Years ago, it didn't even have a fence around it; it simply stood alone in the pasture. It has been such a constant in my life that I'm flooded with a myriad of thoughts, never just one. What do you think about it?"

"It is certainly unique and somewhat peculiar. I never would have expected to find a monument to Confederate soldiers in what was a Union state, especially in a town called Union – especially surrounded by cows."

"My understanding was that the monument's sponsors expected the town to grow up around it. But it never did."

"Uncle Phil says the soldier at the top is a likeness of his great-grandfather, Andy. It makes it more relevant to me somehow that in being part of the same family, I have some link to the Civil War. I always thought of the Civil War as just history to learn in school. Now I think of it in a familial way. It's an odd thought process.

"There's one other aspect to it that I have found quite surprising. I never paid much attention to the weather when I lived in DC. That statue, for some reason, has become a barometer for me. When it is cold, and it is much colder here than in DC, I sense the chill more, feeling what I think old Andy must feel like up there. Sometimes I expect him to hop down from the pedestal and begin a conversation with me, like the Scarecrow did with Dorothy on her way to Oz." Mimicking the Scarecrow, he said, "'That's the trouble! I can't make up my mind. I haven't got a brain.'"

Juliet laughed at his impersonation. They got into the car and drove SR-3 eastward towards Sweet Springs. She said, "We're going to the old Rehoboth Church. It was built in 1786, and it is the oldest church west of the Allegheny Mountains. It's not used by any congregation these days, but is more of a museum used for special events. Rehoboth is Hebrew for 'broad place,' which was the name given to a well dug by Isaac."

Juliet turned left from the highway mile and a half from Union. They crested a small rise on the one-lane road, and Juliet pointed to a log structure, surrounded by modest tombstones. The setting was sheltered from the wind, and there were several earth depressions or sinkholes nearby, indicating karst limestone geology and the presence of caves. "Dad was a Brethren preacher and was always interested in historic churches. When we'd come to Monroe County to visit friends, he would take mom and me here.

"In the day it was built, Indian raids were still a

problem. The builders chose an inconspicuous site. It is a humble, log building with only one room. The logs are small in diameter, and my guess is that it was built quickly. Builders put small ports into the walls where they could shoot outside if attacked.

"By the 20th Century, the original structure was seeing signs of wear. The entire structure was disassembled in 1927 and rebuilt with the same logs, but concrete was used for the chinking instead of mud. The original wood shake roof was replaced with one of similar materials, but the entire structure was covered by the larger tin canopy you see now. The lawn has scores of graves and tombstones. Many are 200 years old."

She parked and got out of the car. "It's getting warmer. I'm going to leave my coat in the car." Under it, she wore a beautiful, traditional Scottish gingham dress. He commented on how nice she looked. She said, "Thanks! There are a couple of things I didn't tell you. One is that I am a bridesmaid. The other is that there will be two brides. My friend is marrying another woman."

Wayne had little time to register his astonishment as they walked across the grass towards the structure, he with his crutches and she rolling his wheelchair. Inside, he saw that someone had thoughtfully brought a portable kerosene heater and the room was comfortably warm. As they walked inside, she positioned his wheelchair near the front, and he sat in it. There were several simple wooden benches arranged in rows on the wooden floor. The pulpit was similarly simple, a wooden elevated platform with a solid railing, the front of which was topped by a sloping surface where the minister could place notes. There was a U-shaped loft, also with rows of simple wooden benches. Juliet commented, "Imagine listening to a two-hour sermon sitting on that hard bench!" Wayne was glad to have his more comfortable wheelchair.

Burton Jones from the Rotary Club was there with his wife. He spoke with Wayne and asked about his recovery. A man wearing jeans, a flannel shirt, and a bolo, sat in the back playing classical music on a mandolin. There were about 30 people there. Everyone sat on benches except Wayne and four elderly guests who sat on lawn chairs. The mandolin player stopped playing for just a moment, then commenced with the Bridal Chorus. Three women entered the room. One was wearing the robes of clergy. The other two wore pleasant, country dresses and identical crowns of silver and roses. Wayne guessed them both to be approximately 40 years old. One had coal-black hair, shoulder length. The other had dark brown hair, trimmed more closely. Juliet stood beside the brown-haired woman. The only light in the room came through two small windows.

The clergywoman said, "We are gathered here today to join in the bonds of holy matrimony Kelly Lee Valentine and Pansy Ann Rankin. When these two women, bound by love everlasting, trade vows to honor, cherish, and hold each other forever, I will pronounce them married, although I have absolutely no power vested in me by the state of West Virginia to do so, at least not yet. But by the authority I have as an ordained minister of the Gospel, I will declare that in the eyes of God, and his loving son Jesus Christ, and this congregation, these two people will be partners in marriage." The two women exchanged otherwise traditional vows. The clergywoman proclaimed them to be married. They shared a deep, meaningful kiss.

Wayne scarcely believed his eyes. The ceremony was exceedingly brief. The musician played and sang a song Wayne recognized but hadn't heard for years.

I see trees of green........ red roses too
I see em bloom..... for me and for you
And I think to myself.... what a wonderful
world.

The bridal couple emerged from the historic, rustic building. Juliet followed Wayne outside. He walked with his crutches and she rolled his wheelchair. Two children threw sunflower seeds at the bridal couple. They walked hand-in-hand to a horse-drawn carriage. The driver, dressed in a tuxedo with a Lincoln stovepipe hat, turned the carriage towards the highway and departed westward towards Union.

Wayne and Juliet got into her Subaru and fell last in line with the procession of cars following the carriage slowly down the highway. Juliet said, "My friend Kelly Lee lost her lover three years ago to breast cancer. It was a long, horrible, debilitating death. Kelly Lee was only 39, but she was certain she'd never find someone else. Pansy was a student nurse at the osteopathic college in Lewisburg. They met a year ago at a concert at Carnegie Hall. Anyway, from the way Kelly describes it, her love for Pansy was at first sight.

"Did you say Carnegie Hall?"

"Yes, there's a Carnegie Hall in Lewisburg. Andrew Carnegie grew up in Scotland with Lewisburg resident James Laing. Laing asked Carnegie to donate money to build the hall as a classroom for the Lewisburg Female Institute, when an earlier building had been destroyed by fire in 1902. The institute was later re-named the Greenbrier College for Women. Carnegie Hall became a regional arts center in the early 1980s and there was some major restoration after a fire in 1996.

"Pansy is from Iowa, where same-sex marriages are legal. Kelly and Pansy are flying to Iowa next week to make everything official. But they felt there was something profound and symbolic to be married here first, in Union. This is the only town in the nation called Union."

"I'm still a bit flabbergasted," admitted Wayne. "What about the sanctity of marriage?"

"What kind of drivel have you been listening to? A foundational tenet of Christianity is to 'love thy neighbor.' Sometimes little girls grow up physically attracted to little boys, an attraction that is mutual. Nobody knows why. Sometimes little girls grow up physically attracted to other girls and little boys to other boys. Nobody knows why. You just saw two deeply religious women in love, committing their lives to Christ and to each other. Should their joy be less than what you felt when you got married?"

"But marriage should be between a man and a woman," Wayne insisted. "God created Adam and Eve, not Adam and Steve. Homosexuality is unnatural. If we make it legal, someday people will be marrying sheep or horses."

"What planet are you from? That's too ridiculous to justify a response. Generally laws are created to protect us. Murder, rape, and thievery all have victims. Same sex marriages have none. What kind of society would we be if we criminalized an act of love? Do you think the state of West Virginia should have these women incarcerated because they dared to marry each other? Tell me how your marriage is threatened by having these two women be married." She paused for a moment to see if he would take the bait. He didn't. "From what I understand, your marriage is about over anyway. I think there are pretty good odds these two women will be together for as long as both are alive.

"There's a national movement afoot to pass a so-called marriage amendment that would ban homosexual marriage forever. It purports to protect not our children, our neighborhoods, or our communities, but merely the integrity of a word."

"How does your dad feel about gay marriage? He was a minister, wasn't he?"

"Yes he was. I only spoke with him once about it. The diocese wanted to place a clergyman in a church near his who was openly gay. Dad was dead-set against it. He thought homosexuality violated the authenticity of the Scripture. He said, 'If the Bible is wrong about homosexuality, how do we know what parts of it are right?' I argued that much of the Bible is routinely ignored by contemporary people, such as the explicit acceptance of slavery, the prohibition of touching pigskin on Sunday, and strict adherence to kosher laws. He finally said, 'Homosexuality is a choice. Gay people should choose heterosexuality.' I guess I knew it would shock him, but I asked, 'Have you ever met a man in your life who would put another man's penis in his mouth by choice, if it didn't excite him sexually?' Needless to say, he was thunderstruck.

"I don't mean to do any moralizing. I've had my share of sin in life. But with all the discrimination and scorn gay people face, nobody chooses homosexuality. It's something people are either born with or not.

"Whether the state of West Virginia recognizes their union as legal and grants them the benefits of marriage or not, you can't deny the joy you saw. What nation, state, or religion would rob these two people of their joy or make them feel any less worthy in the eyes of God? Nobody will ever convince me a compassionate, merciful God would judge what I witnessed this day with contempt or scorn."

Led by the horse-drawn cart, the processional took ten minutes to drive back to Union. Wayne looked behind and saw that several other cars, unconnected to the wedding, were being held up. Nobody honked or attempted to pass. Nobody even seemed to mind. He realized that since his arrival, he'd not heard a traffic report on the radio. He'd never been held up by traffic and never seen anything approximating road rage. More often than not, oncoming drivers on the country roads waved to each other, whether they knew each other or not. He said something about it to Juliet. She said, "Lewisburg has got plenty of traffic, but there's not a single traffic light in Monroe County. We don't have a single mile of 4-lane highways, either. There once was a blinker in the center of town in Union, but the Highway Department decided it was unnecessary and removed it."

The sky was crisp and cobalt blue. Peters Mountain was draped in winter's brown, on the southern horizon. Wayne thought to himself, what a wonderful world!

They went to the Korner Kafé for a reception. A bluegrass band played traditional waltzes and Appalachian swing dances. A dark-haired man in his thirties played the fiddle, and he was incredible. Wayne, unable to dance, hobbled on his crutches to the refreshment table, while Juliet danced. He found himself beside the minister. They introduced themselves. Her name was Fiona McGregor. Trying to make small-talk, he said, "I've never been to a wedding of two women before." He immediately scolded himself, thinking he should have kept his mouth shut.

She said, "Well then, Wayne, I'm glad you came. This is the first one I've ever officiated. If the caretaker of the Rehoboth Church had known I was planning to marry two women, I doubt he'd given us permission. It's a good thing one bride had a unisex name. I'm sure the caretaker assumed we had a bride and a groom."

"Did you have any second thoughts about doing the ceremony?"

"Sure. I can get in a lot of trouble for what I did today..." She seemed lost in thought for a moment. "Where are you from?"

"Virginia. Northern Virginia."

"I don't mean anything negative by this, because Virginia is a great state that has produced many of our nation's most important figures. Virginia is surely a better managed and less corrupt state than is West Virginia. But I am a native West Virginian. We are the brunt of a hundred jokes, but we proud of who we are."

"Are you implying Virginians are different?"

"You probably saw the movie *Braveheart*. Most Virginians – I mean most *white* Virginians – trace their ancestry to the English. The English have always been an orderly, subservient people, bowing to the king. Most West Virginians trace their ancestry to the Scots-Irish. The Scots-Irish are a wild, pugnacious, untamable people, beholden to family and clan. We don't deal well with monarchs. We don't like being told what we can and cannot do.

"We trust in God, but we don't expect God to take care of us. We don't expect the people in Charleston or Washington to take care of us."

"I sympathize with that sentiment."

"There is a lot of controversy about why West Virginia split from Virginia during the Civil War. But Virginia fought to maintain slavery, the act of one human being owning another. Many Virginians who lived in what is now West Virginia were deeply conflicted about this, I'm sure. But the fact is that our state motto is *Montani Semper Liberi* ... Mountaineers Are Always Free. To some, this may be mere symbolism; it's trite or corny. But to me it is *real*. The people of today's Appalachia feel a freedom that most contemporary Americans can't even imagine. The people of America can think whatever they want about us, in our simplicity and poverty. But we are the bravest, most conviction-driven people left in a nation addicted to Whoppers, cocaine, rap music, and *American Idol.* If the world goes to hell in a hand-basket the people of West Virginia will survive.

"From its inception, America has been about religious freedom. I was told many times as a child that sometimes it is better to ask for forgiveness than for permission. I think this is one of those times. I don't think acts of defiance should be solely the realm of long-dead, white-wigged men."

"I can't say I've ever heard a minister talk that way."

She paused, as if returning to the moment from a distant place. "You're in West Virginia now and it is a different kind of place. I'm glad you came today, Wayne."

"I'm glad I came, too."

+ + + +

November 23

During the meal at the following week's Rotary Club meeting, Wayne sat next to Truman. Truman said, "You told me you used to sell cars, but you were thinking of trying something new. Any ideas yet?"

Wayne said, "I spend lots of time on my computer. A few years ago, my computer began to get viruses. I immersed myself in learning about computer security. I think I may pursue providing computer security services for companies."

Truman said, "I once was president of the local bank. Just last night, I had a conversation with the man who replaced me. He told me the woman who managed computer security was beginning to take time off during her pregnancy and they needed some help. If you can prove your ability, he might put you on the payroll."

Wayne said, "That would be great." They arranged to go to the bank at the conclusion of the meeting.

Before the meal, president, Burton Jones spoke a long eulogy for club member Stuart Cummings' deceased son Ansel, thanking him for his military service to the country.

After the meeting, Truman and Wayne walked together to the bank. Wayne thought to himself, the oldest saying in the business book is that it matters less what you know than who you know. Within the hour, he had secured a 20-hour per week job.

+ + + +

November 25, Thanksgiving Day

The week before Thanksgiving, Phil mentioned to Wayne that there would be company coming to share the evening meal. "One of my graduate students years ago at the University of Illinois was from France. After he got his doctorate, he returned to France and has taught at a university there since then. We've stayed in touch. He's teaching for a semester at Virginia Tech. Tech is on break for the holiday. He's got no family here. Since this is a Chautauqua Thursday, he's going to present a short lecture before we eat."

Around 3 p.m., a cold rain was falling outside, and ice coated the limbs of the trees. The pines along the driveway drooped sorrowfully under the weight.

Truman and his wife, Janice, arrived, carrying a cooked turkey in a huge pan. Moments later, Reed and daughter, Juliet, came, with cooked vegetables and stuffing. Gibby Robinson came, saying she couldn't stay for dinner because her family would be eating later on. She brought a man she was dating, saying they'd met in a lab course. Burton James and his wife, Georgina, arrived with pumpkin and apple pies.

Phil said, "Today we're going to hear from one of my old students, Dr. Philippe Voynet. His lecture dovetails on my earlier discussion about energy."

Dr. Voynet began, speaking with a pronounced French accent, "Today I'm going to discuss the concept of that we in biology call bloom and overshoot. The subtitle of this discussion, I say in a flippant way, is why human beings are no smarter than termites.

"As you can imagine, if a tornado blew through the forest on Swoopes Knobs and killed a thousand trees, the termites would expand in numbers quickly. Termites are in existence in every forest on earth. But they only eat dead wood. So the numbers are always kept in check. But with the tornado sweeping through, everything changes. There would be enormous quantities of new food for the termites.

"Almost all animals have the reproductive capability of rapid expansions in their population base. What prevents them from doing so is the absence of available food. If a wasp lays 10,000 eggs, statistically only two of them would live long enough and be nourished well enough to spawn 10,000 more. Otherwise, the world would quickly become overwhelmed with wasps."

Wayne remembered with amusement an old Star Trek television episode called *The Trouble with Tribbles*, where a small, cute, furry animal began reproducing uncontrollably on the Starship Enterprise, much to the consternation of Captain Kirk.

Voynet continued, "A good example of what I am talking about is what happened several decades ago on St. Matthew's Island off the coast of Alaska. Reindeer subsist on lichen which grows on rocks in arctic areas. Throughout thousands of years, St. Matthew's Island did not have any reindeer. Lichens were thick across the island. A herd of 29 reindeer was placed on the island in 1944. Twenty years later they had multiplied to 6000. But by then, the lichens were gone and the population crashed. The following spring, researchers only found 41 females and one apparently dysfunctional male. This is classic bloom and overshoot. The numbers bloom, nourished by surplus energy, and then overshoot the population potential of the energy resource.

"This is the same type of behavior that is seen wherever there is essentially unlimited food. It is the biology of introduced species.

"How does this relate to human beings? Throughout all of human history, there were never more than one billion people on the planet until just over 200 years ago. Today there are almost 7 billion people and the number is still rising. What is it that happened to allow for this phenomenal irruption – a sudden upsurge in numbers – to happen? Just as the termites found excess energy in the form of downed trees in the forest, human beings found a seemingly limitless supply of new energy in fossil fuels, primarily oil, and they turned that energy into food. A farmer outside of Union two hundred years ago could grow enough food to feed 3 to 5 people. Today a Midwest farmer grows enough to feed over 100. The difference is that he uses petroleum energy as slaves. In the way modern food is planted, fertilized, harvested, processed, packaged, and delivered, we almost literally eat oil, as it is required at every step.

"It is axiomatic that as the world begins to peak in fossil fuels, food production will change dramatically – hopefully not catastrophically.

"Today we celebrate the American holiday of Thanksgiving. A traditional Thanksgiving always includes a feast. A century ago, when your ancestors sat down at the Thanksgiving table to enjoy their feast, virtually everything they ate came within a few miles of their home. Americans, and people throughout the industrialized world, obtain food from tremendous distances. I find it ironic as a non-American to see that during this holiday, Americans eat traditional, nutritious, often locally grown food that they should be eating all year. Local food production and consumption not only makes people healthier, but makes farming communities like Monroe County more viable. France has always had a vibrant local food industry, with many specialties like foie gras and truffles. But France is increasingly and tragically following the American model. Speaking of which, I'm getting hungry!"

"How did our current system come to be the way it is? Is it all about energy?" asked Janice Hankins.

"Part of it is political, and I can't answer that unless we delve into your politics. I'm not an expert. I am under the impression that under various administrations beginning decades ago under Richard Nixon, policies were put in place to benefit large, corporate farming at the expense of local farming. Companies like Monsanto, Cargill, Nestles, ADM, and Tysons make huge profits and are able to dictate through market manipulation and advertising what foods are available for us to eat. There is something wrong when a Big Mac is cheaper than a serving of carrots."

Phil said, "It's really heartrending. Most of our farmers here in Monroe County continually struggle to make ends meet. When I was a child, we ate what Monroe County farmers grew. Most farmers were as well-off financially as everyone else. Because central Appalachian farms don't lend themselves to industrial farming, most are small. Few farmers make income commensurate with their effort and risk. Today 25% of our nation's corn crop is being converted to ethanol. We are feeding our cars with food while 800,000,000 people around the world go to bed hungry every night. Particularly on this day of Thanksgiving, this is not something we should be proud of."

Juliet said, "There is a nice farmer's market in town. I'm sure this helps the farmers."

"I'm sure it does, too," said Voynet. "But in spite of the fact that farmer's markets are growing nationally, they still represent a mere fraction of the food industry. They're catching the crumbs that fall from the corporate farmer's cake. In my opinion, the only way to change the system back to the localized, low energy model of the past is to change the policies. What hope do Americans have of doing so with government being so heavily influenced by corporate lobbyists and special interest money?"

As they made their way into the dining room, Wayne said to Dr. Voynet, "That was the most depressing lecture I've ever heard."

Voynet said, "Perhaps, but things are as they are. Reality doesn't negotiate. Knowing what I know, I never take a meal for granted."

+ + + +

November 27

Wayne had never had a massage before. In his prior experience, massages were either what old women got or what was done at whorehouses. But he decided to bury his conceptions and his inhibitions and accept Juliet's offer. The Saturday after Thanksgiving, she arrived carrying a fold-up massage table and a small satchel. They set up the table in the library. Phil and Truman had gone to the new art museum in Roanoke. Wayne found it humorous to think that he and Juliet would be under the watchful eyes of Ruby, the hawk.

After setting up the table, Juliet said, "I'll step outside for a moment and let you disrobe. Here's a blanket. Put this over yourself and lie on the table, face-up. I like to start with faces." She put a CD of Michael Benghiat's acoustic instrumental music on the stereo and left the room.

Wayne, still dealing with limited mobility from his injuries, struggled to remove his clothes. He felt sheepish and awkward, but decided he had no reason for embarrassment. He lay on the table, put the blanket over himself, and listened to the soothing flute music. Juliet returned. She took some scented oil and rubbed it on her hands. She said, "I won't use much oil on your face, as faces already have natural oils. I'm just lubricating my hands a bit and warming them up."

She began to massage his forehead. "You have all kinds of stress built up here. I guess that's not surprising. Try to relax.

"Let's move to your jawbone. I'll be very gentle. I'm sure it still is tender."

As she rubbed his jawbones, he could feel the lingering pain of the accident. She said, "Let my fingers take your pain from you." He closed his eyes and envisioned the bone structure of his face.

The movement of her hands hurt his jaw, but he was inured to pain at this level. This is nothing, he thought to himself.

She worked on his right hand and arm, pushing the muscles towards his shoulders. "You're a muscular man," she said.

"I've been pushing my wheelchair around for months. I think it's really been building my arm muscles. I still have some work rebuilding my leg muscles."

She pulled back the blanket to his waist and said, "What's this round scar?"

He said, "That's where the doctor in Lewisburg shoved a tube into my chest to re-inflate my lung. It hurt like fucking hell."

"Hush," she scolded. "You're on the mend now. Think positive thoughts. For the next hour or so, I am your personal empath. Release your pain into my hands. Breathe deeply. Try to expel as deeply as possible. Envision your pain as something you can banish by your breathing."

His arms tingled. His head felt light, airy. She massaged his shoulders. It felt good.

"Breathe!" she extorted.

She began working on his legs, starting with his right foot and leg, working upwards towards his torso. She expertly slid her fingers on the skin atop the folds of his muscles and tendons. Then she began on his left. "When I get to your hip, let me know if I'm hurting you." She smoothed the scented oil into his legs. He could feel how his muscles had atrophied and how much rebuilding there was yet to do. She stopped and said, "I'll let you rest for a couple of moments, then we'll turn you over and massage your back. How are we doing so far?"

He thought of how Mildred always asked about "we" and how Juliet was doing the same thing.

But he had come to realize this was an affectation of endearment and was no longer offended by it. "We're doing great," he said. "Really great."

She held the blanket slightly aloft as he gingerly turned himself over, away from the injuries on his left side. He said, "How did you learn how to do this?"

She said, "Remember the relationship I mentioned in Guatemala? We had no TV, no radio, and no newspapers. In our free time, we'd practice massaging each other. It was a deeply loving thing. I learned several techniques. For example, I never put massage oil on your body directly. I always put it in my hands first to warm it up. Otherwise, it can be a shock. Once I start, I never remove some part of my body from yours. Did you notice that when I put more oil on my hands, I rested my elbow on your body? If I moved away and came back, it would startle you. I want you fully relaxed."

She began to massage his buttocks and back. "Breathe!"

Minutes passed, maybe hours. He couldn't tell. Finally she quit massaging and covered him again with the blanket. He felt silly-dizzy. "I'm done now," she said. "You rest for awhile. I'll come back tomorrow and pick up the table. Just rest for as long as you like." She covered his back with the blanket.

As she began to gather her stuff into her satchel, he said, "Juliet, I've been meaning to ask you something since the wedding."

"What is it?"

"Are you, you know, gay?"

A smile grew on her face as if she were deciding whether she wanted to tease him. She said, "I'm bi. Everybody turns me on." She chuckled as she pinched him hard through the blanket on his butt. "See you later."

"Thanks," he said. "I left $50 for you on Phil's

desk."

"Thank you! I appreciate the business."

Later that afternoon, he folded the massage table and the blanket and put them carefully in the hallway.

+ + + +

November 28

The next day, Wayne found Uncle Phil reading in the library. Wayne said, "You never finished telling your story about Andy."

Phil said, "That was weeks ago. Where were we?"

Wayne said, "Andy had just returned from the war. I think he was in just as bad shape when he arrived home as I did when I got here! He had some of the same injuries, too."

"Yes," said Phil. "But the medicine in those days was not as advanced as it is now.

"Anyway, by April, 1865, the War finally came to an end with the surrender of the General Lee's Army of Virginia at Appomattox. A few days later, Abraham Lincoln was dead, the victim of an assassin, at a theater in Washington. Lincoln had said in his second inaugural address only a month earlier, 'With malice toward none, with charity for all, with the firmness in the right, as God gives us to see the right, let us strive on to finish the work we are in, to bind up the nation's wounds, to care for him who shall have born the battle, and for his widow and orphan.' I'm not a big fan of Lincoln because of his assaults on Jeffersonian Democracy. Nevertheless, this was a totally magnanimous gesture.

"The remaining soldiers of Monroe County mustered out and began returning home to broken communities, burned mills, bridges and mercantile stores, and fractured families.

"Allie and Andy's son, Bobby, grew straight and tall like his mother but with freckles and facial expressions like his daddy. By age six he was helping in the garden and with the plows, and friends started calling him, 'Little Man,' a moniker which stuck with him even as he passed six feet in height.

"Andy's convalescence continued, and although he regained his health and vigor under Allie's loving care, he was never able to walk more than a few feet without his crutch. His leg was a constant source of pain. You had titanium screws put in your broken hip, but Andy didn't have any of today's modern medical technology. So like so many returning soldiers, he simply had to suffer. He was also unable to regain feeling and strength in his left hand, making it useless for shoemaking, his former profession.

"Andy returned from war filled with rage, livid over his wounds and what would remain lifelong infirmities, with what the Yankees had done to Allie and his baby, and with the deaths of many lifelong friends and his beloved brother-in-law.

"As you know, West Virginia was the only state ever formed from another state without permission from the parent state. Virginia, had it remained in the Union, would never have allowed it. From the perspective of the North, Virginia abdicated its right to determine its borders once it left the Union.

"Anyway, Virginia was enthusiastic about secession. When South Carolina attacked Fort Sumter, Lincoln, in his first strategic move, ordered militias from the North to cross into Virginia to protect the B & O Railroad, the only major east-west trunk line in the nation. Virginians considered this an infringement upon their sovereignty.

"So in the spring of 1861, Union troops were

on Virginia soil, forming a protective barrier to the tracks. Behind Union lines, a series of political leaders, closely affiliated with the B&O, declared themselves the legitimate representatives of the entirety of Virginia to the Federal Government in Washington. Understand that they were never elected; they simply self-selected.

"They set up an office in Alexandria. Congress admitted them as senators and congressmen. Then they gave themselves permission to establish a new state, bypassing all the requirements set forth for such an establishment by the Constitution. They held a plebiscite which supposedly sanctified the process, although only the votes in the counties behind Union lines were counted. None of the counties that are today Southern West Virginia were counted at all. Nobody is sure why these counties down here like our Monroe, or Mercer, McDowell, Greenbrier or many of the others were selected. But it goes without saying that most people didn't want to become part of the new state."

Wayne said, "I thought Lincoln was opposed to secession. Wasn't the splitting of Virginia the same thing as secession?"

"Yes," said Uncle Phil. "Lincoln was supposedly conflicted. Here he was fighting a war to prevent secession, yet allowing West Virginia to form from Virginia. But he was a shrewd politician. The inclusion of this new state gave him supportive senators and congressmen. Many politicians have done constitutionally questionable acts during wartime. Remember George W. Bush's warrantless domestic wiretaps?

"Like most Monroe Countians, Andy was furious over the inclusion of his county in the new state. He was particularly incensed that the state-makers had disenfranchised him and his fellow Confederates. He began venting his frustration at

the Salt and the mill in Centerville in front of anyone who would listen. Before he knew it, crowds
would gather to hear him whenever he spoke. He
talked about the illegal formation of West Virginia
and the craven work of the statemakers.

"The first three governors of the state were Re-
publicans, basically appointees of the Unionist
statemakers. By 1870, the state had been forced by
the federal government to give black men the right
to vote. This meant white men who sympathized
with the Union and black men could vote. White
former Confederate men, and of course all women
couldn't vote. Even the statemakers couldn't for
long have any white men ineligible while black men
were voting. The Flick Amendment was passed in
1870, granting amnesty to the former Confederates and giving them the right to vote.

"Because so many of the southern and eastern
counties were heavily Confederate to begin with,
as soon as this happened, the state swung rapidly
in its political leaning back to being a Confederate
state. When John J. Jacob was elected governor
in 1871, he was the first of six governors almost
through the end of the 19ᵗʰ Century who were Con-
federate-leaning.

"When the incumbent decided not to run again,
Andy was encouraged by the Democratic state
delegate from Union to run for the office of state
senate at that same election. Andy won handily.
My great-grandfather, Andrew Jackson McGranahan, became a state senator. A year later, he moved
from his cabin into a modest house on Pump Street
in Union.

"This new wave of Democrats immediately
undid many of the most important acts of the statemakers. They moved the capital from Wheeling to
Charleston. They discarded the state's constitution and implemented a new one modeled after

the old Virginia constitution, because they felt the original West Virginia Constitution was too heavily biased in favor towards the Unionists. They even tried to dissolve the state and rejoin Virginia, but were rebuffed by the Supreme Court. In a move I can only imagine motivated by pure spite, they assumed what they called an equitable proportion of the pre-war Virginia state debt, strapping their own state.

"Andy himself was instrumental in introducing legislation that restated the rights of property owners outside of West Virginia, allowing significant outside ownership of mineral rights by outsiders. Again, this move was motivated by spite, to handicap the new state, thereby punishing the statemakers. Andy was an angry man.

"Two decades later, Andy admitted in his memoirs that this was done largely out of revenge and that if he had fully understood the long-term ramifications he never would have done it. It has made West Virginia the poor state it is today.

"I have studied Andy's memoirs on several occasions during my long life. He was a man who was deeply scarred, both physically and emotionally, by war. He was haunted by demons for two full decades after his return from war. These days, we'd call what Andy had 'PTSD' or Post Traumatic Stress Disorder, and he'd be given years of psychological treatment at a Veterans Administration hospital. In those days, there were no such services available.

"According to his memoirs, Andy became close to a neighbor's daughter who, at the age of eight, contracted polio. Through empathy with the girl, Andy came to realize that as hobbled as he was by his own injuries, his greatest source of misery was his own angst. As he watched the girl descend into a crippled state, he began to shake his demons and regain his humanity. His relationship with Allie, strained since his return from war, began to improve. His last years of life with her were contented and loving.

"Andy died in the Russian Flu Pandemic in 1889, three days before his 49th birthday, and was buried in the town cemetery on Green Hill, here in Union."

Wayne said, "You are almost twice that age!"

"That's a fact. I never go a day without thanking the Lord for my longevity. Anyway, five years later, in 1894, Monroe County held a reunion of the Confederate soldiers. General John Echols, who had organized the Monroe Guards, the first unit of volunteers in May, 1861, delivered a stirring address. He spoke eloquently of the loyalty and bravery of Monroe Countians. Echols stood an imposing 6-feet 4-inches tall. As he spoke, several veterans hatched the idea of a memorial statue to commemorate the contributions of their peers.

"Echols found the idea enticing and proffered matching funds if a local committee could be formed and could raise its share. Echols died in 1896, but his son, Edward, shared his father's enthusiasm for the project and when the local money had been raised, the younger Echols brought forth the promised contribution.

"Andy and Allie's son, Bobby McGranahan, my grandfather, read the law and passed the bar exam. He married into the wealthy Dawson family and eventually moved into this mansion with his wife, which is how I came to inherit it. Bobby took an active role in the monument committee. When discussion led to the specific nature and style of the monument, the committee decided to create a statue that would feature the form of a common soldier. Bobby offered the photograph of Andy taken at the Salt as he departed for War to be used as a model for the sculptors.

"Mrs. E. F. Bingham and her two children donated a one-eighth acre site for the monument on a grassy knoll on the northern edge of downtown Union, prominently in sight of travelers from both directions through town. The location was also selected as the committee believed that with the rapid growth in population of much of West Virginia, the monument would soon be engulfed in residential or commercial development. A deed was recorded that gave access to the monument site for all persons who may wish to visit in perpetuity. The town has seen little growth, so the statue still stands in the pasture, in the same isolation as a century ago.

"The monument is 20 feet tall, with a 4-foot base of native blue limestone, a 10-foot pedestal of carved Barre granite, and topped with the figure with Andy's likeness. It was carved in Italy of white marble, carefully crated, and sent by ocean liner to Union. The soldier is standing at parade rest, wearing a Confederate slouch cap. A rifle rests in front of him and both his hands rest on the barrel. The words, 'Confederate Soldiers of Monroe County' were chiseled into the base of the pedestal. Just above were the words, 'There is a true glory and a true honor – the glory of duty done, the honor of integrity of principle. R.E. Lee'

"Alison Littletree McGranahan died on September 6, 1898 during the planning process for the memorial. She was buried alongside Andy at the Green Hill Cemetery.

"Two years to the day later on September 6, 1900, a thousand people gathered as the monument's cornerstone was laid. A year later on a sunny Sunday in September 1901, 12,000 people watched the unveiling of the monument. The ceremony started with a parade of dignitaries, soldiers, and marching bands. Maids of Honor represented each of the eleven Confederate States. As the veil dropped, revealing the statue, the news reports said there were shouts of joy, hats thrown into the air, and many in the audience were brought to tears. Old soldiers joined hands around the monument and sang Auld Lang Syne, accompanied by two cornets.

"My grandfather, Robert Isaac McGranahan died of lung cancer on January 21, 1904 at age 46, two weeks after learning of the first successful flight of a contraption called an airplane by two brothers from Dayton, Ohio, on the sand dunes of the North Carolina coast. Bobby was buried alongside his mother and father. His oldest son, Donald, who is my father, and his wife are buried there as well and there's a tombstone there for me already, next to my dear wife Flora who died so many years ago.

"So each day when I look across our lawn, across the highway, and into the pasture, to see a pensive Confederate soldier in white marble, I feel like I'm looking at my great-grandfather, Andy. His portrait here in our library was painted after he moved into town," he said, pointing at it. "I'm sure you can see the family resemblance."

"I can," said Wayne. "It seems to me that Andy faced as many emotional challenges as physical ones, recovering from his war experience. I'm guessing there is a lesson somewhere in this story for me."

Phil smiled peacefully and said, "Life's lessons are wherever we find them."

+ + + +

November 30

At the Rotary club meeting, Wayne saw a new attendee, a man who looked familiar to him. He sat next to him, and he introduced himself. The man said with a Brooklyn accent, "My name is Levi Rubinstein. I am a musician."

Wayne said, "I recognize you! You played the fiddle at the wedding reception of those two women a couple of weeks ago."

Levi said, "Yes, I did. Most of the time I am on the road. But I was happy to be in town to play that gig. Wasn't it fun?"

Wayne wanted to say it was quirky, but instead bypassed his question, "You are an exceptional musician!"

"Thanks very much," he said modestly. "I have been playing stringed instruments since I was nine. I should hope that by now I would be somewhat good at it."

"I'm guessing from your accent that you're not from around here."

"What accent?" he joked. "Seriously, no, I am a newcomer, which locals say is anyone whose father didn't go to high school here! I am from Long Island. I started poking away at the piano when I was four years old. I feel like I was able to read music before I was able to read English sentences. I went to the Juilliard School of music and played professionally with the Boston Symphony Orchestra."

"What the hell are you doing here?" said Wayne.

"I gave it up! I was every Jewish mother's dream. And yet, I was miserable. I hated the regimentation of the orchestra. I hated city life, with its hoards of people, its stress and pretense. Whenever I wasn't practicing my viola or studying for school when I was a teenager, I was growing things in our garden. I have always liked having my fingers in the soil, dirt under my fingernails. This drove my violin teacher crazy!

"Once I was in the orchestra professionally, whenever I would talk to my fellow orchestra members, they were unhappy as well. Our audiences were filled with stoic people of privilege. I never felt appreciated.

"I saved some money and one fall I took a three-month sabbatical. I drove my Toyota 4-Runner down the Appalachian chain. Driving through Union, I stopped just to walk up and down the main street. I looked into the picture window of Red Oak Realty, and I saw an advertisement for a farm and farmhouse. I walked inside and I met with a realtor. He and I drove out to the property. It was just a few miles north of town in a village called Sinks Grove. I put down a deposit that afternoon. I drove back to Boston, and I called my boss at the symphony and told him that I was quitting. He thought I'd gone bananas. He begged me to reconsider. My mother was apoplectic.

"You can imagine how crazy this was. I was a Jewish kid from New York with an accent so thick nobody could understand me. Friends in Boston thought I was entering a scene from *Deliverance*. I was single, and I had no job. I weathered the winter putting some money into the farmhouse to make it more comfortable. I devoured books on carpentry, and I did much of my own work. I joined several local bands, and I began to learn Appalachian and bluegrass music, switching my viola for a violin, what everybody here calls a fiddle. In December, I met a local woman who was home on winter break from pharmacy school. Her dad was the local pharmacist. Her name is Isadora. That was 10 years ago. We were married the following year, and we now have a six year old son."

"I believe I met your wife when I was picking up some pills at the Union Pharmacy."

Levi said, "Yes, you probably did. These days, I make a living by touring with a trio of musicians. We play all kinds of crazy stuff, mixing our roots in classical, traditional American, Blues, bluegrass, and swing music. We even do gospel. Imagine me doing gospel! Our audiences are *raucous*, much more attentive and lively than I ever experienced in the symphony. I'm a member of this Rotary Club, but I don't attend as often as I'd like, since I'm always traveling. I just got back from a tour of six states.

"Enough about me. What the hell are *you* doing here?"

Wayne told him about the crash and about his extended stay with Phil.

"How long do you plan to stay in Union?"

"I haven't decided yet. I am still recovering from my injuries, although I'm perhaps 85 percent well again. I have a part-time job. Frankly, I'm not eager to face some of the situations I left behind."

"The longer you stay the more this place will grow on you, trust me. Many creative people love rural environments. Creative people need long periods of time in peace and solitude. We cannot engage when there is a constant clamor of activity. My mind craves the regenerative power of quiet."

"I think I know what you mean. I'm not what I'd call a creative person. But I have been surprised at the changes in my attitude and approach towards life, being here in such a serene place. I'm not clinging to anger as I once did. I used to be able to spew bile with the best of them. But venting my anger seems increasingly fruitless and frankly, unbecoming. You came here by choice. I came here quite literally by accident. But all the same, this place is growing on me, too."

"I'm playing at Professor Phil's Chautauqua a week from Thursday. You'll be there, won't you?"

"Yes."

+ + + +

December 1

Four months before Wayne's arrival in Union, Phil had sold his house to a couple named Christie and Jim Dickson and had been renting back from them since. The Dicksons had bought it planning to retire to it. Jim had a job with an oil exploration service, and he worked worldwide.

On Wednesday, December 1, the Dicksons were in the States spending time with relatives in New Jersey and came to Union to check on their property. Jim told Phil as Wayne listened nearby, "Our plan was to retire by the end of the year. But with the economy being what it is, we'd like our savings and investments to be a bit stronger before we give up my job. My company would like us to spend at least another year with them, this time in Indonesia. Phil, at your age we're concerned about your health. But if you are still okay and you'd like to stay another year, we'd like you to continue to rent from us."

They worked out a rental rate and a plan to deal with any maintenance issues. Wayne explained the status of his recovery and asked their long-term plans.

Christie said, "Once we get here full-time, we hope to make at least part of the house a guest house or B&B. This house is too special for us alone. What are your plans?"

"Phil and Mildred have nursed me back to health after my accident. Really, the whole community has helped. I'm not sure of my long-term plans. I suppose Phil and I will talk about this soon."

Once they left, Wayne said to Phil, "You've been so good to me since my crash. I'm sure I've over-stayed my welcome."

Phil said, "It's been good having you here. An old man gets lonely in a big house by himself. A pretty, young woman would have been more to my liking, but would have probably landed me in jail!" He laughed. "But you've been good company. I want you to stay as long as you like."

Wayne said, "Some crazy and unexpected things have been going on in my mind since my crash. I think my crash was a metaphor for my life. The pain I endured has helped re-shuffle my emotional deck of cards. I expected to stay in Union for two days and return home the same person as I was before. I've been here three months and if I ever go home, it won't be as the same person."

"You do seem more relaxed."

"I think it is way more than that. If I under-stood it better myself, I'd tell you more."

They worked out an arrangement where Wayne would share the rent, which was less than the small Northern Virginia apartment he'd rented. He wrote Phil a check, retroactively paying his keep since he arrived 80 days earlier. It included all the money coming from Wayne's first paycheck from his job at the bank.

+ + + +

December 9

That Thursday, as advertised, Levi came to Phil's house to play his violin. His wife and son came as well, as did a piano player, a woman in her sixties. While they were tuning up, Wayne introduced himself to Isadora, whose face was familiar to him from the Pharmacy. He said, "My name is Wayne Quarles."

"Yes, I know who you are. Everybody pretty much knows everybody in Union, but I know you because I've filled pain medication prescriptions. The drop in your dosage must mean you're on the mend!" She said cheerfully.

"I met Levi a couple of weeks ago. He told me about moving here. What a great story!"

She had curly, dark hair and a pale complexion. She wore a white Star of David on her necklace that made Wayne think about his erstwhile lover, Cynthia, and her cross medallion. "My mother's mom is a bit of a yenta in Atlanta. When I was in college, she'd ask me over and over again when I was going to find a nice Jewish boy and settle down. I'd always shrug and murmur to myself how improbable that was, living here. Then, wouldn't you know, I met a nice Jewish boy from Long Island right here in Union.

"Like most contemporary Jewish families, we're pretty secular. I come from a rare breed I call 'rural southern Jewry.'"

"Is there any prejudice against you?" Wayne asked innocently.

"Oh, no, absolutely not. I got teased a bit in grade school, but it was innocuous. One snotty boy liked to sing, 'Jesus loves me more than you; I'm a Christian you're a Jew.'

"Perhaps the lack of prejudice results from the fact that my family has been here since the dawn of time, literally since before the Civil War. My maiden name is Mishkin. My dad's family includes a long line of physicians and pharmacists. We're the only Jewish family in Monroe County."

"That's unbelievable!"

"Jews live throughout the world, in almost exclusively minority populations and typically in the larger cities. New York City and Israel are, I think, the only places on earth that have majority, or even significant minority, Jewish populations. The older, bigger cities of the South, like Richmond and Atlanta, have many Jews. Not many of us live in rural Appalachia. But I feel totally at home here. I'm a scruffy, earthy, small-town girl, and I say that without any self-disparagement.

"Jews have borne the brunt of significant oppression and ethnic strife at times and in places around the world. There is no better place in the world to be than West Virginia."

Wayne said, "I'm a bit embarrassed to admit this to you. Before I arrived here, I had an image of Appalachia as an insular, unwelcoming place, almost a gated region turning away anyone who wasn't white, Anglo-Saxon, and Protestant. That notion has been repeatedly dispelled since my arrival. What you've said really shows how wrong I was."

Isadora smiled proudly. "Everybody loves it here. Even my classmates who moved away always look forward to coming home."

The concert was at times quiet and soothing, at times vibrant and energetic. Levi played from a variety of genres, from Mozart to Scott Joplin to Bill Monroe. The 12 people in attendance were ecstatic. The applause was substantial and genuine. After the concert, Levi whispered to Wayne, "See what I mean?"

+ + + +

December 13

On Monday morning, 12 days before Christmas, the phone rang. Phil yelled to Wayne, "It's for you!"

"Wayne, this is Dr. Ramkija. How are you doing?"

"I'm healing pretty well. I'm still using crutches most of the time. My jaw still hurts when I eat and my ribs are a bit sore when I cough or sneeze, but I'm fine. What's going on?"

"I don't know if Phil mentioned it to you, but I ran into him the night before last at a symphony concert at Carnegie Hall in Lewisburg. Wayne, we have a young patient here at the hospital who has renal failure. He is in desperate need of a donated kidney. He has AB negative blood, which is the rarest type. We normally look to get a donor kidney from a family member, but nobody in his family is a match. After seeing Phil, it reminded me that you have AB negative, too. You happen to be the only potential match I could find.

"It is irregular at best and borderline unethical for me to ask someone unrelated to the patient to consider being tested for live donation of an organ, but we're desperate. I'm calling to ask if you'd consider donating a kidney."

Holy Kleenex Batman, Wayne thought! Another under-the-knife experience! "What is involved?" he asked.

"I don't do this type of surgery myself. But if you agree and if there is a match, the hospital will prepare two surgery rooms, one for you and the other for him. This will be done at the Roanoke hospital, as they have better facilities and more experienced doctors. Your surgeon will slice your abdomen and remove one of your two kidneys. Human bodies perform perfectly with only one. While your surgeon begins stitching you up, your kidney will be taken to the recipient. Another surgeon removes the recipient's kidneys and replaces his

two defective kidneys with your one good kidney.
If all goes well, both you and the boy will recover
fully. He will be playing with his friends within a
few weeks.

"It's painful for you, as is any surgery. And it
has the usual risks associated with anesthesia and
surgery. But without a donor, this boy will die."

"I don't know, Doctor Ram. I've been through so
much pain. I'll need to think about it."

"That's the best I could have hoped to hear you
say. Let me know as soon as you can. He's likely
only got a few days to live. If you say 'go' I'll get
things rolling immediately.

"One other thing, Wayne. For what it is worth,
this kid's name is Farooq. His family is Syrian,"
she said.

"Like I said, Dr. Ram, I'll have to think about
it."

"I understand, but please don't take too long or
he'll succumb. Thank you, Wayne. Goodbye."

As Wayne hung up the phone, Phil said to him,
"What was on Dr. Ram's mind?"

Wayne white-lied, "She just called to see how
I was doing." He didn't want to involve Phil in his
decision.

+ + + +

December 14

After the Rotary meeting the next day, Wayne
told Truman he'd walk home rather than catch his
usual lift. He emerged from the Kalico Kitchen and
hobbled towards Ashley's IGA food market. He saw
Peters Mountain in the distance, with a dusting of
white snow at the long summit ridge. He walked
without using his crutches unless he stepped on
or off a curb. As he slowly crossed Main Street,

a tractor-trailer waited patiently. The air was still and cold. The Monroe County Courthouse had tasteful, understated Christmas lights in each window. A small spruce pine tree in the courtyard had white lights. Many of the downtown business-es were decorated as well, with traditional lighting displays and greenery.

Most of the drivers of cars and pickup trucks waved at him, although he only recognized one or two. He turned east on North Street and walked a few hundred yards. He entered the store, planning to buy some beer and soup. He eschewed the chewy snacks he used to crave – chips and jerky – be-cause of lingering soreness in his jaw. He thought it was odd that the store's office sat towards the front of the store beside the two checkout lines, without any walls to shield it from customer glanc-es or provide any security.

Inside the store, he overheard a couple of la-dies talking about a male contestant on *American Idol* from the previous night's show. Three men dressed in Carhartt coveralls and John Deere hats ruminated on the price of hay and when the first snowfall would hit town.

Near the checkout lines was a large, hanging rack filled with cigarettes. Wayne was delighted to no longer be addicted. As he waited his turn in the checkout line, he saw a large glass jar with some coins and several bills in it. Atop it was a hand-written sign asking for donations for a girl with leukemia from nearby Rock Camp.

The woman in front of him had two small chil-dren with her, one standing by her and the other just a few months old in an infant carrier. There was a long, frayed rip in the back of her jacket. She had only a few items to buy, some milk, diapers, flour, rice, toilet paper, and packaged noodles. She took some food stamps from her wallet and some bills and gave them to the cashier. She scrutinized her change carefully and thumbed through the remaining bills in her wallet. Her eyeballs subconsciously went upwards as if she was counting. She took several bills from her wallet and dropped them through the slot in metal lid of the jar.

Wayne paid for his items and dropped the change into the jar. He hobbled outside. In the parking lot, he saw a Ford F-250 pickup truck with two rifles on the gun rack in the back window and a dead deer draped over the tailgate. He watched as a bag-boy helped the woman from the checkout line. He put her groceries in the trunk while she strapped her children into their car seats in her old Plymouth sedan. It had a rear quarter-panel painted in a different color than the rest of the car and rust around the doors. It had decals of Christmas scenes in the back windows, of Santa Claus and snowflakes. Wayne's curiosity overcame him and he walked towards her. "Excuse me, ma'am. I saw that you put a few dollars into a jar on the counter inside. Do you know the girl with leukemia?"

"No sir, I don't," she said, unfazed by being addressed by a stranger holding crutches. "But I recognize the family name. I wish I had more to give." She looked at his crutches, and then continued, "People would be there for us if we needed them."

"Merry Christmas to you."

"Merry Christmas to you, too."

A man in his forties driving a Mazda rolled down his window and asked Wayne if he wanted a lift. Wayne said, "I appreciate the offer, but I think I'll walk. Thanks for asking."

He crossed the street and had gone another 50 feet when another unknown driver, this one in an old Honda Accord, rolled down the window and asked Wayne if he wanted a ride. He declined politely again. "No, thank you."

Rather than going directly home to *Serenus*, Wayne aimed towards the Confederate Monument. Leaving Main Street, he walked through the small parking lot of the Union Presbyterian Church, a tan brick building with four white columns supporting its front portico. He walked towards a stone entranceway to a paved sidewalk, flanked by white fence. He ambled towards the fence-enclosed park and rested on a bench. He looked at the visage of his ancestor. It stood casually yet impressively on a 14-foot tall pedestal, inscribed with "Confederate Soldiers of Monroe County," and "There is a true glory and a true honor – the glory of duty done, the honor of integrity of principle. Robert E. Lee." He pulled his harmonica from his pocket and played *When Johnny Comes Marching Home* and then *Dixie*. It was a peaceful, timeless, reverent moment. For the first time he could ever remember, Wayne thought shamefully about his own honor and resolved to improve it.

Arriving back at *Serenus*, he called Juliet, leaving a message for her to call him. When she returned his call that evening, he told her about Dr. Ramkija's call and the urgent need for a donated kidney.

"I need some advice," he said.

"What can I do or say?" she asked sympathetically.

"I want you to say I should donate a kidney. Or, I want you to say I should not donate a kidney."

"What does your heart say?"

"I'm not used to listening to my heart. I'm used to listening to my head, more often than not, the devil in my head. My head says, 'Don't subject yourself to any more pain.' If I never see another operating room in my life, it'll be too soon."

"And your heart?"

"My heart tells me that everything I've ever done in my life has been for me. *Obey my thirst. Look out for Number 1. I deserve a break today.* Everything has been about me, me, and me. I am a self-absorbed, bitter, insensitive ass. The last time I remember doing a completely selfless thing was more than 20 years ago when I helped an old woman change a flat tire on Route 7 during rush hour. I stopped only because I thought she was a friend of my mom's, and by the time I realized I was mistaken, it was too late to leave her there. Do you know what decades of selfishness have earned me? They have earned me a broken marriage, a couple of kids who think I'm a jerk, an extended unemployment, and a broken body. What few friends I ever had have largely abandoned me.

"Today I stood in line behind a woman at the grocery store. I'm guessing she was perhaps 30. She obviously had little money. And yet when somebody she didn't know needed some money to combat a terrible illness, she was willing to give. It occurred to me that she looked as happy as anyone I'd ever seen."

"Listen to your heart, Wayne. Let your heart do something other than push some blood around."

"What my singular devotion to me has earned me is nothing, absolutely nothing. Maybe I should try another approach. Maybe I should try something else, a Plan B. I need to do something selfless, something I'll be proud of."

"Now what was it that you called me for?" she said, mockingly.

"I think I called to ask if you'd drive me to Roanoke tomorrow. I'm going to call Dr. Ramkija right now and see if we can make a date in the morning."

Juliet said, "Tell you what, big guy. One good

turn leads to another. Give this boy a kidney and I'll give you six month's worth of massages, gratis. Just let me know when you're up to it."

"You've got yourself a deal," he said.

Not surprisingly, when Wayne scanned the Union phone book, there was only one listing for Ramkija, with a first name of Vijay. He dialed. Nobody was home but he left a message. "Dr. Ram, this is Wayne Quarles. I can be in Roanoke as soon as the surgeons are ready for me."

When she called back, he and she discussed plans for the morning. She reminded him, "I won't be doing the surgery myself, but tomorrow is my day off and I'd like to meet you in Roanoke and tell the surgeon that you're doing me a special favor. Oh, don't eat or drink anything after midnight just in case the surgery is a go."

+ + + +

December 15

Wayne was prepped for surgery at 8:50 a.m. the next morning at Roanoke's Community Hospital, where Juliet had delivered him.

The young boy, Farooq, was already under anesthesia when Wayne arrived. As the anesthesiologist prepared Wayne's dose, Wayne asked Dr. Ram and his surgeon if he could see the boy. He took one quick look at the dark-haired, angel-faced boy. Wayne's eyes glazed over for a moment, and he envisioned seeing Eddie, his son, lying there. Wayne pursed his lips, nodded his head, and in his best hillbilly accent said to the surgeon and Dr. Ram, "Okay, let's get 'er done!"

♥

+ + + +

Three hours after surgery, the surgeon called on Wayne to see how he was doing. The doctor said, "Farooq's parents are here. If it's okay with you, they'd like to come in. They wanted to express their gratitude."

"Sure."

A Middle-Eastern man and woman entered Wayne's room. In broken English Wayne remembered none of later, they poured out their emotions, overwhelming him with thankfulness and appreciation. Wayne thought again of Eddie and how he would feel if a stranger had saved his life.

By 10 o'clock the next morning, Wayne was back at *Serenus*. Phil said to him, "You did a good thing yesterday, a selfless thing. You have made our family proud."

Wayne thought how good hearing that felt.

+ + + +

December 25

On Christmas day, Phil McGranahan had invited Reed and Juliet Rathmell, Truman Hankins and his wife Janice, and Levi and Isadora Rubenstein and their son for dinner.

Wayne had bought a nice shirt to wear on Christmas day. He shaved for the first time since his accident, revealing the healed scar that made its way from the left edge of his mouth to below his chin.

Reed and Juliet arrived first. Wayne gave Juliet a hand-made scarf he'd bought at the Country Creations store and gallery. Juliet gave Wayne a pair of binoculars she'd bought at a pawn shop in Lewisburg and a book on the birds of Eastern United States. Wayne gave Uncle Phil a set of suspenders and Phil gave Wayne a subscription to *Cycle World* magazine – Wayne had been telling Phil his interest in motorcycling was recovering along with his body.

When the Rubensteins arrived, Levi said to Wayne, "Because we're Jewish, we don't celebrate a religious Christmas. But we always appreciate it when Phil invites us over to share dinner." Levi played his violin for a half-hour before dinner and everyone sang Christmas carols. Levi's instrumental version of *Oh, Holy Night* was breathtaking! Wayne played *Stop the Calvary* on his harmonica, less than breathtaking but still to the delight of everyone.

Juliet and Reed brought a glazed ham. Janice Hankins made two vegetable casseroles. Isadora brought a rum cake for dessert. Wayne cooked a turkey and made stove-top stuffing while Phil tossed some greens he'd grown in the greenhouse for a salad.

After dinner, Juliet and Wayne hand-washed the dishes while everyone else retired to the living room. Juliet said, "You look so different without your beard. I'm not sure what to think of your scar."

"I consider it to be my war wound. It is a lasting symbol of the guy I once was."

As Juliet handed him some silverware, Wayne said, "I've found I like washing dishes. It's become my favorite chore. Union's winter is much colder than what I'm used to in NoVA, and I haven't gotten into the habit of wearing enough clothes to stay warm. I like having my hands in warm water."

He handed her a plate to dry, but she dropped it. "I'm sorry," she said, accepting responsibility. She reached for a broom to sweep up the chards. "How clumsy of me! I've been dropping a lot of things lately.

"According to the Weather Channel, we're sup-posed to get unseasonably warm weather for the next few days. Are you well enough to take a short hike with me on Monday?"

"How hard a hike is it?" he asked.

"It's an easy, mountain ridge walk. It's only about one mile each way. For anyone in good shape, it's no problem. I'd like to talk with you. How's your recovery?"

"It's okay. I'll be slow but I should be fine."

"Great. I'll pick you up around 9 a.m."

+ + + +

December 27

As advertised, Monday dawned surprisingly mild, with the outside thermometer at 48F. Wayne checked www.weather.com and saw that for Union, the forecast was for a high of 60F, almost 20-degrees above average. Juliet arrived on the dot.

"Where are we going?" Wayne asked.

"Do you remember me mentioning the raptor observatory on Peters Mountain, called Hanging Rock? I'm taking you there. Bring your heaviest jacket and hat. It will be colder on the mountain."

Wayne borrowed a down jacket from Phil. He took a water bottle. He had made two sandwiches of turkey and lettuce, leftover from Christmas dinner. Juliet carried a large day-pack and shoved Wayne's jacket inside. She said, "I brought dad's trekking poles for you. I think you may find these easier to use on the trail than crutches. I brought a set for myself as well."

She drove southward on Main Street through Union and continued southward on Willow Bend Road. She drove much slower than he would have, and she seemed unrushed. Past Willow Bend, they turned left on Zenith Road and drove through Zenith. Juliet turned right on SR-15 and they began ascending Peters Mountain on the steep, lay-over road Wayne had ridden two months earlier in Ansel's pickup truck. "At the top of the mountain, the Allegheny Trail crosses. You've heard of the Appalachian Trial, which goes over 2100 miles from Georgia to Maine. The Allegheny Trail is the poor woman's Appalachian Trail. It goes 300 miles through West Virginia. Around 500 people hike the entirety of the Appalachian Trail each year, but only a few dozen do the Allegheny Trail. The trails share the same route for about 20 miles on Peters Mountain near here, but the portion we're walking is on the Allegheny Trail alone."

At the top of the mountain was a sign that said "Hanging Rock." Someone had draped a dead raccoon over it. Juliet said, "Damn! Sometimes this state has too many redneck West Virginians!"

She parked the car at a gravel lot at the crest of the mountain. It looked large enough for four or five cars. It was empty. "Hanging Rock Raptor Observatory was a former firefighting lookout tower, built back in the 1950s. It was burned by vandals in the 1990s while I was overseas. People were infuriated. The Forest Service was all for having it rebuilt, but they never have enough money to properly maintain their facilities. So a small army of volunteers gathered quickly, including my dad, to rebuild it. The new one was dedicated in 1991."

They began hiking a well-beaten trail through a hardwood forest. It seemed ten degrees colder on the mountain, but still not uncomfortable. Wayne struggled up the gentle grade and was impatient with himself, but Juliet seemed to be in no hurry whatsoever. There were patches of snow still on the ground from a snowfall a week earlier, but most spots had melted off. Everything was painted in winter earthtones.

They crested a small rise, still in the forest, and then descended to a gap where a side-trail merged from the right. They stopped to take a break. Juliet said, "Peters Mountain crests at just over 3200 feet. It is famous for producing what meteorologists call the 'Peters Mountain Roar,' a unique phenomenon that occurs when conditions are right, typically in the spring, when wet, Atlantic easterly winds flow over the mountain and accelerate in speed and force. Sometimes locals find ocean gulls and other waterfowl carried here by the winds. It has been described to me like the sound of waves crashing over a rocky shoreline. Now is the wrong season and the winds are calm today, but it makes a nice story."

A row of rock outcroppings appeared on their left, reminding Wayne of teeth emanating from a gum. They came to a sign with arrows saying, "AL-LEGHENY TRAIL" (straight) and "FIRE TOWER" (left). They went left and walked through a cleft in the rock. The going became much rockier on the south side of the crest. Wayne saw a set of wooden stairs leading to a cedar-clad lookout tower, some 15 feet above. He hobbled up the stairs with Juliet inching up behind him. They stood on the landing that encircled the cedar-shake clad room. The view was breathtaking! To the north the topography was gentle, with rolling hills and small mountains. The mountains were forested while the flatter areas were grassy pastures. There were few habitations in sight, although he was able to see the town of Union. Long contrails streaked white across the deep blue sky.

Juliet said, pointing northward, "See that band of grey pollutants to the northern horizon? I think most of that comes from the coal-fired power plants on the Ohio River on the other side of the state." They walked the landing to the south side of the building. Sheltered from the wind and facing direct sunlight, it seemed much warmer. "In the valley below is where Waiteville is located."

"Yes," Wayne said. "That's where Ansel Cummings lives. Lived. I went to his cabin once." Wayne's ears rang with the memory of the percussion of Ansel's assault rifle.

"Across that is Potts Mountain. Peters and Potts Mountains run parallel to each other for over fifty miles. Beyond that – see all those crenulated ridgelines? – are the other ridge-and-valley mountains of Western Virginia. On the horizon there you can see the Peaks of Otter on the Blue Ridge, with Sharp Top on the right and Flat Top on the left. The first settlers to see the Blue Ridge Mountains thought the Peaks of Otter were the tallest in the state, but Mount Rogers and Whitetop Mountains in the far southwest turned out to be the tallest." The mountains seemed painted in taupes and umbers, with gentle, wave-like ridges. Small stands of green pine trees interrupted the russet earthtones.

"I've been coming up here since I was a girl. Even before becoming a falconer, Dad has always been interested in hawks. Peters Mountain has forever been a superhighway for migratory raptors. The location and position creates updrafts they use to soar sometimes more than a hundred miles in a day. This is not migration season. That ended in November. But the view is great any time."

They went inside the glass-walled building and sat at the table inside. While eating the turkey sandwiches Wayne brought, they looked over several logbooks, one with printed forms where watchers could document their raptor sightings. Another was a blank notebook where visitors could record any thoughts or ideas. Children had left drawings in it, primarily of soaring birds. A poster of raptors, with photographs of each type: eagles, vultures, owls, and hawks, was attached to the wall along with a tally of sightings over the past twenty years. It showed a dramatic decline of broad-winged hawks, from over 10,000 annually to 1500 in the most recent year. Happily, almost all other species had increased, including bald and golden eagles and peregrine falcons.

"The timelessness of this place has let it become a fixture in my life. Some of my best memories with Dad are from here. We'd sit for hours, listening to the wind, watching the hawks glide along, wishing we could fly with them. We would talk about things in our lives. At various times in our lives, we came here every week and at other times not for several years. But the feeling we had together was always the same. I'm sure there are generation gaps in every family, but dad and I have always adored each other. At dad's age, he can't make the trek any more. Father Time marches on."

They were silent for awhile, taking in that view and enjoying the comfort of the solar heated room.

"Was there something you wanted to talk to me about?" he asked.

"Yes. Several weeks ago, I started feeling excess fatigue. I was stumbling, and I felt awkward when I walked. I could barely run any more. I went to my doctor to see if I had a virus or something. When things didn't improve, she sent me to a specialist in Roanoke. Bottom line; I've been diagnosed with ALS."

"Lou Gehrig's disease?" he asked.

"Yes, that's right. The full name is amyotrophic lateral sclerosis."

"I don't know much about it. I thought only men contracted it."

"It's much more common in men. Around

20,000 people in America have it. It's a disease of the neurological system that attacks the nerve cells – the neurons – that are responsible for controlling the muscles. My impression is that the muscles themselves are fine, at least initially, but the brain loses the ability to instruct them. If they aren't given instructions, they don't do any work and they begin to atrophy.

"There is no cure. It's invariably fatal, often within two to five years. Most victims have respiratory failure as the brain can no longer instruct the lungs to breathe. Strangely, the disease seldom impairs the mind. Stephen Hawking, the physicist, is one of the most famous victims in the world. His brain is amazing.

"Fortunately, it won't affect my ability to see, smell, hear, taste, or recognize touch. That is, until it kills me.

"So my doctors have told me to live my life the best I can and prepare for the end. That's why I'm here today. I'm laboring as much as you are. Since we've known each other, you've gotten stronger and healthier and I've gotten weaker. I've been inspired by your recovery, how you have rejuvenated yourself both in body and in spirit. I'm certain this will be my last trip to Hanging Rock. Forever."

He was dumbfounded by her tragic kismet. He felt woefully inadequate at every level to respond or sympathize in any way. They sat and watched the motionless scene in front of them. A jet spewed a contrail high above streaking westward. He stammered out, "I am so, so sorry!"

"You know, we all are going to die. I just have a better idea when than most people."

"You are facing this with such resolve."

"What other options do I have? After a few weeks of crying almost non-stop, I sat down a few days ago to develop a long list of plausible responses.

After about a half-hour of thinking it through, I had discounted suicide, despair, and self-pity. In fact, my list had only one entry: deal with it the best I can.

"When I was a Girl Scout, I had a Scoutmaster who asked each of us to list our goals for life. I had three. First, I wanted to visit 20 countries and live for a least a month in three of them. Second, I wanted to have a child. Finally, I wanted to earn a PhD. Since then, I've at least set foot in 27 countries and I've lived in five. I'm just a few months from my doctorate. Being successful will mean more to me than you can ever imagine. I want those three letters, PhD, chiseled on my tombstone."

"Look," Wayne said, pointing in the distance. "I see something soaring." Juliet withdrew her pair of binoculars from her backpack, and they walked outside to the landing. Wayne lifted to his eyes the pair Juliet had given him for Christmas. As he watched, it flew motionless towards the observatory. It grew closer and closer and then hung seemingly immobile perhaps 70 feet above them, pointed to the west, primary feathers fluttering lightly in the wind. With its auburn tail feathers, Wayne knew it was a red tailed hawk. He delighted in thinking it was a progeny of Ruby. It was bold and free against the azure sky.

As he watched, he thought about Juliet. He had grown exceedingly fond of her. Nothing had crossed their lips in terms of a relationship. Now he knew she would be gone too soon. Would he embrace her more fully in her few remaining months? Or would he selfishly withdraw? He implored the right answer from himself.

Juliet interrupted their reverie by saying, "One of the most interesting tasks I've ever taken on is writing my own obituary. As dad and I discussed my fate, he suggested it to me. When he was a preacher, he comforted many people facing death. Confronting my mortality and writing about my impending death has forced a deep reflection on me. Even if I live several more years, I think it is a good exercise."

"I bet so!"

"Have you written yours?"

"No, the thought has never occurred to me."

"You might try it."

"Did he give you any pointers?"

"He said to start with the compulsory things, like your family, education, and life experiences. The meat of it is in coming to terms with the person you are and the person you want to be. I've been working on it for a few weeks. I'll share it with you next time we get together."

Wayne's attention drifted back to watching the hawk. Juliet continued, "None of us can know what the future will bring us. They say life isn't fair. I hoped I'd be able to come to Hanging Rock to watch hawks as I aged into my seventies and eighties. It is not to be. But I have no regrets." She reached over and kissed him lightly on the lips. "With the experiences I've had and the family and friends I hold dear, my life has been blessed."

+ + + +

December 29

Two days later, three days before New Year's Day, the Public Service Authority held a public hearing on the wind turbines. A governor-selected panel of businesspeople, environmentalists, and politicians were to be in attendance, and this group would settle the fate of the turbine project. It was held at the James Monroe High School auditorium, which was the largest assembly hall in the county. The county's consolidated high school was in Linside, 18 miles south of Union. Even the kids from Waiteville went there, on a bus trip that took 1-1/2 hours each way. It was the longest ride of any students in West Virginia.

Reed and Juliet offered to pick up Wayne and Phil. Phil declined, saying he didn't feel well. Wayne went partially to please Juliet and partially out of curiosity. Although he was walking almost normally, he brought his wheelchair along to ensure himself a comfortable place to sit. It was cold and well after dark when they left Phil's house at just after 7 p.m.

Almost 250 people crowded the room, the largest single meeting the county had seen that entire year. Delegate Spencer Cahill introduced the panel. "We are here to take public input regarding the application of Bedford Energy Company to put 20 wind turbines atop Peters Mountain. They will provide electrical power to the grid, which the company will sell at prevailing rates. I now open the floor to speakers."

Former state senator Franklin McRoberts III was the first to speak. "Our county needs the money this project will provide. There will be several hundred construction jobs and a few dozen permanent jobs in maintenance. Our county needs growth! Plus, it will reduce our dependence on foreign energy. These are things everyone can agree on. I think the environmental issues are overblown."

A professor from West Virginia University spoke about impending bird and bat kills.

Another professor from Virginia Tech spoke about the potential for the displacement of groundwater that the immense foundations for the turbines would require. "Water is one of this county's most precious resources. I caution against doing anything that could adversely impact it."

Most speakers were everyday citizens from the county. One woman from Zenith said, "It is a bastardization of terminology that we call this project a farm. Farms are places where we grow food. Nobody can eat a wind turbine." Several audience members chuckled.

A bookish-looking man with a blue bow-tie said, "Hanging Rock Raptor Observatory is one of the treasures of West Virginia. These wind turbines will be on both sides of it and will destroy everything it is about. It is unconscionable that we even consider this proposal."

One woman wearing the most professional power-suit Wayne had seen since his arrival in West Virginia said she was on the County Board of Supervisors. "We constantly struggle with revenue. It would help everyone in this county to have a new, consistent source of revenue for our schools, social services, and fire and rescue teams."

An older man wearing a cap with an aircraft carrier logo on it said, "I fought for our country during World War II. I know how important energy is to the security of our country. We have men and women in uniform fighting today and in some cases losing their life over energy. Let's bring these men and women home by generating our own energy here."

One man with a long braid of hair said, "I have seen mountaintop removal mines, and I have seen excessive timbering. A row of propellers on top of a mountain does not constitute a problem on this scale as far as I am concerned."

It was difficult for Wayne to get a read on the direction things were going. He began to think about his own life, the experience he'd just had on Peters Mountain, and what the wind turbines would mean. He rolled his wheelchair forward to look at a wall clock. Momentarily, there was nobody at the speaker's podium. Delegate Cahill mistook Wayne's intention and said, "You, sir. Do you intend to speak?"

Wayne thought to himself, why not? He said, "Yes, please, I do." He rolled himself forward. He carefully lifted himself to a standing position, realizing this was unintentionally creating drama and apprehension. He said, "I am new in this community, and an accidental resident." A few people guffawed at his pun. "I arrived here broken, wretched, homeless, and filled with anger and despair. In the past four months, I have confronted the elemental issues of life and humanity.

"All my life, I have been a selfish, egocentric, consumptive lout, a *Drill, baby, drill,* kind of guy. But I am seeing things now in a new way. West Virginia has been asked for 150 years to provide the resources our nation has demanded. Why should these people who have done so much to make America great have received so little in return? Metropolitan America sees West Virginia as nothing more than a limitless ATM resource machine. Your children and grandchildren will judge you not by what you develop but by what you preserve." He thought of the red-tailed hawk he's seen from the Hanging Rock Observatory, and said, "No amount of money can ever piece back together a soaring hawk."

Wayne turned from the podium and sat back down in his chair, which he wheeled away from the speaker's stand. The room was deathly quiet. Juliet smiled at him and nodded, as did several other people in the crowd.

Delegate Spencer Cahill saw that nobody else from the crowd wanted to speak and said, "Thank you all for coming. Our committee will be in deliberations for four weeks. We will issue a public announcement of our decision then." He adjourned the meeting.

Reed, Juliet, and Wayne began the trip back to Union. Juliet said, "Wayne, what you said really struck a nerve in that room. I am convinced the decision makers were moved. I am proud of you."

"Thank you." Wayne lost himself in thought, realizing this was the second time in two weeks someone was proud of him. He could never recall that happening before.

+ + + +

Flurries of snow danced around the headlights of their car as Reed and Juliet arrived with Wayne at Phil's place around 9:30 p.m. Wayne said, "I'll let myself in." Before emerging from the passenger's seat, he shook Reed's hand and said, "Thank you for taking me tonight." He met Juliet outside the car as she moved to his seat from the back. They hugged and he nuzzled her nose and cheeks with his. "G'night."

He removed his wheelchair from the trunk and unfolded it. As he walked behind it up the ramp, he noticed that Phil had left a light on in the library.

Wayne looked upwards into the cold sky, at a sliver of the moon overhead. He waved at Juliet as she and Reed drove away, and then let himself into the front door and hung his thrift-store coat on the hook in the hallway.

He walked into the library to turn off the light Phil left on. As he walked past Phil's favorite chair, he saw Phil's body, lying in a fetal position, on the floor. The carpet was soiled under him. Wayne stepped towards him and saw that his face was white and pale, and that his eyelids were open but his stare was vacant. Wayne took Phil's left wrist and felt futilely for a pulse. It felt cold, rubbery, unnatural.

Wayne fell backwards into the chair, stunned and crestfallen. He stared at the body of his uncle and wondered what to do. He had never seen a dead body before. Whom should he call? What should he say? It was already late at night. He didn't relish the intrusion of police, undertakers, or investigators. As he pondered the compulsory logistics, his emotions took over and his eyes began to moisten. "I'm so, so sorry to see you go, Phil. You were a wonderful man," he said to the corpse. His jaw began to quiver, his eyes moistened, and he began to weep. Waves of penitence permeated his psyche as he grasped the loss of this man he'd come to love and admire, and the link to his past that only 4 months earlier he had no idea about.

He remembered Phil's story of Allie and Andy's dead baby, when friends and family of the deceased sat with the body overnight. He went upstairs to the bathroom and brushed his teeth. He changed into pajamas. Then he got two blankets and his harmonica. He went back downstairs. He gently turned Uncle Phil's body on its back and straightened the legs and arms, finding them still supple. He closed Phil's eyelids. He covered Phil's body with one of the blankets, understanding the futility. He sat in Phil's favorite chair and covered himself with the other blanket. He alternatively dozed and played his harmonica.

Phil and Andy, Walking, garden, forest of birds, deer. Allie, dark Allie & Willa, long white dress, dancing. Wayne dancing with Willa. Donna. Beautiful Allie. Donna smiling. Phil and Andy embracing . Ruby soaring, rivers of milk. Pristine land super of white, creamy white snow.

+ + + +

The grandfather clock in the hallway chimed midnight. Wayne got up to stretch his legs. He ambled towards the portrait of Robert E. Lee. Lee had a full, white beard, dark eyebrows, and grey hair, and looked regal and serene in his double-breasted jacket. Wayne understood why his soldiers looked upon him so reverentially. He looked the blue-grey eyes in the portrait of Stonewall Jackson, and thought of Andy and his reverence for Jackson.

Wayne moved to the portrait of Nathan Bedford Forrest, still covered with a towel. Wayne removed the clothespins and removed the towel. He folded it gently and laid it on the bookshelf. Wayne looked at Forrest, squarely eye to eye. Forrest's pupils began to morph, to darken and quiver. A sneer began to form in his vile face. Wayne's arms prickled. He took a deep breath, feeling the pain in his ribcage, but knowing he'd overcome it, and said, "Go to hell, Forrest. Your spell on me is over. Find someone else to terrorize."

Wayne narrowed his eyes and stared back as if locked in mortal combat. To his astonishment, a horizontal tear formed in the canvas, slowly fraying like the knee of a child's jeans, directly across Forrest's eyes. Wayne felt as if he's been victorious over a vanquished foe. "Take THAT you asshole," he said, smugly, puffing his chest.

Wayne decided he'd had all he could stand of the haunting, overpowering influence of Forrest's portrait. Phil was dead. The portrait was torn.

Wayne lifted it from the wall. He carefully opened the backside of the portrait, intending to liberate the canvas from the impressive frame which he would salvage. He removed the brads and worked through the layers of antique cardboard. There he found, tucked between the cardboard sheets, a dozen freshly minted $100 Confederate States of America bills. Mouth agape, he was hesitant to speculate what they may be worth. He took an envelope from Phil's desk and stashed the bills inside, wondering who, given Phil's demise, they would belong to. He rolled up the torn canvas and placed it on the smoldering embers in the fireplace. Within moments, the portrait of Nathan Bedford Forrest was a pile of ashes.

He stared at the portrait of his great-great-great-great grandfather, Andrew Jackson McGranahan. Wayne stood up and walked to the portrait, attempting physiognomy. The visage had a kind familiarity Wayne had never noticed. As he looked closer, he saw a faint imperfection in the portrait that he previously thought was a flaw in the canvas. A scar ran from the left corner of Andy's mouth down to his chin. Wayne placed his right hand on the portrait, over the scar, and his left hand over his own healing left jaw. A tear drifted from his eye onto the tip of his index finger.

Something resting on the shelf beside the portrait caught Wayne's attention. He wondered why he hadn't seen it before. From partially hidden behind a book he withdrew an old, cracked leather strap to which was affixed an exquisite pearl-white arrowhead. He picked it up and turned it over again and again in his hand. He tried to envision what it would have looked like against young Allie McGranahan's bosom, as she tended her garden and watched a boy with freckles fall from his horse after running into the branch of an overhanging tree. He decided he would string it with a silver chain and give it to his daughter, Willa, at her high school graduation. He wondered what she, a child of Target and The Gap would think of it and whether she would ever wear it.

Wayne took the perch where Ruby, the stuffed hawk, stood, and placed it on the floor where Ruby's glass eyes pointed towards the deceased patriarch. Wayne sat back in his chair and played Auld Lang Syne on his harmonica.

+ + + +

December 30

Wayne shook himself awake as a bright sun reflected brightly on new-fallen snow, illuminating the library including Ruby, still standing where he placed her to watch over Uncle Phil. Wayne placed the arrowhead he'd held all night on a coffee table. He urinated and brushed his teeth, in no hurry to make the requisite phone calls. He made himself some coffee. First he called Truman. "Uncle Phil died last night. Will you please come over? I'd like you to be here when the authorities come."

Truman said he'd be there in 20 minutes. Wayne waited ten before calling the Monroe County Sheriff and the Union Funeral Home.

Truman arrived first. He pulled back the blanket and took a look at Phil's corpse. He stood up and he and Wayne embraced. Wayne walked into the kitchen without crutches and returned with a cup of coffee for Truman. Soon thereafter, the Sheriff arrived and knocked on the front door. Wayne told him about Phil's death. The sheriff removed the blanket and concluded there had been no foul play. The undertaker arrived and the body was removed from the house. While Truman found a can of carpet cleaner and did his best to clean the soiled rug, Wayne dialed Mildred's number and told her of Phil's death.

+ + + +

January 1

Two afternoons later, on New Year's Day, there was a memorial service for Phil at his Monroe Methodist Church. Reed Rathmell and Juliet had given Wayne a ride to the church. Everyone Wayne had seen at the Rotary Club meetings was there, as were dozens of people he recognized from town, including Renu Ramkija with her husband, Stuart Cummings, the *Monroe Watchman* editor, along with his wife and the daughter of his dead son's fiancée, Basil and Sarah Foster from Sweet Springs, Burton Jones and Franklin McRoberts III from the Rotary Club, with their wives, and Levi and Isadora Rubenstein. Gibby Robinson, the young guitar player and her boyfriend and parents were there. Mildred and Sherwood Webb were there. Mildred sobbed uncontrollably.

The minister gave a traditional sermon about life and death, interspersing references to the promise of the New Year. He concluded by saying, "Philip McGranahan was one of this community's most intelligent people. I suspect the education of Heaven will get a boost from his presence there. We give him now to his late wife Flora and to God."

The American flag draped casket was carried by Truman and seven other men from the Rotary Club to the awaiting hearse and driven to the town graveyard. The cemetery was in a sublime setting, atop a small hill just east of town. Reed's car passed under a simple, metal arch with the words "Green Hill Cemetery" marked the entrance. To the north Wayne could see *Serenus*, his home for the past four months and the home to which he would return alone after the burial. A brisk wind blew from the northwest, from the direction of Swoopes Knobs.

Wayne counted 90 people in attendance. It had snowed overnight, leaving three inches on the ground. It sparkled with a lustrous, luminous intensity and softened the corners of the fence-posts. The air had a crystalline chill that pinched his nostrils as he breathed. The funeral home had shoveled a path from the ring road to the grave. Wayne thought how lovely the snowfall looked on the tombstones and the pine trees on the memorial park's south perimeter. Two red-tailed hawks circled overhead.

Wayne, standing with Juliet and Reed, watched as the casket was lowered into the ground. He looked at Burton Jones and Franklin McRoberts and wondered if they were thinking of their own mortality. He looked at Levi and Isadora Ruben-stein and sensed the deep love they felt for each other. He watched as Sherwood Webb comforted his wife Mildred in her loss. He gazed at tiny Renu Ramkija, the foreign woman who saved his life, and felt a warm sense of gratitude towards her. He looked at enchanting Gibby Robinson and thought of the beauty of young people in love. Finally, he looked beside him and saw that Reed Rathmell's gaze drifted towards his beloved daughter, Juliet, and wondered at his deep, personal grief over her heartbreaking situation.

Behind the burial hole was a tombstone with "Flora McGranahan" with her birth and death dates on one side and "Philip McGranahan, PhD" on the other. The dates of his birth and death had not yet been chiseled. A soldier of the West Virginia National Guard played taps as the minister, working with Truman, took the American flag from the coffin, folded it, and gave it to Wayne. As a shadow of a soaring bird hovered momentarily over the coffin, the soul of Phil McGranahan was delivered to eternity.

As mourners filed away, Wayne asked Reed and Juliet to give him a few moments to himself before the short ride home. He sat for a time in a chair near the tombstone. He was about to depart, when he was compelled to visit the tombstone again. He spent a moment staring at it. He got up from his chair and walked behind the tombstone, to the east. He noticed a smaller, older and more weathered stone. He brushed some snow from the lettering. It said "Here lies Andrew Jackson McGranahan, B November 5, 1840 D November 2, 1889 and wife Alison Littletree McGranahan, B Mar 2, 1842, D September 6, 1898. RIP."

As Wayne walked to Reed's car, he could see in the distance a statue atop a solitary monument, standing in a pasture, a memorial to the Confederate Soldiers of Monroe County. Wayne remembered the words of Robert E. Lee inscribed on it, "There is a true glory and a true honor – the glory of duty done, the honor of integrity of principle."

+ + + +

January 2

The following day, Wayne awoke to a field of new-fallen snow. He wandered about the big house, thinking how empty it felt. He downloaded his email and found a message from Donna's address sent the previous day.

> Hi Daddy. I hope you are having a
> happy New Year's Day. We are having a

party today. We miss you. Please come
home soon. I love you. Willa

He hit the "reply" button and wrote,

Dear Willa, I hope you had a happy
New Year's Day, too. I miss you too and
will be coming home as soon as I can.
Please tell Eddie and Mom how much I
miss them, too. Love, Dad

He hit the "send" button.

He thought about Juliet and her suggestion to
write his own obituary. He opened a new document
in his word processor. He picked up his harmonica and played a few bars of Woody Guthrie's *This
Land Is Your Land.* Then he began to type.

> *Wayne Derek Quarles died yesterday
> peacefully in the library of his home. He
> was 90 years old.*
>
> *He was pre-deceased by his longsuf-
> fering wife, Donna Brickman Quarles. He
> was survived by two children, Willa Quarles
> Schwartz and her husband, and Edmund
> Quarles and his wife Felecia, four grand-
> children and three great grandchildren.*
>
> *He attended the University of Virginia
> but was expelled due to Honor Code Viola-
> tions. Twenty years later, after issuing
> an essay of apology and remorse, he was
> given the opportunity to return and complete
> a bachelor's degree in American History
> with an emphasis on the Civil War.*
>
> *Wayne struggled with emotional issues
> and suffered a nearly fatal accident in his
> early adulthood. But with the help of caring
> strangers, friends and family, was able to*

*overcome his problems and live a successful
and blessed life with many endearing and
treasured friendships. He was a member of
Rotary International for four decades and
was an active volunteer in community chari-
ties and international aid. He was always
mindful of those less fortunate.*

*In his fifties, Wayne became a licensed
falconer, the sport of kings. He kept several
birds of prey during his golden years and
looked to them for courage and inspiration.*

*He will be interred in the Green Hill
Cemetery in Union, West Virginia, alongside
his wife and ancestors. Any gifts should
be made to The Hawk Project, a non-profit
organization working towards the understanding and preservation of wild raptors.*

+ + + +

January 5

Early in the morning four days later, Wayne
wrote an e-mail to Jim and Christie Dickson, owners of the house, to inform them of Phil's death.
He assured them he was still occupying the house
and would be responsible for upkeep and for paying the heating and electric bills. He asked them to
reply indicating their willingness to allow the con-
tinuation of plans discussed during their visit with
Phil.

Around 10 a.m., Wayne got a call from Truman.
"I'd like to come by and discuss Phil's estate with
you."

When he arrived an hour later, Truman sat
with Wayne in the library under the watchful glass
eyes of Ruby. Truman took a sip of the tea Wayne
had given him and said, "How are you doing?"

"I'm okay. I miss Phil, and it feels really strange to be here alone in his house. But I have Ruby to keep me company." Both men smiled.

"Wayne, I am the executor of Phil's estate. I have studied his will and have met with his lawyer. Phil bequeathed most of his liquid assets and his few remaining investment funds to the Nature Conservancy. The Conservancy obtains land of special biological significance and preserves it in perpetuity. The Conservancy has one preserve in Monroe County, called Slaty Mountain, near Sweet Springs. The Slaty Mountain shale barrens have steep, dry, south-facing shale slopes that harbor several rare plant species. Phil specified that the money be used for education and trail building at Slaty Mountain.

"He left the rest to Mildred Webb, who took such good care of him for so long. That includes all the furnishings in this house. As you might imagine, he never re-wrote the will with you in mind.

"I met with Mildred yesterday. She said there were three paintings in the dining room she'd always admired. She took down one of the pieces artwork hanging in her house and said, 'I'll put that gorgeous landscape painting right here! I'll think of him every time I see it.' She said that not being family and seeing how much you had meant to Phil these past few months, she didn't feel right about taking anything else from the house. She said that if you could work out paying the rent, she would leave everything in place for you to use as long as you wished. When the owners decide to occupy or if you decide to move on sooner than that, she would meet with you to deal with everything else.

"She also said you were welcome to keep Phil's car. She bought a new car a couple of years ago, and she's doing less driving these days. She knew you would need one. She said if you'd take over the title and insurance, you can have it."

"What a completely magnanimous gesture," Wayne said. "She has every reason to despise me."

"You should know better than that by now. She doesn't work that way." Truman took another sip of tea. "Oh, as I was leaving her house, she told me to tell you that you can keep the portraits of all those dead Civil War people. She said they've always given her the creeps."

Breinigsville, PA USA
09 August 2010
243234BV00004B/1/P